# ALMOST GLORY

# ALMOST GLORY

A Novel by

F. BENEDICT

DUELL, SLOAN AND PEARCE

NEW YORK

To
CHARLES DE VERTEUIL
in memory of the old days and
those midnight sessions with the
typewriter

# CHAPTER ONE

ANTON Jankowski smoked one cheap cigarette after another and silently cursed. He cursed the discomfort of the Polish trains; he cursed the tragic reason for this return; above all he cursed the years—from infancy to manhood—that had dragged him over the sordid dust of life.

Loznan, Starogin, Zblevow—the long journey across the flat lands dwindled away—Kilana, Milunken, Gora; he felt that there should have been a change in these places after six years, but there was none. What was the journey to him? But the mere change of scene on the homeless passage of his life. It was not even mildly exciting as he had hoped it would be, nor graced by profound and holy thought, as should be the return to the land of one's birth, a journey in the nature of a pilgrimage. The land and the birth were deplorable. A futile, illegitimate birth: and what a land! For hours he had watched it reel by; under the dead sky its decayed hovels showed like the blotches of some plague on the gaunt, melancholy face of the landscape. Half-melted snow spread away in squalid monotony to the unchanging skyline.

He knew that in summer it would have a different spirit, a different mood. He recalled the stillness of pine-woods broken by the desultory piping of a bird, the undulating sand, the perfect blueness of the sky. Melancholy always, but a landscape like a god, placid and beautiful, asleep in an inscrutable peace.

Fragmentary conversations in the carriage fell with a

strange foreignness on his ears. The woman sitting opposite hugged a bulging shopping-bag, her face was lean and brown, her anxious voice had persistently disturbed his thoughts.

"Yes, yes I see—but a burn, I told the poor little thing and she wouldn't stop crying. Now Lena—that's the youngest——"

He listened to her weary recital. A picture of these little Poles—Lena and the one who had been burnt—formed in his mind. With fair plaits and bare feet he imagined them chasing through the warm, dusty sand of the roads in summer, or singing while they toyed with those blue flowers that grew in the places where they watched their father's geese.

The landscape changed; the train roared through the fringe of a forest. Jankowski leaned forward in his seat and tried to explore with his eyes the vista of gloomy tree-trunks. This was his own district; he had felled trees here; picked berries for his mother. Alphonse and Joseph Nacek might be there to-day with their faces flushed before the blaze of one of those great fires. Perhaps they were singing their favourite song—what a song it had been! They had sung it in the evening going home together, their axes slung over their shoulders. It would be good to hear that song again as they had sung it—wildly, passionately, but with the natural harmony of Poles.

The train came out into the open country again. Looking at the isolated homesteads, the patches of pines and remote landmarks on the skyline, he had the recollection of a wind-buffeted boy spreading dung over an immense field, the snow caking on his ragged clothes. Even in those days he had sung on the homeward path, his song inspired by the prospects of steaming coffee and warmth, above all the restful, blessed atmosphere of home.

Far away he saw the grey streak which was the lake of Lokau; he looked away hurriedly—the sight of that lake had taken him back to an incident of his childhood which lurked tenacious and vivid in his memory. It had happened when he was returning from one of those dreaded, begging visits to Poznan, visits to a grandfather who had never forgiven his mother her wild love for his father. He had left the train at Lokau, partly to save money, partly to delay telling his mother that her father, as usual, had refused to see him. Yachts were coming in over the blue water of the lake, their white sails furling as they approached the green shore. The wide, clean street, lined by chestnut trees in blossom, stretched away with a promise of romance and change. A boy and girl came towards him, their heads lifted, smiling.

"Look at the colour, the white—the yachts are lovely, absurdly lovely." Her clear voice, her grace, every pose and movement of her was enchanting. To attract her attention, he began throwing stones at a pole that stuck out of the water. She glanced at him as they passed; he felt that his accuracy had impressed her. He heard her say, "You saw him, that ragged boy throwing stones at the pole? They say he's got no father; well, at least that if he has . . ." He heard no more as the couple sauntered away under the sunlit trees, her tawny hair catching the light, catching the glances of the loitering youths who stared at her dumbly; aloof, graceful, she turned the corner and was gone, leaving the street desolate, and in the street the ragged lad who was an expert at stone throwing, and upon whom was borne, for the first time, the realisation that he was unwanted, illegitimate, a pariah. Though he never consciously understood it, at that moment there was born the bitterness that grew and crystallised in his mind.

The train began to slow down; Jankowski reached for his suit-case. He was tired and not in the mood for Jan's yellow teeth and futile exuberance but on seeing the round-shouldered figure waiting for him on the platform, he felt thankful—it had been good of his cousin to offer a home.

The other's eyes flickered over the train's length and passed Jankowski without a sign of recognition; the half-formed smile of welcome faded.

Jankowski alighted and crossed towards him.

"Hey! Jan! Jan Domohoski——"

Jan's cigarette fell to the damp platform and expired with a faint sizzle. He peered at Jankowski with comical perplexity.

"Anton? No, it's unbelievable——"

Half-incredulously he reached for Jankowski's hand.

"Six years is a long time Jan."

"Our little Anton Jankowski, but what a change! Six years, yes, you must be twenty-three. You look older than that Anton. But come on, let's get home—the family are longing to hear all about it—England, what you've been doing——"

Jankowski looked at the weather-beaten face with its high cheekbones and wide mouth. He remembered that years ago Jan had seemed magnificent, with his strength and air of indifference—like some tameless bandit, now, under the disillusioned eye of manhood, Jan stood unadorned by romance, a work-weary Pole who existed by the incessant war against the bad soil of his thirty acres.

There was the ghost of a red sunset as their little

waggon left the straggling outskirts of Likora and turned into the lonely Malkow road. Jankowski felt the impersonal touch of the wind which blew the pony's mane into its eyes; he tried to light a cigarette as the waggon bumped and jarred. He felt childishly happy; perhaps this stretch of road, this exact time of day, these same bumps had suddenly gladdened him as a boy because it had been the last stage on the journey home, and now the combination of these things raised the ghost of that gladness.

The tree-lined road ran between two lakes, then rose with a graceful sweep until it dipped, as if it had dropped over the rim of the World; in the distance, where it was highest, the trees were outlined against the sky in a half-wild symmetry, making the road look Godlike and everlasting and melancholy, with a noble sympathy for the forms of earth and sky.

A chaise drawn by four grey horses came over the hill. The reddish glow of the evening was on the gleaming bodywork. Large and serene it whirled towards the little waggon; Jankowski caught a glimpse of the woman who sat between two army officers, of her pale forehead and long lashed eyes.

The aristocratic aloofness of its passing was shattered by the most penetrating 'Hi!' Jan's pony flung its head back at the unexpected sound. The officer who had shouted, frantically waved his cap through the window.

"Jankowski! You blind rat! Don't you remember me? Hi! Franek, stop!"

"The Markenskis," Jan Domohoski gasped, "they know you—I never thought——"

He pulled the pony to a standstill.

"No, that man's name is Radek," Jankowski answered.

The face of the man had been in shadow but he had recognised the voice; with the recognition came a fleeting impression of unreality—it had been uttered so far from that peculiar environment to which it had once belonged, to the atmosphere of an English river, the mists, the scraping of rowlocks across the still water at dusk, the crying of the gulls. In England, by the Thames at Gravesend, he had first met Zygmus Radek, an artist of sorts, a patriotic ass too—they had argued far into the night, perched on some bales in old Neelon's gloomy store-room; the solitary candle had burnt itself out but they had continued to rave at each other in the darkness; over some remark interpreted by Radek as 'an insult to his native land' they had nearly fought. In London too, where Radek had been connected in some mysterious way with Lenski & Son, the Polish Jew financiers, they had occasionally met, curiously enough mostly by chance, as though the Gods arranged it merely to contemplate the futility of their endless conflicts.

Radek's sudden appearance on this Polish highway was tinged with the fantastic; Jankowski had the impression that the other played a part, that he had donned that uniform to typify, for the benefit of an unseen audience, a gallant Polish officer, leaping out of an elegant chaise into the slush of a Polish road.

"Hi, what is this?" demanded Radek with humorously exaggerated bewilderment. "Fate, an evil omen, or are you merely commissioned to haunt me, Jankowski? Yes, we'll shake hands now, before we start the usual argument——" he went on, taking Jankowski's hand.

"I thought you lived in Warsaw," replied Jankowski. "Had I known you were the local squire here I might

12

have returned sooner. This is my cousin Jan Domohoski."

"But I knew him—he is the kind man who gave me a
lift from Mass once. Your cousin? Amazing! Oh, I do
live in Warsaw, I'm on the way back now, those two in
the chaise are my friends the Markenskis. Do you
know them? I remember you telling me that you used to
live somewhere in Pomorze—they live at Malkow."

"I used to live at Struga, about seven kilometres
away. I have heard of them," Jankowski answered.

He noticed that the two occupants of the chaise were
getting impatient. The girl looked out of the window
and the evening light fell on her face, on the pale, clear
complexion and fine eyes; but the face at first glance was
not beautiful, the forehead was too wide, the mouth too
large.

"Zygmus, we are giving you one more minute—the
train will be almost in by now. One more minute," she
repeated severely.

"Yes," shouted the other officer, poking his young,
ingenuous face over her shoulder, "we'll go without
you, Zygmus."

"What a family," groaned Radek. He indicated
Jankowski with a spectacular wave. "I haven't seen this
man for two years—this is the great Anton Jankowski,
the man without a faith, without a conscience, a cynical
menace to our native land and the only man who has
ever drunk me under the table! Jump out, Jankowski,
meet my friends Stepha and Leo Markenski, they'll
hate you like poison of course, but come on——"

Jankowski climbed down from the waggon. He
wondered how a man could go through life and change
so little; Radek had always been like this—a fount of
enthusiastically uttered irrelevancies.

"Anna Jankowski was your mother. I knew you would come back," was the girl's extraordinary greeting.

"Anna Jankowski was my mother. I have come back," he affirmed with a suggestion of ridicule, but her statement, the curious solemnity of its utterance, had startled him.

She looked down and murmured a word he did not catch; he felt vaguely ashamed of his own curtness.

Radek laughed.

"Anna Jankowski was his mother. He has come back—what is this? A kind of litany, a game, a joke—look here, have you two met before?"

"No, no, we have never met before," she said slowly, "never so far as I know." She looked at Jankowski. "But even so, I have heard so much—about your father I mean, I wish I'd known him, they still talk about the 'mad Englishman'—the people round here, yes they do, really. Prisoner of war Lestimer—John Lestimer. You see, even I remember that name, and I wasn't born in those days. The older people round here remember him well, they have told me how he escaped—but of course you know all about it; you must think me quite mad, talking like this, but you see, I have wanted to meet you."

He made no reply. He felt confused, exasperated. These futile efforts to stimulate good-will jarred upon his mood.

"Stepha," interrupted Leo Markenski gently, "we must drive on, you know, the train will be almost in by now. Your friend will excuse us, Zygmus, though I suspect he is really bursting with impatience to get home himself."

14

He looked at Jankowski with unaffected good-humour.

"One moment," begged Radek, "Jankowski, you are not going just to fade away again. Where are you living now?"

"Nowhere in particular. I only arrived to-day—I shall stay with my cousin for a time."

"But why are you back? I thought you were going to stay in England until those long-suffering devils kicked you out, or hanged you. Don't tell me old Neelon gave you the sack after all!"

"No," Jankowski answered, "my mother died—I tried to get here in time. God knows," he burst out with sudden violence, "why I left her in such a place—abandoned her, the only one——" he ceased abruptly.

"I see," murmured Radek, "of course, you will go back? To England I mean——"

"I have no plans," Jankowski explained in a subdued voice. "I might stay in Warsaw until the summer. But there are rumours—I cannot concieve a more fantastic fate than getting involved in a war for Poland's freedom," he concluded sententiously.

"But what do you mean?" asked Stepha Markenski softly.

Her voice was as cold as the atmosphere created by his words. These people were patriots, he should have known. He turned away with weary exasperation.

"You're hopeless, Jankowski, absolutely hopeless," Radek muttered. "Thank God you are half-English."

"I do," replied Jankowski. "Good-night."

Radek opened the door of the chaise.

"Hopeless, hopeless——" he repeated with fervent conviction. "Good-night, Jankowski, we'll meet again, it's inevitable. When you come to Warsaw look me up. You know where I live? Szpitalna street—the same place. Good-night."

The chaise moved; the young coachman having calmly accepted their 'good-nights' as his cue to drive on.

"Who are they, Jan—these Markenskis?" Jankowski asked, as he climbed up beside his cousin. "The name is familiar enough."

"You don't remember the Markenskis! What a fellow you are, Anton—six years away and all us poor Poles are forgotten. Lucien Markenski owns nearly all the land between Malkow and Likora, part of the Struga forest is his——"

"I remember him vaguely—you can't expect me to remember all about these local racketeers."

"Racketeers!" exclaimed Domohoski hotly, "he is the most God-fearing man. They are a fine family, everybody loves them. Leo is a captain now, you saw him, and Stepha—I think she has a lovely face, the kind of beauty men kill and die for," he concluded with animation.

"Fools have killed and died for less," Jankowski answered. "They die in millions for less."

"Was it your father she was talking about?"

"Yes."

Neither spoke for a while. Jankowski looked at the forest that receded Southwards in shadowy expanses; he tried to piece together the fragmentary, elusive story of the father he had never known. No realistic personality had ever emerged from the cloud of fancy under which the romantic Poles had hidden it. The 'mad Englishman' had remained a kind of legend in Struga, where he had been a splash of colour in a dull place, the gust of a more vital life. And this was the forest into which that

fantastic prisoner of war had escaped in the summer of
1916. Jankowski remembered how the accounts of that
exploit had enthralled him by an absurd tinge of romance. Lestimer and a thorough-bred mare had disappeared at dusk; the mare had returned the next morning with a note pinned to its saddle—an apology to
Max Kassel to whom it belonged and an I.O.U. for its
hire. Lestimer never returned.

The thought of that exploit did not enthrall
Jankowski now. It had been an act of scorn for an unshakable devotion. Through increasing hardships his
mother had loved on, he remembered the tales she had
told about his father's wonderful personality; he knew
the path, high above the lake in the Struga forest, where
his parents used to meet. Where the path wound
between the tall, dark trees there was little sound but
the dry rustle of reeds and the call of water birds. He
imagined his father striding through the secretive trees
to keep a midnight tryst. Had it ever occurred to the
man that he would leave a son to this God-forsaken
land? It would not have occurred to himself; perhaps he
took after this father he had never met.

He too had gone from that same unshakable devotion.
His craving to go abroad might have been inspired by
his father's own glamorous accounts of England which
his mother had cherished. And of course, there had
been Kenar with his wild notions of joining some fabulous uncle in Perth, this rich, romantic figure—though
transpiring to be a product of Kenar's great imagination
—had done much to lure them into the fortunate unknown. He remembered the Danzig quayside where
Kenar's cheerful assurances had been hollow, comfort-
less nothings, swallowed up in the looming prospects of
an unfriendly sea, even as Kenar himself had been swal-

lowed up, completely, in the crowds of London eleven days later.

Hunger had been a familiar spectre during those first days in England, eventually it had been replaced by the dread of being unable to send the monthly allowance to his mother.

He turned to Jan Domohoski.

"How far is Pallow from here? It was Pallow you mentioned in your letter?"

"Pallow, yes. It's almost sixteen kilometres from Struga—of course, I shall take you there myself," he sighed pityingly. "Poor Anna, you know how sorry I am, Anton——" he twisted the reins round in his hand with embarrassment. Almost incoherently, he burst forth again. "Yes, yes your poor mother, Anton—if only my letter had reached you in time . . . but she had the best burial—the old man came from Poznan—he treated us like dirt, you know what he's like, I often wonder how he could have had a daughter as gentle as your mother—but he insisted on the best burial, the finest gravestone, if he'd been a Catholic she would have been buried at Struga instead of a Jewish church-yard. We could do nothing—you know what he's like."

"I know," Jankowski said. "But it doesn't matter, Jan. I should have been there myself."

"We shall go to Pallow to-morrow whatever happens."

Jankowski did not answer. His eyes were held by a solitary farmstead that had come into view a mile away. It was on a hill and outlined dimly against the fading sky. How many times had he seen it thus, a lonely deformed building which crouched on the brink of a ruined sunset? No change. The five ragged trees by the barn looked as remote and strange as ever, like brushwood brooms stuck slantwise into the earth. It had been his home. He would not go near it again. It seemed unnatural that its transition to an empty shell should leave no outward sign. The place had no significance now. Those days were dead.

They turned right where a cart-track led towards Domohoski's lake-side home. Long before they reached the house Jankowski fancied he smelt burning peat and heard laughter. The past surged back to him at the sight of the house, so old and derelict, boards were missing from the sides of the out-buildings; to him they had always suggested missing teeth. The place seemed more lonely than ever, cramped here between the brambled-matted slopes of the little valley, the roof of the old Mill which stood between the house and the lake had almost fallen in. But the mill-stream flowed into the lake as clear and as fresh as on the day he had come down here to say good-bye. The small boat was still moored in the reeds; unpainted and rotting, it harmonised with the general dereliction.

"It's getting late," Domohoski said. "I hope Antek has put some hay in the racks."

A fitful March wind came over the lake and whirled scraps of straw into their faces. Jankowski began to scrape the frozen lumps of snow from his shoes on a spoke of the waggon wheel. The untidy yard, the broken ploughs, the ancient, rotting buildings and the smell of peat reminded him of his birthplace. They stirred a fleeting image of that room with its brick stove, cracked and smoke-blackened, the steaming potatoes, the fir-cones drying and always that defective lamp discharging its reeking smoke towards the ceiling, but finding a glorious reflection on the dark gloss of his

19

mother's hair. She had never been too tired to sit up at night and rub fat into his aching hands.

The sudden memory of these things filled him with an immense, unutterable sadness; it overflowed from his heart and seemed to darken the sad, passionate land which was all around him, the night coming down on its lonely homes. It was all so utterly forsaken now by the blessing of that irreplaceable love.

He would go to Pallow to-morrow; next week he would leave for Warsaw. He knew that if he stayed here he would get absorbed into this atmosphere, this place where there was no change but the gradual turn of the seasons, the melting and freezing of the lake, the corn turning from green to gold and finally being carried away; not a sound but the stream or the wind.

# CHAPTER TWO

JANKOWSKI watched the reflection of his rod in the still water and smiled. What would the Markenskis do if they caught him here, fishing in their lake? He was curious to know; during his five months stay in Warsaw he had heard so much about their generosity, after colliding into Radek on the Poniatowski Bridge he had heard of little else. Radek idolised the family; had stayed for weeks at the old white house at Malkow, for so long apparently, that he could go to bed there now without cursing the murmur of the aspens or the music of a stream which fell into the garden pond.

Whenever he had met Radek at the little café in Praga, the conversation had been steered round towards Stanislaw Markenski's bees, Stepha's paint-boxes and birds' eggs, Leo's skates or the father—Lucien Markenski—whom Jankowski could now picture as a gentle, humorous eccentric, who liked to pick his way through the languid cats and twisted fly-papers of the old kitchen in order to catch flies. Markenski would wander round, his well-shaped hands swooping over the sugar, or the jam; he would take the catch into the loggia where two evil-looking spiders had apparently grown to rely upon the benevolent aristocrat for sustenance.

Radek had spoken of a painting done by Stepha Markenski, a view of the lake which hung in the hall at Malkow, between the landscapes of a great artist. The family had refused to believe that 'little Stepha's' picture was inferior to the others. Jankowski wondered whether her youthful effort had been inspired by the

21

view which lay before him now, the autumnal forests that separated the shimmery grey of the lake from the clear sky, the many colours that quivered across the water from the other shore. Radek had also spoken of the 'Masterpiece'—a statue in the garden with the unique distinction of being the one work Zygmus Radek had finished. A statue of a little girl with an open book and a hand raised, as if reciting—an effigy of Stepha Markenski as Radek had met her five years ago. Only her charm, he had pointed out, could have inspired him to finish anything.

Jankowski slid his rod into the reeds and turned to watch the Malkow girls who were binding corn in the field behind him. Along the path at the other side of the fields, a girl was riding, for a moment he saw her plainly under the open sky, then she passed into the shadow of the limes and began to flick the leaves away in showers with her riding whip—it was the Markenski girl riding home over her father's estate.

She left the dust of the path and rode downhill between the sheaves. She was fairer than he had thought, under the bright sun the loose strands of her hair looked like gold. He watched her ride towards him; he wondered why he had not thought her beautiful when he had seen her five months ago. But then he had not seen her graceful figure, her shining hair, the noble set of her head.

She seemed preoccupied. The bird she had watched drifting over the lake had gone, but her eyes were still fixed on the spot where it had dipped away over the Struga woods. It occurred to him that she was shy, that her pre-occupation was feigned. Perhaps she regretted taking a path which must involve her recognition of such a dubious character as himself? Not until she was close enough for him to see the little medal hanging round her neck, did she turn towards him. As she pulled at the reins her eyes wandered down to his home-made rod. Now she would tell him that fishing in the lake was not allowed.

"So you are tired of Warsaw———" she began, then she laughed and indicated his empty basket, "it's hopeless here, really—this spot; do you know that lake in the woods on the other side of the Likora road? My father fishes there often and he catches all kinds of fish."

"It's a long way to go," Jankowski answered thoughtfully, "I shall try it some day."

"But I don't believe you'll ever catch anything—you are the kind that never does," she said seriously. "Of course you met Zygmus in Warsaw; he wrote and told me. In the central Station, wasn't it?"

She looked down at him intently, as if his answer was of great importance.

"No, on the Poniatowski Bridge," he answered slowly.

With her intent air she seemed to ponder this trivial information.

"What are they saying in Warsaw?—the people, do they think this crisis means anything really? What do you think?"

He remembered the undercurrent of excitement in the capital, but the people did not think war was coming, he was sure of that. Before he could answer, she began talking in her soft, enthusiastic voice.

"Stanislaw is at home—he is my brother—and he is quite certain there will be a war. But surely not . . . people are not so mad, I mean———"

"They are."

"You sound very certain," she said slowly. She turned away from him and looked across at the binders

23

coming towards the lake, moving in line, their arms brown like gipsies, their dresses vivid and picturesque against the mellow fields. The men were in front, mowing in tireless harmony.

"The children," she said suddenly, "look at them all, it must be tea-time."

From the direction of the village a troop of little children had appeared. They came over the slope of the field, carrying their coffee-cans and little baskets with a quaint air of responsibility. They were very neat; gay ribbons adorned their diminutive plaits. Stepha Markenski waved to them, but they were too shy to wave back and only smiled.

Watching them, Jankowski thought of the war which had begun to loom below the horizon of Europe. What would it mean to these people who rose at dawn to milk their cows, to bake their bread? They had slaved on through centuries of devastating wars; the little children were reared to inherit the yoke of their forefathers.

He pulled his rod out of the reeds and rose. This girl was right; he would catch nothing in such a bad spot. The shadow of the horse fell across the water in front of him; he was conscious of the rider watching him. Then he heard her voice, level, confidential.

"Zygmus Radek is coming to see us this week, he turns up at all hours—he might be there now, in fact I am almost sure he will be there now. Would you like to see him?"

"Yes, I suppose so," he answered carelessly, "he knows where I live."

She began to bend the twig she held into the shape of a bow.

"I wonder, perhaps, if you like—come back with me. Leo is in Torun—you remember him? He was in the coach when we met. Stanislaw is older, he would really like to meet you I know—he is always talking about going to England but he never will. *You* look English I think—at least, my idea of an Englishman."

As she looked down at him he thought how her pure complexion was set off by her hair, her lips.

"In England I was always mistaken for a Frenchman," he replied, with an assumption of gloomy indifference. But he was attracted; in the loneliness of his heart there lurked the disturbing notion that of all the persons he had met, she alone was capable of understanding him. He could not resist the invitation to go back to Malkow. He told her so. To his surprise, she dismounted without a word.

"I cannot ride while you walk," she explained.

He persuaded her to mount again and they followed the shore of the lake until it met the Likora road.

A line of waggons rumbled home with coal from the station. The drivers, their faces black with coal-dust, stood on boards and cracked their long whips; as Stepha Markenski appeared over the bank they touched their peaked caps and grinned. The cracking whips grew louder than ever. She looked down at Jankowski and smiled. He smiled too, knowing how the drivers were trying to impress her with this one thing in which they excelled.

She began to talk of her father, of how he rode with her sometimes during the first fall of the leaves, of how exhilarating it was to ride at night against the West wind. He would take her where they could see miles and miles, where the undulations of forest-land looked shadowy and immense under the moon, like the backs of great lizards fading away into the dimness of the horizon.

"He is wonderful, he knows the name of every bird, every tree even," she said. "My mother died years ago —I hardly remember her . . . my father, he is hard to describe, I think he is a dreamer—people make fun of him sometimes but he is loved by them, they know he is good, they know—well, if somebody is ill, if anything is wrong, along they come, hat in hand. He is too soft I suppose but thank God he *is* like that. Though really——" she paused with a slight frown, unable to express her thoughts. "To you, what will he seem?" she went on, with a vague, depreciatory gesture and a strange smile. "Very ordinary—to be seen and forgotten; after all, I suppose it's only the knowledge, the understanding of another—the sympathy . . . if these go deep enough, they can only end in love."

Jankowski remained silent, yet he had the impression that she expected some kind of reply.

Suddenly she reached for the scarlet berries of one of the mountain-ash trees lining the road; she held them in her hand and looked at them closely, as at something strange and wonderful. The sun slanted through the boughs to her face, giving an inscrutable depth to her dark blue eyes. The little oblong medal dangling between her breasts glittered brightly.

"And your father—you never saw him again?" she inquired with that ghost of a frown. "Not even in England?"

"I never looked for him. I had no idea where he lived. But who cares anyway? Who cares?"

"Well I don't," was the unexpected retort.

He glanced at her quickly. She was staring straight down the road, and by the set of her full lips conveyed scorn. He had offended her, God alone knew how! How long did this preposterous girl expect him to pace

26

through the dust at her side, while she rode aloof, her eyes fixed inflexibly ahead?

He walked beside her for a while, waiting for her to look round and speak, but she only turned when it was necessary to murmur a solemn 'for ever' in reply to the 'praised be Jesus Christ' of a little peasant boy who passed. Jankowski decided to return—he could not go on any further in this absurd way. But while he tried to think of some excuse for leaving her, she glanced down at him. On her face he glimpsed the shadow of conflicting emotions, before it vanished miraculously, melted as it were, by the warm glow of her smile.

"As for sympathy, understanding—oh, we seem an excellent pair," she laughed softly. "I *was* angry; I thought—the way you spoke—that you wanted to snub me. I care. I was interested—your mother and father . . . that was a romance—you don't understand. I know how you feel," she added hastily. Her eyes were solemn again.

"Interesting? Romantic? Nobody thought so in those days. My grandfather—he was a lawyer in Poznan— he never found it romantic."

He spoke gently, he did not want to offend her again. He expected her to ask him more about his grandfather, but she did not.

They had reached the end of the fir avenue which connected the farmyard with the Likora road. She was taking a last look at the lake, it was very still under the late-summer sky.

"I know it sounds incredible," she said, "but Leo and Stanislaw can swim right across it—I never could, never. Ah, but when it freezes——"

The thought of the lake freezing filled her with delight. At once, with great enthusiasm, she began to tell him about the gay times she had had there. Every Christmas the entire Markenski family would go down there to skate. Last year Radek and somebody called Morecki had joined them.

He hardly listened. White dust lingered over the road where army lorries passed at regular intervals. His mind would dwell on war and its implications. Nearly everyone to whom he had spoken in Warsaw professed a passionate love for their land, but what was patriotism to him, who had no land? He remembered Radek outside the Boguslawski Theatre, his black eyes full of the excitement some critical news had awoken. "*Jesu Maria*, what use is a man who cannot love his land?" he had almost shouted, "and what land is there like this—our Poland. Where else can you find such forests, such lakes, such glorious women, such strong men! If I die for Poland I die happy. They cannot keep us down! They have tried—my God, how they have tried—they cannot keep us down, Poland that fights with no wall at her back. Jankowski, you dog, you should be eager to fight for our dear old, poor old, passionate Poland——"

Radek had proclaimed his patriotism thus in England too, but in those days Jankowski had believed that the depth of it accorded with the potency of the cheap wines they used to drink.

"You must be tired, walking in the dust like that; I do wish you would ride."

He looked up at the girl who rode at his side, recalled to his senses by the imperative tone of her voice.

Solemn, reflective, her eyes met his.

"I am not tired," he answered, "anyway, it's not far to go now."

He was confused by her steadfast regard.

"You were not very interested in my account of the

skating, it seems," she said slowly, as if talking to herself.

He did not answer. Her manner suddenly angered him—of course, she was accustomed to the rapt attention of those within hearing of her seductive voice.

"Oh, I am hopeless," she said, low and fervently, so low that he hardly heard what she said above the dull thud of the hoof-beats on the road. "Skating! Why should you be interested? Look here," she went on eagerly, "tell me something about yourself, your life, your days in England——"

"My life is not interesting—it has been a most sordid affair."

He smiled, wondering how he could have been angry; she was sensitive; so had he been five years ago.

"No, no, your life *must* be interesting, even mine has been, please——" she was leaning towards him, one hand on the pommel of the saddle. Her lips parted and her eyes bright under their dark brows.

"The truth is," he said gravely, "I like to hear you talk but my mind will dwell on war to-day."

"I know. That's it," she said. "If only this Hitler man knew that Poland will stand no nonsense—of course, our army could be in Berlin within a month."

"Of course."

She leant forward in the saddle to brush the flies away from the head of her horse.

"Can you ride?" she asked suddenly.

"That's something all Poles can do."

"I was just thinking about that escape. I suppose in a place like this people remember things of that kind—there's little else to talk about. But it must have been pure joy, galloping away like that—almost worth being a prisoner. You know, I don't believe you take after

29

your father—not in appearances anyway. They say he was fair, his hair was wavy too . . . all the girls fell in love with him——"

"They don't fall in love with me," Jankowski answered, "I am not fair. I have never galloped into forests on other persons' horses. It seems I don't take after him. I wish you would tell me about your painting."

"Oh, I don't really do much painting. Zygmus gave me a box of paints once; I have done a few pictures— the only one who believes they are good is Hugo Kassel. Do you know him? He is a German, his father is Max Kassel—of course you have heard of Max Kassel—it was his mare your father took. Hugo is a kind, sentimental boy—very proper, but I'm afraid he's quite a Nazi now. He can't talk about anything else but rallies and all that kind of thing. How Zygmus used to laugh at him! But Zygmus laughs at everybody—even father."

She told him about the history of Poland her father was writing; he had been writing it for years, for as long as she could remember, but he could not drag on any further than the reign of the first Boleslaw. Radek joked about it, saying what a tragedy it was that such stuff should divert a man's attention from his land. He admitted that the estate was going to the dogs anyway.

Its condition certainly indicated a magnificent scorn for any kind of administration. They had reached the yard, and it was the time of day when every animal there was determined to make itself heard. The cows, quite imperturbed by the cowman and his boys who tried to drive them in for milking, were in every corner; drinking at the pond, pulling at the heaps of green-fodder outside the stable door, even chewing the mangolds piled under the opening in the sheep-stall wall. The cowman's wife, with a milking stool in her hand, was cursing the dog, whose assistance had degenerated to futile yapping from the centre of the yard.

"What a noise!" Stepha Markenski exclaimed, "even the pigs sound as if they were being murdered. As for that dog——"

An excited, heterogeneous crowd of hens dived for the grain scattered by a little girl who was obviously more concerned with something going on above the sheep-stall. Jankowski looked to see what it was and saw the stork trying to induce its doubtful youngster to leave the ancient, reed-thatched roof. Its mate wheeled high over the yard, distinct against the blue remoteness of the sky.

"You are thinking that everything is in a terrible state," Stepha Markenski said, as they went over towards the stable. "I know. A few more generations of Markenskis——" she shook her head sadly.

"My cousin told me that the Markenskis have always been greatly loved."

"I don't know——" she answered vaguely. "Do you notice how everyone is looking at us? They wonder who you are."

She was right. He saw that the carpenter scrutinised him from behind a half-closed door, that the man in a blue shirt who had been unloading straw into the cow-stall loft had stopped work to watch them, that the grimy, bowed form of the smith emerged for a moment then turned and hurried back into the forge, as if struck by the realisation that time is too precious to be wasted.

"Well, that bloodthirsty old character knows who I am," Jankowski answered, nodding towards the forge, "he used to tell me tales about the old days, of murders and insurrections. I doubt if he'd recognise me now."

They came to the stable door, where three peasant boys tussled round the head of her horse for the right to hold it while she dismounted. Their shrill voices rose in a frenzy of eagerness.

"Bruno!—let go, *I* was here first——"

"Oh no you don't—little devil you——"

"Miss Stepha, look—tell him!"

"Tad! Bruno! Steph!" she beseeched. "Stop fighting like that—now you can all hold him, surely."

Laughing, she dismounted. At once they clustered round her. Where had she been? Had she seen those aeroplanes? Would she come berry picking with them? So they questioned in their high, insistent voices. Yes, she would come berry picking with them, she had seen the planes. Jankowski smiled at her promises and random replies.

"I do hope Zygmus is here," she said, watching the children take her horse into the stable.

She sounded confused, apprehensive. The invitation to return with her had been impulsive, he was certain that she regretted it already—of course her father would object—a stranger walking in.

"I can wait here while you go and see," he suggested.

"Oh no, you can't do that—don't be foolish. But I *do* hope he is there—you have come so far. We can go through the garden."

She opened the small gate at the end of the stables. He followed her erect figure under the old trees, where shafts of sunlight fell on her glossy hair. When they passed the sunny back of the cow-stall she looked round and nodded towards the bees buzzing about a line of hives.

"Don't worry about Stanislaw's bees," she said with a smile, "they have never stung anybody in their lives."

32

She crossed a path in front of the house and disappeared into the shadow of an open doorway. He followed.

They were in the long, dim kitchen; fly-papers dangled from the low ceiling; a clock ticked . . .

"Mind the cats. I don't know why we have so many —they get trodden on——" his companion murmured in a sad voice.

She picked up a copy of the *Express Poranny* from the table; once again he felt that she was confused. For a moment she stood with her head on one side, as if listening to the water that gushed from some unseen tap in the scullery. Behind her, outside the open window, pale leaves glanced and murmured. Yellow sunlight revealed dust on an old brass crucifix, a first Communion picture. The sound of gushing water ceased. A shadow crept across the beam of sunlight shining through the scullery door. He watched it, fascinated.

A plump young woman with a red band round her head emerged with extraordinary caution; in her hand was a half-peeled potato and her attitude was one of ludicrous menace. Stepha Markenski laughed. The maid's hand flew to her mouth in dismay.

"Oh! Miss Stepha!—I thought it was that rascal Bruno with the milk——" the bewildered face was almost as red as the head-dress.

"Does the poor Bruno deserve such treatment, Sofia?" Stepha Markenski inquired with unexpected gravity. "Well, perhaps he does, you should know," she added. "Never mind. Is Master Zygmus here?"

"Master Zygmus? No. No, Miss Stepha——"

Jankowski did not know whether to be pleased or disappointed. Radek had been the excuse for his presence here, he would have to go.

He told her so.  She said that it would be absurd to leave without a cup of coffee, without even meeting Stanislaw or her father.  Oh no, he would have to stay a little longer—she would never forgive him if he left so soon.

Somewhere in the house a door slammed and rapid footsteps sounded in the passage.  The door opened and a slim young man in the uniform of a Cavalry officer came in, his blue eyes radiant with excitement.

"Stepha!—come on, we've waited for you.  Didn't you know?  It's a celebration—by rights the whole country should celebrate——"

"Stanislaw, this is Zygmus Radek's friend, Anton Jankowski," she interrupted gently.  "Zygmus knew Mister Jankowski in England; I think I told you about him, you remember?"

Jankowski was certain that the other did not remember, but Stanislaw Markenski, remarkably genial in his excitement, greeted him like an old friend.

"Of course, of course—come into the library."

They went into a room where the French windows were wide open, where an immense bunch of yellow leaves rustled on the table.  To Jankowski it was a pleasant place, with its volumes of poetry and Polish history, its sporting pictures.  He noticed that somebody had left a straw hat and a basket of blue-berries on the window sill.  The room was steeped in that spirit of the late Polish summer, full of its colour and tranquillity.

"I am so sorry we just missed father," Stepha Markenski spoke as if it were a great tragedy, "he has gone out to see them threshing, Sofia told me—we *would* miss him . . . if we had only arrived a few minutes sooner——"

Stanislaw Markenski was already bending down by the sideboard.

"Ah, now this is the stuff!" he said joyfully, taking out a long bottle. "Zygmus calls it the spirit of life or something, he said he stole it from some drunken sailor in Danzig—the man he got that parrot from, do you remember, Stepha?"

"I wish you would tell us what you are trying to celebrate, Stanislaw."

"Haven't you read the papers? Don't you take any interest in what's going on in the world?" he inquired with exaggerated pity. He turned to Jankowski. "Well, at least *you* will remember those declarations in the spring, those guarantees between us and Great Britain? They were signed yesterday, the papers are full of it."

Jankowski, recalling no such guarantees or declarations, murmured, "thank you" as he took the greenish drink the other was offering. It occurred to him, as he sipped it, that the sailor in Danzig had not been worried by its loss.

"And what do they mean exactly? These guarantees——" Stepha Markenski asked without much interest. "I am not sure that you know yourself, Stanislaw."

She had been standing by the window with a glass in her hand, but having spoken she turned to the bowl of leaves on the table; many had fallen to the yellow cloth and she began to collect them one by one. She was like her brother; Jankowski noticed it for the first time. Much darker of course, more thoughful, and without quite such a wide, smiling mouth, but the eyes were the same—gentle, under rather disdainful brows. In her there were traces of deeper passion, of greater energy.

"But everybody knows what these guarantees mean," her brother protested. "It means there won't be a war. This crisis will blow over. If it doesn't——" he looked at her steadily, solemnly, "we shall give them 'Nazis'," he said at last, "with allies like Britain and France it would be over in a month," he turned to Jankowski and smiled. "It seems you've come back to Poland for nothing after all, but it's just like a Pole to come back at such a time—they would have all come back to fight——"

"Don't mistake me for that kind of fool," Jankowski answered. "I have nothing to fight for."

For a moment there was complete silence; the withered leaves in the girl's hand did not rustle; even the cowman's dog in the yard had stopped barking. Brother and sister stood perfectly still and looked at him.

"No," he added softly, "I am not the fighting kind."

"I don't understand," Stanislaw Markenski murmured, "you mean——?"

"Only that I haven't come back to fight. As I said before, I am not the fighting kind."

They regarded him in silence, solemnly, coldly, as though frozen by the intensity of their immense disdain.

He had a craving to say something scornful, to tell them that Poland had no chance against Germany. But what was the good of telling them anything now? Like all the rest they had reached that primitive, blind state that sweeps a nation to the exhilarating brink of war— they were invincible, they were the best fighters, they were the best statesmen, they were the greatest race— their cause was God's. Then there would be the aftermath, bewildered despair on stupid faces as the realisation of their own vast madness dawned upon victor and vanquished alike. A trivial weed like himself, sprung from the last abysmal farce, could tell them nothing.

"It is unbelievable."

With this disdainful observation, Stanislaw Marken-ski turned away and sauntered over towards the window. He noticed his cap on the sill, he changed the position of the Polish eagle badge, then held the cap at arm's length to admire the effect.

His sister stood by the table, twisting an empty wine-glass in her hand. Her self-absorption appeared complete, but the curve of her full under lip, the line of her dark brows betrayed her anger and contempt. While Jankowski was wondering dispassionately whether she would ever speak to him again, she looked him straight in the face. It was the solemn, unfathomable regard with which he was already familiar.

"And you call yourself a Pole?"

She spoke slowly, with cold restraint.

He heard somebody knock on the door behind him and enter.

"No," he answered, without turning to see who it was, "I am half-English as I think you know."

She never answered. The plump maid had come in with a telegram. It was an order recalling Stanislaw Markenski to his unit.

"Gruziadz again——" Jankowski heard him murmur, "of all the dreary places——"

He turned over the slip of pink paper, as though he expected to find something even more depressing on the other side.

"Well, I told them—the fools round here—I've been telling them since the spring, and now? In a few days! In a few days we shall be in the thick of it——"

Jankowski finished his glass of wine.

"It is late," he said, "good-night."

He stepped out through the French windows.

# CHAPTER THREE

WE shall give them "Nazis"!' the shuddering blast of a German bomb on Starogin recalled the words to Jankowski's mind; they had sounded impressive nine days ago, in the comfortable Malkow library, as though 'giving them Nazis' was a small, personal favour. But to-day he had watched the dust-whitened Nazi columns sweep into Poland; his head still ached with the petrol fumes, the roar of tank-tracks, of motor-cycles. He wondered where Stanislaw Markenski was now. All round him lay the land ravished by war. What sight could be so soulless, so weary? He longed to see somebody ploughing on the fields, doing some common daily task, but there was only a great stillness now. The hatred, the anguish, the diabolical madness, the death which had saturated the earth and gone, seemed to have drawn away its life and goodness. Silence. The very birds had gone. The white road stretched away, no longer with the promise of life and change, but into the heart of an immense despair.

He wandered on, with no clear idea where he was going, only desiring to get away from the grey faces, the vacant eyes of those who listened, chilled by the infinite menace of that sound:—the enemy on the roads of their land. It was defeat here; it would always be defeat. Why had he come back to this land! Why could he not have forgotten it? Cast off the shadow of its sombre memories forever?

He hurried on, keeping to the grass verge because his feet were tiréd; he passed a line of abandoned cottages, the windows were smashed and the interiors wrecked;

one cottage had been burnt out, under the charred beams an old woman rummaged among the litter. Again, from somewhere behind a belt of forest, he heard the low roar of armoured columns and realised that he must be going towards the Likora road. The only sound of fighting was the distant boom of artillery in the East.

Taking a path through the woods, he came out on the main road, where the endless blue-grey column was tearing Eastward, the motor-cycles, covered in white dust, racing ahead of the armoured vehicles; sometimes a soldier waved, his face distorted by the intoxication of victory.

Jankowski could not take his eyes from the evacuees, the small farm-waggons, the men pushing prams. One waggon had turned over; an old man with a bandaged head was picking peas up from the dust and putting them into a tin. He crawled too near to the advancing columns and furious curses were hurled at him from the windows of staff-cars, but he was deaf to it all, his bird-like hands darting for peas from right under the sprawling carcase of his horse.

Jankowski went on, through the petrol fumes and dust, until he came to a little group who watched where the road turned towards Malkow. Most of them he recognised. A woman's voice was choked by sobs.

"Oh, God, God—our poor boys—what can we do . . . what have we done to deserve this? Dear Jesus, what have we done to deserve this misery? It was a massacre . . . my poor little Alphonse. . . ."

With the flames of rage and hate round his heart, Jankowski turned towards her. It was the plump maid he had seen in the kitchen at Malkow nine days ago.

"If they take our cows and that meal I put away," she went on, between her sobs, "why must we have these devilish wars?—it's not God's will—the children, little Vitek—what will they do with the children?"

"Nothing," Jankowski snapped at her in his exasperation. "They are men like us. Can't you see they are men like us?"

There was no answer to his scornful question. He asked her how the Markenskis were.

"The house is full of them now—these beasts, I ran away, they might have done terrible things . . . these swine . . . they took the horses too . . . I ran away . . ." Jankowski did not ask again after the Markenskis. Nothing must drag him down from the pinnacle of his dispassionate contemplation. He must remain apart from it all.

"It was hopeless from the start," remarked a fat man with a fair moustache, "look at them, revolvers, machine-guns, field-glasses, hand-grenades in their boots—what was the good?"

"What was the good!" a gaunt youth turned on him passionately. "You can say that? Just wait—we'll drive these swine out yet—there's England and France remember . . . just wait—and we'll string the Kassels up too—throwing flowers on the tanks! I saw them, I heard them—'we're German, we're German, we're German'. Traitors! I shall go into the forests," he went on in a voice which was suddenly soft and thoughtful, "I could live in the forests, there are plenty of berries——" he clutched Jankowski's sleeve, "you're young and strong, you're not going to stick this, are you? I know a place, and there are birds, deer—we could live."

Jankowski looked into the glowing black eyes.

"No doubt we could live until the winter came, and then?"

The other stared at the yellow leaves at his feet.

"God knows what the future holds," he muttered.

Further down the road, four German soldiers were laughing and chatting with some civilians from Likora. A man left the group and came over to Jankowski.

"They are just like ourselves," he said, in surprise, "they don't want this war any more than we do——"

Jankowski did not answer; he was watching a column of prisoners being marched back, weary, unshaven, they had little resemblance to the Polish soldiers he had known.

"These front-line Germans are not bad fellows," the other went on, "it's the civilians that come after I'm afraid of, the *Gauleiters*, the secret police, the S.A.—but these lads are human enough, that one with the long nose speaks perfect Polish, his aunt lives in Torun, he says."

"Why are we standing here like a lot of fools?" the old smith from Malkow demanded suddenly. "It is finished, finished——" he repeated, as if the word had been invested with the force of a divine prophecy. He raised his stick in a gesture of farewell. "May God have mercy on us."

Like an answer came three great thuds from the East. The little group began to disperse. Only the gaunt youth remained to watch the invader sweep into Poland.

On the way back to his cousin's Mill, Jankowski met two German soldiers who swaggered down the path from the direction of Struga. They walked in step and their helmets swung in their hands, the field-grey uniforms were blotched by the shadows of the trees. The taller of the two smiled at Jankowski; it was a strange smile of pride and embarrassment.

"What do you think of our Führer now?" he shouted in Polish. He did not wait for an answer, he seemed eager to be friendly, to show that he hated nobody. "I come from Marienwerder," he went on, "I cannot understand you fellows—why do you strive against us? We don't want to do this—bomb towns, kill civilians —we're trying to kick out Capitalists, trying to make a better world. The Führer devotes his life to it——"

"Why talk to these Polish pigs? What's the matter with you!" came the savage interruption from the other German, "we're not here to be lady-like. It's nearly four o'clock."

They marched on; he heard them laughing further down the path.

He followed the lonely track round the shore of the lake and came to his cousin's Mill; during the past week he had been thankful for the remoteness of this place in which he lived.

"Your friend is here," Jan greeted him in the yard, "that officer—he's hiding here——" he glanced at the Mill.

Behind the dust of an upper window Jankowski saw a familiar face.

"Of course, the great Radek," he murmured. They would have to be careful; when the Germans found time to think hidden soldiers would be routed out and those who had hidden them put against the wall.

It seemed that Radek had not thought of these things. Hay was clinging to his black hair and one of his boots was off; he was as cheerful and enthusiastic as ever.

"My God, Jankowski! Make yourself at home, brother, but first, have you any good razor-blades? I feel like a

bandit. Lord, but I had a shock last night! I went to
Malkow. I crawled up that little path by the stables—
not quite crawled but you know what I mean—the
dining-room window was wide open, madman that I
am I went right up to it, I must have been deaf—the
place was full of them, drinking, laughing—thank God
they were drinking, the table was littered with bottles.
It was a dark night . . ."

Radek paused and listened. There was a lull in the
sound of traffic on the road; they heard the yapping of
the dog and the far-off guns.

"But this place is ideal," he continued enthusiastically, "who would come here? Why it's completely
hidden from the road. And that boat—does it leak? I
mean that little boat in the reeds, don't you see what a
short cut it is, across the lake to that fringe of rushes?
It's mostly marsh I think, but if one could reach those
bigger trees the ground must be firm—we could be in
Malkow in an hour. Hark at those damned Germans on
the road again! I wanted to get back to our boys but the
front is miles to the East now, I was taken at some place
called Klona—it was a massacre! Directly they started
to march us back I decided to escape—I thanked my
guardian angel when I recognised this district——"

Radek went over to the little window and peered out.
Outside the dog was barking madly, demented by the
renewed roar on the distant Likora road.

"My God, Jankowski, think of it—not so long ago we
were sitting in that little café in Praga—what a fantastic life! But nothing seems to shake you," he turned
from the window. "I want you to go to the Markenskis,
Jankowski—go at night and for God's sake be careful—
my ankle's sprained or I'd go—tell them where I am."

"And what will they do?" inquired Jankowski.

"Why, we can talk—arrange something——"

"Listen," Jankowski interrupted, "the place is full of Germans. Get it into your head that Poland is finished. Some fools still think that it's not. Before long there will be German administration everywhere—it's no time to be gallant."

"No time to be gallant? What do you mean? You think we should submit to everything—give up the fight? There is something wrong with you, Jankowski. I am a Pole. I shall go on as every Pole will I hope—resist, resist, resist. Listen! Can you hear the guns?—Poles fighting for their land, their freedom—Jankowski, I believe that you would fight for nothing on earth. Never mind, God forbid that I should stay here——"

He turned away and limped over to peer through the cracks in the boarding. Jankowski looked at his torn jacket, his swollen ankle, something in the man's attitude impelled him to go up and put a hand on his shoulder.

"It would be insane," he said, "the Markenskis might have left Malkow. Anyway, Germans are in the village, German patrols—it's insane to try it. I went there in August, a few days before the invasion; I am not very popular there; they don't trust—in fact they hate me. Stay here until your ankle is well, and then——"

"Oh never mind, never mind. Can you row me over the lake to-night?"

"I can do that."

"Could you take this empty bowl down, and thank your cousin very much for the soup. They are fine people, Jankowski."

That night the little boat slipped out of the reeds. A waggon rumbled on the Likora road; they heard the faint boom of guns, but under the night the land slept.

"You are not coming with me?" Radek asked softly, as they drew into the other shore; as if he already knew the answer he prepared to moor the boat to one of the alder stumps.

"I will come," Jankowski muttered, "though God knows why; unless it's the chance of tasting some more of that putrid wine you stole in Danzig——" It was Radek's ankle of course; the thought of him limping on alone would have killed his sleep.

The boat rocked as Radek leant forward impulsively.

"Brother, I knew you would! I knew it— I know you better than you do yourself, Jankowski. Now, listen to my plan——" he was eager and friendly now, "the Kenars work for Markenski; we can go there first, they live over by the school, away from the village——"

They left the boat and blundered on through the dim trees; through the damp leaves of the dells, over the firm ground of the higher glades where they could see the outline of neighbouring woods and the misty purple of night beyond. Sometimes Radek spoke, but Jankowski could not catch all his words; the words he did catch irritated him; Radek might have been addressing a convert to a new faith.

"No giving in now—never! We Poles must never forget our history——"

"Do you know where you are going, Radek?"

"You see, our roads have shaken under the feet of an invader before . . . other men of our race . . . in these great forests have hidden and fought . . . Poland lives . . . my intention, to hide out here, to form a band, if somebody like you could join me, I know, I know, your heart is not in this thing as mine is—yet, you're half-English, that means something . . . unshakable fidelity to the ideas of justice——"

They skirted a lake that Jankowski had known well as a boy; to-night its misty sheen awoke a strange elation; danger lurked along its sombre shores, brooded over the shadowy expanses of forest. The enemy? He smiled at the thought—just poor fools like himself, greater, blinder fools to be dragged by their noses into death and mutilation for their 'sacred rights', their sacred causes, their 'freedom'. How many Poles and Germans were dying to-night, for the freedom which they neither knew nor loved?

Fragments of Radek's conversation came and went across his thoughts:

". . . the sand, the pine-woods, oh, I knew the place, and that grey tower in the distance—so pale it merges in with the sky—their hateful, vivid flag flickered above it, a dominant fleck of colour—a threat! Little children with bare feet were trying to give us bread . . ."

What place was Radek describing so sadly? Somewhere through which he had been marched as a prisoner perhaps, Klona or wherever it was.

"I have skated here," Radek waved his hand towards the lake, "with Stepha and Leo—I think that young fool Kassel was there too—I would sell my soul to see her skate again; she was the best for miles round here—perfect, with that figure, that natural grace—ah, wonderful! Stepha I mean. I hope these cursed Germans have left her alone——"

Unexpectedly they came upon the open sky. They were out on the Malkow fields, among the deformed, unfinished corn-stacks and dark sheaves.

"The village is somewhere over there," Radek said, "I can hear the dogs."

The Kenars' cottage was in darkness and silence. They watched it for a while then Radek rapped on a window. Almost immediately and without warning, the pale, unshaven features of a very old man showed behind the glass. Jankowski stared back at that face which was there without movement or sound, a foot away from his own; he felt that he stood before an intense scrutiny, a judgment.

When the voice came it was startlingly loud; it asked them what they wanted—if it was bread he could spare a little; he had been in the Army himself, had been through it; he knew. He knew. He had fought for Poland. If only he were young now—why even yet—!

The old man's excitement rose; his voice cracked. Jankowski half-expected him to break into the National Anthem.

Radek gently intervened. They had come to ask after the Markenskis; to find out whether Germans were still in the village; whether the Markenskis had left.

Markenskis? The name was repeated stupidly behind the glass. They thought he had forgotten it, but he had not—of course the Master was still at Malkow, but there were Germans there. There was no news of Stanislaw or Leo, Miss Stepha was at Palukin with the Naceks; she was out of the way there.

Jankowski thought how well out of the way she was there. He knew the Naceks well; he had often been to their red-tiled house on the edge of the Struga Forest. As a boy he had been intrigued by the icons, the large, brilliant pictures of Christ and Our Lady that gave a holy air to the place. And the Naceks were holy people, good people.

They had thanked the old man, said good-night and

were out on the road again when Radek put the question Jankowski expected.

"Do you know these people—these Naceks?"

"They live at least two kilometres away."

"I could limp ten times that distance in pursuit of the golden girl," was the answer.

Irritated, for no reason he could think of, Jankowski almost told him to limp on, but even while he framed the words he realised that he wanted to go himself.

"There's a cart-track further up the road—it goes left into the woods," was all he said.

Long before they reached the house a dog began barking furiously. The sound was startling; Jankowski cursed it and tried to go more silently along the path.

The old woman opened the door in answer to his knock. She flung it wide as if in defiance. Somebody was stooping just behind her, trying to stifle the barking of a little dog. While she peered out at him, another door opened and he saw into the room behind the kitchen. There were several persons there but only one face stood out clearly, a face he seemed to have known for a long time, though in the lamp-light it had a subtle difference—the eyes looked larger and deeper set.

"Hey! Stepha! Oh, curse this dog——"

Apparently Radek could see into the room as well.

Jankowski spoke his name loudly and clearly then stepped into the light.

Little Anton Jankowski! They could not believe it, why he had had short trousers on when they had seen him last! They became excited and cheerful; they laughed and shook his hand, as if it were a celebration. Old Mrs Nacek hurried to and fro with her two daughters, getting food and coffee. Stepha Markenski rose from the table where she had been looking at a picture book with a small boy; she shook hands with Radek and looked at Jankowski with lingering bewilderment; she seemed about to come forward and greet him, but she only smiled.

"God has spared our home at least," Anna Nacek told him, "but all the terrible suffering—poor, poor Poland——"

"Don't listen to these girls, Anton," old Nacek said hotly, "they talk as if we were beaten—our army is still fighting; just because the Germans are here, it doesn't mean that Poland has fallen——"

He produced an antique map. He would just show them how things were going at the front, he said, the news was good; a fellow in Likora could get the latest bulletins . . . some fools believed the German propaganda; believed that Poland was all occupied! Well, here was the map; they could see for themselves. Here by Lodz, Kutrzeba was counter-attacking—throwing the Germans back; Bortnowski was by no means beaten in Pomorze—it might be a matter of days now before the Polish Army was back; the Germans fleeing before them. There was a reference to it in the Bible even.

Jankowski stooped over the map and followed the moving finger. He had always liked the old man for his simplicity and kindness. Seven years had not changed him much; the cheeks were less chubby perhaps, the moustache even larger, but the round blue eyes were as bright and as interested as ever. Sometimes he made stupid mistakes over the names of Generals or statesmen and his wife would snap at him in disgust, then she would try to engage Jankowski or Radek in another conversation, as if in disdain for the old man. He would only stoop lower over the map and ramble on, pretending that he had not heard her.

"We had nothing to fight them with—they were much too strong," Anna Nacek murmured to Jankowski. "Father does not understand. All I pray for now is peace; I can't help thinking about those poor refugees. May God have mercy on them——"

"May God have mercy on all of us," old Mrs Nacek said fervently, "we shall be enslaved again——"

Radek put his arm round her shoulder.

"Please, don't be so downhearted, mother—don't for one moment believe that our soldiers have given in. We shall fight on."

All the evening Radek was most attentive and polite; he gave the impression that he had come expressly for their opinions on the war. His dark eyes glowed in response to the old man's enthusiasm; then he began telling them his own fantastic adventures; describing frightful scenes, unbelievable hardships, but his voice was calm and humorous; sometimes he passed his hand through his hair and shrugged.

"Oh, but it made life sweet, that constant fear of death, slinking along that path, senses alert, the black night peopled with untold terrors, and of course those fools shooting blindly, a few bullets seemed a positive luxury after that first day at Klona, I quite believed then, you know, that the great German offensive was directed against me personally—that's what it seemed like, I felt quite important but very scared I am afraid," he laughed and sipped his coffee. "Ah, but life was so sweet when I recognised the Struga lake—I had been three days on the run, I remember there was a little tree, in the mist that had come up from the lake I mistook it for some silent watcher—I came upon it suddenly, my heart missed a beat——"

He paused; they waited in silence for him to continue,

but he laughed softly and congratulated the Naceks on their fine coffee.

Jankowski smiled; how well he knew this queer tendency of Radek to leave a subject abruptly; he was uncertain whether it was a deliberate trick to create a halo of drama and mystery round himself or an unconscious habit. Not that it mattered; it always had a great effect.

"Ah well, that's all over now."

Jankowski heard the tense, unexpected comment of the boy, who had come to his side, unsuspected and silent. Jankowski looked down at him, wondering who he was. The boy surprised him again by saying that he remembered him coming into the house with Alphonse and Joseph Nacek; there had been axes slung on their shoulders; they had put on the gramophone . . . oh it was years ago now!

"You must remember," the boy said, "I remember it all so well—you wrestled with Joseph and knocked a bowl of milk over——"

The scene came to Jankowski, and other scenes. Of course there had been a little boy in the Naceks' home . . . a little boy—Leo! That was it. He had never known from where the child had come.

"I remember you," he said, "I remember you well. But Alphonse and Joseph?—I thought . . . but of course, with the war—the Army has——"

In confusion he broke off; he inwardly cursed himself. The others had heard the names mentioned and fallen silent; the smiles had left their faces. Why had he asked after the two sons! He should have known.

Yes, Alphonse had been at Czestochowa, Joseph at Kutno. God alone knew where they were now.

"Zygmus Radek tells me that he is going to hide out

in the forests, that he is going to resist—fight on against the Germans."

For a while he had been conscious of Stepha Markenski's eyes upon him, her words, slow and insinuating, came to him like a subtle threat, a judgment pronounced on his lack of faith, his secret impartiality.

They all looked at him, waiting for his answer.

"There would be more than the Germans to fight against in the forests," he said as calmly as he could, "the cold, the hunger . . . the monotony."

"Monotony? Oh no, Jankowski!" said Radek cheerfully.

"But what will you do?" Stepha Markenski went on, "we are all slaves now, you know; we shall all be put to work."

"I have worked before."

"Oh yes, of course, I know, but never as a slave under the Germans."

"As a slave," he answered.

"Surely not—where could you have done? Don't tell me it was in England——"

"No, in Poland."

She looked at him. Her dark blue eyes seemed nearly black in the lamplight and contrasted strangely with her hair which glinted just above her forehead, where it had been bleached by the sun; there was neither wonder nor disgust in her regard, only a kind of reflective sadness.

"You don't belong here," she said at last.

"Stepha, you must not take him so seriously," Radek broke into the silence that followed her words, "you don't know him as well as I do—he speaks like a traitor, he only does it for effect. But you will not find a truer friend than Anton Jankowski—he's like our pal

Morecki, Stepha; do you remember that he always tried so hard to be cynical? Isn't that so, Jankowski—Come on, admit it——"

Jankowski laughed.

"Unlike your friend Morecki," he said, "I try so hard not to be."

"You have given up fishing in the lake now, I suppose?" Stepha Markenski asked suddenly, "or did you ever try that place in the wood I told you of?"

"I never tried it."

"And now it is too late——" she said slowly, most sorrowfully, giving the words a wide significance. He knew that she was not thinking of the fishing in the lake, but of her home, the sudden breaking up of her family, the ruinous change in her life, of all the things it was too late to do now.

"But it's not too late for me," Radek put in joyfully, "it's just what I want—in the forest too—fish for breakfast every morning—wonderful!" he laughed, at the notion that he had been developing a joke against himself, "here's to Zygmus Radek—the Terror of the Nazis!" he raised the cup of coffee above his head: "to the Terrible Radek!"

His act made them all cheerful again and brought a magic change to the atmosphere; the boy laughed as if he would never stop, the old man waved and said, "Yes, yes, that's it!" with fervent conviction; the two daughters and the old woman watched Radek's reckless, vital face with tenderness and admiration.

"Well, at least I shall pray for you, Zygmus," Stepha Markenski told him solemnly.

"Stepha, if you think of me it will be enough——" he took her hand gently from the table and began to raise it to his lips. He let it go suddenly.

The dog was barking furiously outside.

"It's them——" the old woman whispered, "dear Jesus——"

Somebody tried the outer door.

"I must hide quickly," Radek said, "but there is no need to panic."

Jankowski jerked up the trap-door in the floor, under which potatoes were stored.

"In here—quick!"

"Fine!" Radek said, as he squeezed himself under.

Somebody banged on the outer door.

Jankowski closed the trap-door and dragged the table over; he removed Radek's cup of coffee then sat down next to the boy.

The door was banged and shaken.

"I must unlock it . . . I must let them in . . ." Franceska Nacek said in a small voice.

"I'll let them in!" the boy shouted suddenly, rising from the table, "why is everybody so terrified?" He rushed from the room.

Stepha Markenski touched Jankowski's arm.

"You may be mistaken for a soldier——"

"God forbid!" he answered.

They heard voices and heavy footsteps. Two German soldiers entered the room.

"*Heil Hitler.*"

"Praised be Jesus Christ," the old man mumbled automatically.

There was a short silence while the Germans, well-armed, large and formidable, stood just inside the door and looked about them, their hands on their hips. Their eyes wandered over the brilliant prints of Our Lord, the First Communion pictures, the last year's calendar— wandered into every corner of the room, not searchingly, but with a weary distaste that had in it something possessive, something sinister.

The eyes of the soldier with the red face, finally rested on the collar of Jankowski's jacket.

"Stand up, you Polish pig!"

Jankowski did not move.

"Get up!"

"Please . . . please, Anton . . . " Anna Nacek begged him, "oh, this is terrible——!"

The other German took his companion's arm.

"Don't start that stuff here," he said masterfully, "you might be in the mood for it—I am not."

"Well, they ought to get up——"

"Let it be, let it be——" his comrade answered; he looked round the room with a friendly smile. "Please seat yourselves—I hope you understand some German, I have noticed that nearly everybody in the district does; of course it is a German district as you know—this is really West Prussia——"

"Oh, for God's sake, Willi, spare us all that," the red-faced soldier interrupted; he winked at Stepha Markenski and grinned: "They breed fine wenches here, wherever it is," he said, and was suddenly embarrassed by his own words; he blushed; his eyes wandered round the room again.

"I want you to believe the *Wehrmacht* is not here to harm any of you," the tall youth went on earnestly, "unless you hinder us. The war will soon be over—Poland is done for, a few fools are still fighting of course; we are mopping them up as quickly as possible——"

"What is he saying, Anton?" Leo asked.

Jankowski told him.

"I must warn you against hiding Polish soldiers," the

55

young German went on in the same friendly voice, "I have seen so many families shot for it——"

"And who the devil are you?" the red-faced soldier demanded suddenly of Jankowski, "you're young and fit enough! Hiding, eh?"

"I was never in the Polish army."

"You speak rotten German——" the other commented, "I don't like the look of you. What do you make of him, Willi?"

"He'll get picked up soon enough," the tall one answered, "anyway, we didn't come here to hunt prisoners——"

"We came here to ask the way to Gora," the other said, "but you had to give the usual speech—which these uncultured savages don't understand anyway——" he turned to old Nacek. "Hi! wake up, you—where's Gora?"

Old Nacek explained.

"If that's not the right way, we'll be back," the soldier threatened. "Let's march, Willi."

"Good-night," the tall youth said as he went out. "*Heil Hitler.*"

They stamped out. The outer door closed with a bang.

"All this is not good for the nerves——" Stepha Markenski's words broke the silence that followed their exit. She smiled faintly as she spoke.

"All clear?" they heard Radek's voice.

"Just a moment, Zygmus——" She went out and locked the outer door.

They all began talking at once.

"Another ten minutes among the potatoes—it would have been enough," Radek said as he emerged, "when that fool started shouting I thought trouble was coming.

But look here, we must go," he was suddenly serious, "it is much too great a risk for you all—you understand? An escaped prisoner——"

His voice was lost in their ardent protests—how, could he say such things? As if that mattered! He was a Pole; that was enough. Anything they could do—food or perhaps a blanket—it would be an honour——

"Why doesn't he stay here?" the boy asked.

The suggestion was pressed by them all. Under the straw in the barn would be an ideal hiding place, they said, until his ankle was well again; until he was fit enough to go into the forests.

Jankowski realised that he would have to return alone.

Before he went out into the darkness he looked again at the colourful prints of Our Lord, the icons, the white cloth embroidered with yellow flowers, the First Communion pictures. All the faces in the warm light were turned to him, it seemed with an infinite kindness. All their eyes, young and old, were on his face. They seemed to accept him joyfully—as a brother or a trusted friend—into the precious shadow of their mutual disaster.

"Come and see us again, Anton," old Nacek said, "at any time of the day or night——"

"Don't go through Malkow," Stepha Markenski told him, "it is full of Germans——"

"Don't worry——" he mumbled stupidly, "goodnight."

But he went out with anger stirring in him. He would not return to this place—they had mistaken him for such a good comrade, ready for the wildest adventures on behalf of their prostrate land.

# CHAPTER FOUR

AS he clambered down from the cattle-truck in which he had travelled from Danzig, Jankowski felt the East wind lash his face. He dropped his suit-case and breathed into his hands; stamped his feet on the frozen ground. The sun was sinking, one side of the little East Prussian station glowed with an illusion of warmth.

He began to walk down the siding where a gang of Poles were unloading the railway waggons, throwing off long, quivering boards that were covered with a feathery frost. They were singing, but in a painful, determined way—trying to combat in deadly seriousness that diabolical wind. Watching them, he suddenly recognised her, balancing precariously on the boards, her pale face tilted upwards, wisps of hair escaping from her close-fitting cap. For a moment he watched her; he felt embarrassed, as though her ragged, flapping garments, her bluish face and tired eyes had been his fault. But he knew why the sight of her moved him—she typified the defencelessness of a land; its utter humiliation. And the name Markenski had been woven into the background of his childhood; he remembered the grey horses, the gleaming coach that used to pass serenely under the mountain-ash trees of the Likora road. And now Stepha Markenski wore a man's boots, laced with string.

He went up to the tin plate hanging from the farm-sledge they were loading. Yes, there is was—the name and address he had expected to read with such a strange certainty—Hans Tieson, Klein-Heinrichau, Ost Pruessen.

He looked up. She was looking down at him with a smile half-eager, slightly incredulous.

"I thought I recognised you——" she began, then broke off; she seemed unsure of him, uncertain how he would respond to the cheerful spirit with which she was eager to invest the occasion.

"I am glad you recognised me. It was a year ago you remember, at the Naceks——" he said.

"Yes, over a year," she answered lightly. Too lightly, as if in fidelity to a standard of conduct, an aristocratic standard, demanding the concealment of how much she might have appreciated the tragic significance of that year.

"How long have you been working for Tieson?" he asked hurriedly.

"Oh, since the spring. I had been in Cracow—do you know it? I think it's a wonderful place—it really is. The Palace . . . and in the spring too. I had never been there before; and the times my aunt had invited me before the war! You can see the mountains too . . . I suppose you were just rounded-up like I was? Just rounded-up like—like cattle. Still, I missed the prison and Majdanek——"

She ceased abruptly on the name, as if the associations it recalled had killed the source of her speech.

He began to tell her how he had registered with the Labour Office at the beginning of the year, of all the farms he had been sent to in East Prussia—at Rosenberg, Elbing, Danzig—and how it was Hans Tieson, of Klein-Heinrichau.

She stood motionless. She had not heard a word, he was sure of it. He noticed that the five girls and the little boy on the waggon had stopped work and were looking at him with a faint interest. Perhaps he had a vague, dubious distinction in their eyes because he knew Stepha Markenski; no doubt they were convinced that the class from which she came teemed with cultured and romantic personalities.

He nearly laughed—cultured and romantic! What a cold, ragged, and morose fool he must look, shivering by a railway-waggon, with his cracked boots, with his cousin Jan's old army over-coat which had a jagged fringe where he had cut two feet of cloth to make a scarf. He had the collar of the coat turned up, it over-lapped the pulled down flaps of his long-peaked cap.

The Foreman watched them with mournful intensity —cadaverous, with little drops of ice clinging to his moustache—his long face was fixed in an expression of abject misery. The young driver stamped up and down by the sledge, a hand over his mouth and his eyes fixed on the ground.

"Hans Tieson——" Jankowski murmured, "what is the place like? Plenty of sugar-beet——"

The name Tieson awoke a passionate outburst. He was a swine! A swine, a swine—a miser; too mean to live, their work was never finished. Sugar? It was a sugar-beet farm.

The young driver ceased his furious pacing.

"Have you been sent here, brother?" he asked.

"Yes."

"Then run away—bolt for it, brother. You should have seen the bread we got this morning! Green. Green, I tell you—we live like dogs . . . like rats. Can you play the accordion?"

"No."

"What a pity; you could have taught me. I've just bought one."

"And you are learning? That's the worst news of all—I think I shall bolt for it!" Jankowski answered.

They all smiled. The driver laughed and offered him a cigarette; "only a *Junak*, brother."

"Come back with us," Stepha Markenski said, "this is our last load—it's much too long a walk and there will be room on the sledge."

She looked down at him; he smiled back, gladdened by the eagerness and simplicity of her youth; it seemed surprising and wonderful that she had not changed, that there was no disenchantment in her blue eyes.

"Good," he answered, "but I thought that was Klein-Heinrichau," he nodded towards a cluster of dark and squalid cottages half-a-mile away.

"No, no, that is Gross-Heinrichau," she explained, "our village is almost six kilometres down the road, but it's much the same."

He nodded. They were all the same, these squat, exposed habitations, huddled together on either side of the straight East Prussian highways. But for the dark smoke escaping from the chimneys and being snatched away by the wind, Gross-Heinrichau looked as dead as the frozen flatness of the land.

Jankowski shivered and put his hands deep into the pockets of his coat.

"This seems the coldest spot on earth," he muttered, "how large is Tieson's farm?"

"Three thousand acres perhaps," she answered; she turned to the driver; "how large do you think it is, Franek?"

"It's like the Sahara desert," was the answer.

The five girls and the little boy were already clambering aboard the wood stacked on the sledge; they were light-hearted and excited now; their eyes glistened in the snow-reflected light.

"It's getting dark," Franek muttered to himself. "I hope little Stephan has put the straw down."

Jankowski wedged his suit-case between the boards and sprang up beside the others. He held out his hand to Stepha Markenski; she clambered up beside him as the horse jerked the sledge forward. They started to glide over the frozen puddles and trampled snow.

They began to sing and he sat up in amazement. It was his favourite song! The one he used to sing himself years ago. They sing it beautifully, he thought in fervent appreciation, it sounds really wonderful now.

What other song could they have sung into the teeth of such a merciless wind? It was their song, nobody else but Poles could sing it in that way, and it had to be inspired by images of steaming coffee, relaxation, warmth.

He looked at the hand resting next to his own on the frosty boards, at the broken finger-nails showing through her glove. He glanced at her face. She was singing like the rest, but something in the set of her head made him wonder. Where were the signs of a year's degradation and hopelessness? He saw that her eyes were tired, but they still held their audacity and aloofness. She had more fortitude than he had realised; he knew these East Prussian farms, he had shared the dark, lousy shacks with his fellow slaves too often. All these large farms were the same—Sammerau, Freystadt, Peterwitz—the rough table between two layers of beds, the black stove plastered with pictures cut from ancient magazines—the wretchedness of unending toil. She would need her fortitude.

He looked at the beet-fields that stretched away into

the distance on either side of the road. He cursed the luck that had brought him here in time for the beet harvest; he had hoped for a job in some town—Torun or Bydgoszoz—but he had known in his heart that it was a forlorn hope—they were rounding up men now in Polish towns for the harvest.

The sound of her voice singing made him turn towards her again; he wondered why she had not mended the holes in her glove; he wanted to talk to her, to ask her how her family was, but Poles rarely put that question to each other now—too often it brought tears to the eyes, there were places, Stuthoff, Majdanek . . . He could imagine tears in her eyes but the idea of them falling was fantastic, incompatible with her fidelity to that aristocratic standard of conduct. Perhaps that was her strength, her defence against the slow corruption, the degradation, the wretchedness.

The nagging wind seemed to have been cut off. They were gliding over straw and frozen dung, between two red-brick buildings; he could see the yard of Klein-Heinrichau. They had stopped singing.

"How is your family?" he asked hastily.

"My family——" she repeated slowly, as if she had not quite understood his meaning.

"I was told about Stanislaw——" he muttered. God! Why had he not held his tongue.

"Yes, he fell at Grudziadz——" she paused as they turned into the yard: "they took my father away in January—I don't know whether you heard . . . and do you remember Leo? He was reported missing—that doesn't mean that I won't see him again, I am almost sure he is a prisoner, but where he is, what camp——? I have tried hard to find out—there were some parcels I wanted to send—but nobody seems to know where he is."

He wondered what she could possibly have to send.

The sledge stopped with a jerk and she sprang off.

"And what about your cousin?" she asked suddenly, as if realising a breach of courtesy.

"I haven't seen him for a year," he answered, "but he is quite well as far as I know. Do you know what happened to Radek?"

She came very close to him before she replied.

"He joined the Partisans—as he said he would," she said softly, "I get notes from him sometimes, of course he can't say very much. But what a life it must be! But I can't help thinking that he will get caught—the risk is terrible. You know, we mustn't talk about him here. Come on, let's go and get our coffee and bread, and I believe there is jam to-night—it's strange meeting you again, but I had an idea I would; you haven't changed very much, considering . . ."

"Neither have you."

"Oh, but I have, surely?" she stopped and looked at him. "Do you really think that? Or are you just trying to cheer me up——"

"I was not consciously paying you a compliment," he answered, "but I realise now that it is a compliment— the greatest compliment."

To his surprise she blushed.

"I thought you were one who never paid compliment——"

"I am," he said, "I'm afraid to—my compliments sound like veiled insults; it's my tone, somebody told me once that I couldn't keep the sneer out of my voice——"

"I think I know what they mean, but they made a mistake—it's not a sneer."

She never told him what it was. Two men were coming towards them from the stable.

"Tieson," she said softly, "and the other one is Lenski—that's the Inspector."

Jankowski had guessed who they were. Their eyes were on him and he knew the look—suspicious, calculating. They were hurrying forward to inspect that for which they had paid. What kind of cattle had the Labour Office sent them this time?

The younger of the two—blond, energetic and obviously Tieson—had a slip of paper in his hand.

"Jankowski yes? The Anton?"

"Yes." Jankowski spoke sharply, even this small word might betray the fury in his heart.

"Do you understand land work?"

"Yes."

The bulky Inspector was muttering behind his moustache:

". . . he looks strong, what we have wanted since Mania left—useful when the threshing starts——" his voice changed as he addressed Jankowski. "You will find your bread, and a margarine ration for three days in the quarters, your blanket is on the palliasse. We start pulling beet to-morrow——" he paused and began to scrape some scraps of straw together with his stick.

"Understand?" Tieson's harsh voice broke in, as if to banish any illusion of familiarity or goodwill Lenski's information might have induced. "You are expected to work. Go and get some food. And don't stand staring at me!" he concluded with sudden ferocity.

Jankowski picked up his suit-case and walked slowly away. He knew they were watching him, knew they were smiling. He tried to smile too, to keep calm—to smile from the pinnacle of his detachment, but he was muttering "the swine, the swine, the swine:" What had they said? Nothing much; threatened nothing, but before them he had felt the cold, unspoken threat under which the soul of a country rotted.

That first night at Klein-Heinrichau he could not sleep. Round the two-roomed shack there raged a maddening, persistent wind, drumming its futile fury into his brain, like a lunatic determined to press home some entangled, meaningless argument.

The smell of damp straw and dirty clothes had succumbed to fumes from the room's extinguished carbide lamp. He listened to the breathing of his sixteen fellows and thought of the great beet-fields he had seen. Already the thought of his last farm was like a memory of home; it had been a small place, they had understood him there, old Bergmann had been kind, the food good. Yes, that harvest had finished too soon. But in this place, with sixteen men and eleven women, it would last until Christmas.

Reaching over to his trousers on the end of the bunk, he took a cigarette-end from the pocket. He lit it and lay back.

"Can't you sleep, brother?" he heard the voice of Franek, the young driver, "is it your conscience? I noticed that you never said your prayers to-night."

"I never do," Jankowski answered. "No, I can't sleep to-night, brother."

"Have you heard about the prisoners of war? Lenski's son told me—they're coming from Marienberg, Englishmen or Frenchmen, he said—poor devils. That's why Kubek has been putting barbed-wire round the old forge. I hope they are Englishmen—I've never met any. Stepha told me that you had been in England. You knew Stepha before, didn't you?"

Jankowski murmured "yes" into the darkness.

"I shall never forget the day I fetched them from the Station—there were five of them. My God, it was pathetic! Thin? Half-starved . . . but she stood out, it was her eyes——" Franek's dreamy voice ceased; he was silent for so long that Jankowski thought that he had fallen off to sleep.

"No, no, this is not the life for a girl like that," the words were almost inaudible, as though the driver had sighed deeply and turned over in his bed while speaking, "so very generous, so good-hearted . . . I feel like killing Lenski when he shouts at her. Did you know her well? You weren't her lover, were you?"

"No."

"The girls say that she's still a virgin. I think so too. There are not many on this farm—it's the life, demoralising, soulless, I have been here a year now; I lived in Kalisz once, had a good job in an office too— I'll go back there like a clod of earth. You had better be careful, brother, Lenski's got his eyes on you for sack-carrying, you're the right build. Schacter is a good fellow, he's the Foreman—he treats us as well as he can. But Lenski——!" the driver hissed the name venomously, "I'm going to kill him when the British Army comes—if he hasn't died of old age by then. Well, I must get to sleep, see you in the morning. By the way, what's your name?"

"Anton."

"Good-night, Anton."

Jankowski was still awake when the old watchman came in to rouse the drivers at five o'clock in the morning.

On his third day at Klein-Heinrichau he found Stepha Markenski working beside him on the field, topping the beet, on the row next to his own. They were well behind the others but Tieson had ceased to rage at them; he stood ten yards away and glared. His hands were on his hips and his head was slightly forward; by the power of his glance he tried to bring on their heads the threat of unspeakable degradations, floggings, concentration camps—the defilement of their very souls. Twenty yards behind a guard, in an almost identical pose, stood over seven British prisoners of war.

Jankowski worked slowly on, laying the beet he had dug in a neat row behind him.

"Yes, you must miss it all, the comfort, the gay times," he spoke loudly; he knew how Tieson reacted to the Polish language, but he had a reckless urge to provoke, to enrage—damn the swine; it was his own voice!

"Oh no," she murmured, "it's not that; when I think of home I think of the peace . . . the peace of it——" she halted the regular swoop of her knife at the beet, "I wonder if those trees are still growing? I planted some silver-birch trees."

He was baffled by the look she gave him—pre-occupied and very young. He glanced at her as she knelt there in her ragged clothes. Her hands looked cold as she fingered the rusty cutting-knife. She had had everything: beauty, breeding, wealth, the love and shelter of her family. Her wealth was gone, her brothers killed; her father? God only knew. But after all, beauty and breeding were still worth something, and courage too. She had that.

"You know, I don't like you much," she said unexpectedly, "there's something wrong with you; you've got no . . . no core, you would never love anything enough to die for it. I believe you don't even hate these people."

68

"Such deluded mugs are not worth it. And every place is not like this—my last farm for instance, I was treated well, it was a little place near Elbing, the farmer was one of the kindest men I have met. Of course you hate the Germans like poison, they have taken so much from you. But what have they taken from me? Freedom, I suppose, and a pair of English boots——"

"Is that all you worry about! What about your poor, suffering land—Poland? Don't you know it's in chains, it's enslaved—our people are getting murdered! You have some spirit surely?" she looked at him tensely, as if his answer meant everything to her.

"Not much," he admitted, "I loved my mother, but as you know, she is dead."

"Yes," she paused and her eyes dropped as if in deference for the dead, "but Poland?" she continued earnestly. "Surely—it is your land—your mother's land—don't you feel like doing something about it? The Polish Aristocracy—where is it? Murdered, tortured . . . oh how I hate these people!"

"But I don't belong to the Polish Aristocracy," he answered mildly.

"No," she said slowly.

"And after all, I am an outcast," he went on quickly, "an altogether useless dog. Why should I care? I had a bad enough time before we dreamed of the Germans taking Poland—your so beautiful Poland."

"Don't you think it is beautiful then?"

He smiled at the childish astonishment in her voice, even though it was mixed with anger and contempt.

"No," he answered, "at times I've hated it; as you know, I went away as a boy. God alone knows why I came back. But we have had this argument——"

"Then why did you come back?" she interrupted.

"My own opinion is that Poland can do without your kind."

He realised that she was trembling. Seeing her put down her knife, he picked it up and began scraping it with a piece of stone; the jarring screech of stone against steel filled the strained pause in their conversation. He noticed that the other Poles were far ahead, urged on by the cold, inexorable fear of the modern slave. He threw the stone away into the line of beet in front and gave her the knife. He began pulling the beet slowly.

"You are young," he remarked sadly, as if it were an incurable illness, "and I must seem a low specimen. You are sensitive, too easily sickened by the greeds, the jealousies, the petty, soul-killing things that seem to constitute our fantastic life——" he was conscious of her watching him; he wondered whether it was with contempt or pity. "Yes," he went on, "I can imagine you in that fine house, riding, dancing, having such a sweet, untroubled time in your beautiful Poland. But where was I?" he broke off and stared at the ground, "no, I never knew any of that," he said at last, "but I dreamed fine dreams too, once—what a great, unselfish fellow I fancied myself then! But——" he shrugged. "You asked me why I came back? As you know, it was to see my mother's grave," he mentioned finally.

"And did you?" her contempt subsided before a feeling of curiosity.

"More than once," he said, "she was buried at Pallow—the Jewish graveyard is on the hill there; you might have seen it——"

He paused and listened. Voices were being raised behind them. He looked round and saw that Tieson was wrangling with the prisoners' guard.

"But you are not a Jew," she said slowly.

"No, but my grandfather seems to have scared my cousin into burying her there—he was half-Jewish—he paid for the gravestone. It stands well out on that hill; it has permanence and peace there. I shall go there again." He ceased with the disturbing conviction that he had said too much, that she was secretly laughing at him.

Her voice reassured him.

"I see, I understand." After a pause, she looked up again from the beet. "I think you called me young just now, and how old are you?"

"Twenty-five."

"So young! You seem much older——"

"No, still young, still healthy—a useful slave in fact."

"Yes," she nodded thoughtfully. "I suppose I am too—but really, we don't work very hard, do we? Even the prisoners are catching us up." She looked over her shoulder with a smile.

"You look very cold."

"Only my hands and feet—my body keeps warm. When do you think it will all end?"

"God knows."

They worked slowly on, leaving in their wake a long line of beet severed from their tops. They could hear English voices joking a few yards behind.

It was cold, the leaves of the beet were stiff with frost; he decided to run up and down until the blood circulated in his feet—Tieson would be screaming at them soon in any case for falling behind. The thought drove him to spring up; he stamped his feet and swung his arms but that cold fear was at his heart—he was so much at their mercy.

An English prisoner said: "Good old Anton, he never

71

gives a damn!" Another one—the one with curly hair —shouted: "How is it going, Anton boy? Ignore that square-head, you could wring his neck with a hand behind your back!"

"Quiet!" roared the guard.

"Och, away——" came the disgusted retaliation from a short Scotsman.

Jankowski looked at them and smiled. Ragged, thin, clad in the worn-out uniforms of every occupied land, they grinned back. He was thankful for their humorous sallies, their laughter, and their shouts of encouragement cheered him disproportionately; touched his vanity like a compliment, like an award.

Then it came, the infuriated scream of Tieson.

"*Teufel nochmals!* Move! Work, you lazy dog!"

Jankowski bent down and grasped the frosted leaves again.

"Doncher worry cock," came the advice from behind, "our time's coming."

"Hadn't we better work a little faster?" Stepha Markenski suggested, "Tieson won't stand much more. As for those prisoners—he can't understand what they say and that makes him worse; he hates you too."

"I had half-suspected that."

"There is nothing funny about it," she turned troubled eyes towards him, "he's gone to fetch Lenski from the yard."

"He can shout even louder perhaps?"

"No. He uses his stick. I know because I felt it during the harvest."

For a while there was only the sound of her knife falling and the swish of the leaves, then the prisoners started talking again; he heard their conversation in disjointed fragments.

"We were in a farm-waggon," the one with the woollen cap was saying, "a smashing day . . . remember some damn Jerry shouting 'good luck Sonny-boys!' . . . sounded funny, as if he wanted to come with us—seemed to envy us almost, pleasant looking bloke too——"

". . . four days in a cattle truck—no grub," the tall one drawled, "oh, they heaved some bread in at one place but I never saw it. Our truck had been used for coal—we staggered out like a shower of wogs . . . must have looked a desperate bunch. God knows why they stopped us at Berlin—might have been some propaganda stunt . . . show us off, cheer the Hun up a bit. I won't forget that tart either. Showy bit of stuff. Well made too, but you should have seen her face when we all peered out! Talk about contempt—and she kept walking up and down to make sure we didn't miss the expression. Some fool started singing the *Siegfried Line*——"

The bell in the yard creaked and clanged.

"Why it's like magic!" he heard Stepha's fervent voice, "the smiling faces—just look at them!" she threw down her knife and sprang up.

The prisoners shouted breakfast as if proclaiming great news, though they would spend the ten minutes searching through their pockets for cigarette-ends.

"Let's eat our sandwiches here," she said, "it's too far to the edge of the field."

He stood with her and unwrapped his sandwich of brown bread and ersatz Margarine. Further down the field the other Poles were in a group, stamping their feet, their misty breath showing up against their dark forms. A few yards behind him the British prisoners chatted as if in a public bar of an English inn.

"Torun? Yeah, I was there," the one with the woollen cap said. "I lost my mates there in a sorting-out parade; you know the carry-on—swede-bashers fall out here; brickies fall out somewhere else. I was a dairyman right away, don't you worry—Pictured myself knocking back pints of it. I wound up on some lousy spud farm by Deutsch-Eylau—not a cow in the place—" he frowned and blew into his cupped hands. "God what a frost! Roll on the boat!"

"Roll on Willenberg," put in the one with curly hair, "I've had enough of this dump."

"Willenburg? I was only there nine days and I crawled out like a ruptured monkey——"

Jankowski munched his sandwich and listened. He longed to ignore the guard, to walk over and talk to them about England, about the places he knew. The curly headed Englishman looked at him and winked.

"Alright, you lucky devil, I can see you and your girl friend there. Boy, what a figure!"

"No talking with civilians!" the guard shouted.

"Speak Latin, we might understand you, laddy," was the answer.

Stepha Markenski touched Jankowski's arm.

"They are coming back," she nodded towards the yard. "I'm not afraid of course," she added looking round at him quickly, "but the sight of them—I can't help it—it gives me that feeling——"

He saw Tieson and Lenski hurrying past the straw-stacks, Tieson's black dog running ahead; he knew what she had meant: their appearances had cast a nameless dread over the fields, over the peaceful farm-buildings where plumes of pinkish smoke were rising above the barn, the red-brick stables, the trees—the dread of something unknown but always expected. The other

Poles were silent, but the Englishman with the woollen cap talked on loudly; he was unable to forget the 'lousy spud-farm by Deutsch-Eylau'.

". . . one decent bloke—sort of cousin to the Frau I think he was—educated gink, speak better English than we can . . . used to drone on about Shakespeare. 'Our soldiers call you Tommies,' he said to Bert, 'what do you call us?' Bert told him . . . I thought our feet wouldn't touch, but he was a gent that bloke——"

The bell clanged. The prisoners cursed it, they cursed the man who rang it, the man who had made it, the entire family of Tieson to whom it belonged.

"He's coming," Stepha Markenski said in a low voice, as she picked up her knife. "I wish we weren't quite so far behind."

Her words trailed off as Lenski stormed up to them.

"You are here to work!" he shrieked, "what do you think we feed you for?"

The high-pitched voice from a man of Lenski's bulk struck Jankowski as theatrical and bizarre. He smiled back, wondering at his own calmness.

"Work, you insolent swine! Look where the others are—you've been talking all the morning, talking, talking . . . Move!"

Lenski raised his stick, but let it fall again; his fury seemed to have given out, leaving him frustrated.

"God! Why can't somebody else take this cursed job on!" he exclaimed bitterly. He glared at Jankowski: "You work during the dinner-hour. You too, Stepha."

The prisoners booed as he stamped away up the field.

Stepha Markenski sighed deeply, giving Jankowski a side-long glance. He noticed that her face was pale.

"We must never fall behind again," she murmured.

He did not answer, but they worked on a little faster.

"The sun has come over those trees at last!" she burst out after a while, "I have been watching, oh thank God—five more months now, five more—then it's Spring!"

"Is the Spring so pleasant here?"

"It's not that," she said quickly, "you see, I might get a chance to do some painting—I used to paint, you know; I long to do it again."

She went on cutting with renewed energy.

# CHAPTER FIVE

FROM the bank, where he watched the cows with Stepha Markenski, he could see the low cottages of Klein-Heinrichau, the great black barn in Tieson's yard rising above the plane-trees. The village was not squalid now, the Spring sun was on it, on the white hens wandering over the fields, on the geese, on the patches of new thatch in the roofs. The voices of the children sounded clearly and Jankowski heard the rattle of buckets as a woman went to the pump at the end of the village street. The birch leaves under which they sat were silk against the remoteness of the sky. The sheen of an enchanted sunlight was on the world, on the countless wild flowers; it had struck the distant clouds and the white wings that took a strange bird unerringly sunwards.

"Jack's accordion must madden the others on Sundays," he remarked, nodding towards the British lager; he wondered whether she could hear the faint, reeling strains of *South of the Border*.

For a moment she did not reply. With her back against the tree she gazed into the boughs through which the sunlight came. How familiar was the youthful face on which it fell! Familiar, and yet—by a subtle disharmony between the eyes and lips, by some provocative hint of passion—how strange it was still. Her hair was plaited, parted in the middle and already bleached to a reddish gold by the sun. With the self-absorption which was peculiarly hers, she seemed hardly to breathe, the rise and fall of her breasts was barely perceptible.

77

"At times like this," she said softly, "when we are not worried, when it's peaceful, it should be easy to forget all the bad things, all that has happened—I mean my father . . . and, well the heart gets very sick at times——"

She paused. Her silence disturbed him more than the unconcealed despair of her voice had done. He waited with a vague dread.

"Oh God," she said in a low, hopeless voice, "that terrible little room, the ceaseless, meaningless voices, that's all I long for now—peace, to get away."

He did not reply. He could not; he was appalled by her words, as if they had been the admission of some monstrous defeat.

"What a sordid puzzle it all is," she went on, with the same cold dread in her voice, "human company has become almost intolerable to me now, at times my mind feels like an open wound—every human voice, every glance even, touches it and I nearly wince. Would you call that madness, Anton? You see, there's no escape, no solitude, always that ceaseless babble, and something seems to be fluttering in my mind like the irritation of the wound. Could you understand that I wonder?"

"It will all end sometime," he mumbled.

"It must, it must—something is dead already," she said very low, "I must get away . . . there is a place—I don't know whether I have been there or whether it is a place I have pictured but somewhere on high ground, where one can look on forest and marshland and not see a vestige of human things; the wound would heal there —I know it would! There must be such places. It would take long perhaps, and only by the grace of God," her voice trailed off into a profound silence.

He looked at her in dismay and indignation.

"There is——" he began shakily; he made an inane gesture towards the village, "perhaps I——"

He could not go on—it was damnable. What right had she to inflict such moments of her despair on him. It was like a sordid betrayal of her great dignity. He was familiar with her changing moods, her unquenchable enthusiasms, those beliefs expounded with enchanted eyes, the wild plans to liberate people from Stuthoff, Majdanek—he had heard them all; they had been like dust in his throat. She had even associated him with herself as the champions of some hopeless cause—certain proof of her supreme simplicity.

But never once before had she given him the merest hint of her own hopelessness.

He looked at her again, tenderly; for five months she had attracted and exasperated him with a faith in human nature that was pathetic, unbelieveable. How could he help her? Did she expect him to tell her where peace could be found for a Pole in occupied Europe? Or anywhere else for one who contemplated sufferings that extended to the uttermost ends of the earth? He had seen her eyes at the sight of a whipped horse; she felt such things. And she worried about her father, believing that he was still alive, perhaps tortured.

"If you could paint again," he said suddenly, "I think it would comfort you."

"And do you really think I could ever paint any more?" she asked, "without—oh you don't know what a refined torture it is to long for the solitude and peace the mind needs. Do you think our trampled minds will respond any more to that something in life which is poetry, which is love . . .?"

She was silent for a long time.

"I want to paint again, Anton," she said at last, "you seem to understand. Try to forget this mood I'm in."

"It will pass."

"It is good of you to help me watch the cows on Sunday, forgive me for feeling so fed-up," she went on in a low tone.

"There's not one man in the village who wouldn't do as much for you," he answered, "all the prisoners are in love with you. They call you Madonna, did you know?"

"Zygmus did what he said he would after all," she said, staring into the distance, "he went into the forests and it's the Spring now—there must be plenty of eggs round the shores of Struga Lake. It can't be so bad."

"It will be if he goes on sending us those notes— the Gestapo are not altogether fools."

"He mentioned a gramophone and a wonderful record called *Adio Venezia* . . . the trees are all out now—the people help them too. I wonder who the other three are? Oh, the times I have ridden through those woods."

In the silence that followed her words he remembered the day he had seen her, carefree and beautiful under a blue sky, riding home over her father's land; she had whirled her cane at the yellow leaves and gloried in the colour and peace of the late Polish summer.

"It reaches for miles and miles that forest," she went on, "and he is so clever—how could they know, how could they ever suspect? They couldn't look every- where, and it's so thick in parts. And the adventure— by the way he writes, compared with this slavery, he makes it sound like——" she brought her eyes down from the boughs to his face, as if to make sure that he was not laughing, "almost like paradise."

"He could make hell sound almost like paradise."

He recalled Radek's last dramatic note, the narrow escapes, the astounding adventures on dark nights—oh, life was worth living again! Life was wonderful. The police were already terrified of going into the forest after sunset. And as for food—they lived like Rajahs.

The note had concluded with a passionate appeal for cigarette-ends.

"That sound on the roads," she said suddenly, "it never stops now."

By her voice he knew that her old enthusiasms had returned, and he knew, without looking, that her eyes had brightened, that she listened in a passion of attention. It was that subdued roar from the Deutsch-Eylau road, the familiar sound of an army moving. She listened as though it were an enchanted voice, as if she found in it some note of hope, the promise of a fortunate change.

For days a mighty column had been moving East, tanks and armoured vehicles, gun-carriages, superb horses beneath energetic officers in fine uniforms, smiling, sun-bronzed soldiers, grey staff-cars; Jankowski had watched them raise the dust of the straight, tree-lined roads.

He remembered the day when the first tanks had passed through Klein-Heinrichau, how each tank had been pelted with flowers; he had been returning from work behind the British prisoners and their guard.

"You will never see a sight like this again," Schacter the Foreman had exclaimed, with pride and sadness in his voice. "Look! That is the glory of war, what a fine army going up to fight, with everything to win, with the world before them—conquering! You will never see such an army again—and it fights the worlds, it has the glory, like Napoleon, like Cæsar—how splendid, our glorious *Wehrmacht*—the last real army to go into battle! Look, my friend, look hard, the last—the last time an army will look glorious in the history of Mankind—ah, what horses, and how the officers ride. They are Prussians, those officers, most of them, the best of them! But I am afraid . . . the East, they are going East——"

"Do you think Russia will go to war with Germany?" Jankowski had asked.

"The papers say nothing about it—I don't know," old Schacter would reveal nothing. "I was a prisoner in Russia during the last war—the people seemed kind enough."

Jankowski remembered that all the children had been paraded outside the school and that their lanky teacher had stood with his shaven head held back and his narrow shoulders braced. As if the passing of each tank had released a spring, his long arm had jerked up: 'Heil Hit-lah!' The British prisoners marching in front of Jankowski had started laughing. The one they called Curly had shouted: "Get that hair cut! You sloppy-looking bastard."

A report had been sent into Marienberg about it.

"Lenski's son told Anna that all these troops are going to go through Russia and into India," Stepha Markenski said, "and that Russia has given them permission."

She spoke reluctantly, as if it were almost too indelicate or stupid to mention.

"Most of them believe that," he replied, "they must."

"It's such a long and terrible war, I can see no end to it, but there can only be one end—the love of God is on our side," she said with perfect conviction.

82

For a moment he accepted her words, as he accepted the truth of the blue sky and the sun, the return of Spring. His eyes were on the flat, pale distances of the land. Something was running, or it was a crow flying close to the fields, and there was the far-off line of trees that marked the Deutsch-Eylau road. He saw the dove-coloured steeple of Schonau Church and heard the very faint, but clear peal of its bells.

"The love of God might be on their side," he suggested.

"Oh no," she answered simply, "how can you say that? By the things they have done they have renounced God—as for love, they have renounced that too, love to them is just a tiresome word, a word at which one smiles and sneers and curses. Where could love lodge in such dry, dusty hearts?"

"No," he answered. "They love, and their loves are your loves, their hates your hates."

"No, no, no, you are quite wrong. How could you of all people be right? You say yourself that you neither hate nor love, I have tried to explain to you so often, to explain the love I have for my land, for . . . for mercy and justice——" she paused.

He was astonished at her sudden anger and impatience.

"How can I ever make you understand the meaning of the word love?" she went on in a subdued voice, looking away from him. "I can't give life to the dead. I couldn't show that white cloud to the blind."

He looked at her; she was very close to him, the repose of her supple figure seemed to enhance her youth, her vitality. The sun slanted down upon her, the silver trunk behind her head looked aglow, her face was slightly averted, but the sunrays fell on her neck, making the thin gold chain of her crucifix glint against the white skin. Small winds coming over the meadow stirred the strands of her tawny hair, moved the collar of her blue shirt. He wondered whether, in her simplicity, she was aware of her great temptation.

"I know the meaning of the word," he replied evenly.

"And yet you can say that they love the things that we love: Mercy and freedom . . . justice!" she looked at him with infinite pity.

"Love, justice, freedom," he repeated with exasperation and disgust, "is it love that has plunged the world into misery? Love for the motherland, love for freedom, love for justice! Is that why justice is almost a meaningless word now? And freedom—where is it? Where is this fabulous fruit for which Man is willing to rot his soul until it stinks, stinks before Nature and God? Is this love——?"

"Is what love?"

"You can read the papers," he went on, disregarding her interruption, "there is so much love in the papers now—love of justice, right, freedom; freedom, right, justice—can man hide his festering little soul under these words that grow more shadowy every day? Have you heard the leaders of nations, leaders of Germany, England—their souls are bursting with love, freedom, right, justice; they will fight to the last man for these things, to the last woman—to the last little child for these things that they have turned into shades, shades that come and mock the slaughtered man in his last agonies. Do soldiers talk about these things in the face of death, of mutilation? Freedom and right and their shadowy little brother justice? They know in their hearts. They know, they know——"

"And yet they fight on——"

"Oh yes, they fight, they come; they cheer and polish their boots. Freedom is in peril! They must answer the call as their forefathers did before them; the fire of youth, the force of a tradition that they accept as noble: St. George must slay the Dragon. Listen! Can you hear that low rumble on the Deutsch-Eylau road? Where St. George goes on his way? You can't see from here, it's a little too far, but his sword is flashing, his jack-boots shining, he puffs out his be-ribboned chest and reads in the *Danziger Vorposten* all about the wicked Dragon, and English roads are blocked by St. George going on his way, playing the mouth-organ— reading in the *Daily Mirror* all about the wicked Dragon. At last they confront the Dragon and find themselves staring into their own stupid, bewildered faces——"

"You have lost your temper, you are talking nonsense," she said severely. "Is there no such thing as right and wrong then? Ask somebody who has spent a year in Stuthoff! I cannot understand the twist in your mind, Anton. I cannot . . . yet, perhaps I can—you need a faith, any faith——"

"Even a false one, even faith in the sword, faith in the power of words to excite hate in the name of love? And I never lose my temper by the way."

But he had lost his temper; and had he talked a lot of nonsense? These absurd arguments.

"How can I make you see, I wonder," she murmured. "I know people are dying, I know too well— the thought sickens me, but I know why they die, and all the poor people who are trampled on in Europe, they know why too, if my father is still alive he will know why. Evil must be fought, there are certain ideals on earth, you know—things worth fighting for."

"Ideals!" said Jankowski in disgust. "And you think that every soldier that is dragged into this ghastly farce is possessed by the fire of truth and fine ideals! Every obscure Pole, Frenchman, Englishman—can you believe such nonsense!"

He paused for a moment while he rolled a cigarette; he spilt some of the tobacco and when he looked up he found that she was smiling at him. He was not sure whether she was amused by his arguments or by his clumsy method of making cigarettes.

"By a mere political intrigue Poland might have been dragged into a war against some other land," he went on calmly, "some remote, little known land, or even a land of which the Poles knew nothing—what then? St. George would have gone with his chest puffed out, his conscience clear, as for ideals—he could get them un-rationed in the *Gazeta Polska* or the *Express Poranny* and anything he wanted to know about the wicked Dragon. So wicked that it's quite liable to come on the stage against the glorious, gallant Ally within five years."

"I shall not say any more," she announced, with a mournful shake of her head, "you will never compre-hend Anton—you cannot comprehend—the loves, the deep-rooted loyalties that are part of ourselves, that make us what we are." She ceased, her voice fell with the ring of finality.

He waited, knowing that she would be unable to leave the matter there.

"And yet you loved your mother," she said after a long silence, "very greatly too, I know you did—by the way you speak of her I know. Can your logic explain that away I wonder? Would you have considered the right or wrong if she had been in danger? Poland is my land. I am a Pole, I never can be anything else. It is all

I have now. And you? How terrible! you haven't even got that."

"I would answer that I have the entire world," he said wearily, "if I had the slightest love for it, the slightest loyalty towards the poor fools who devote their time scarring its surface, in their mad-dog efforts to slaughter their own brothers."

"They are coming, it is milking time," she interrupted gently, "I just saw the *Schweizer* go past the Lager—and his wife, I saw that red scarf she wears round her head. I must drive the cows nearer the path. And——"

She paused; he thought that she was about to comment on the stork that relentlessly sought out frogs a few yards away in the meadow, but she sighed and stood up.

"You will never comprehend," she stated simply.

She looked down at him for a moment, as if trying to gauge the extent of his soul's decay.

"Never, never, never," she repeated sadly, and walked away.

One day in the late June of that year, he saw a line of German planes flying Eastwards; they stretched as far as he could see but he had no time to watch them—he was loading hay in the meadow that ran along the edge of a stream, as he sunk his fork into each heap the waggon jerked forward.

"*Holab!*" it stopped again at the next heap. "*Weiter!*" and it moved again. Tieson set the pace, following the waggon like a porpoise in the wake of a ship.

The sound of planes sunk to a murmur, the mere buzzing of an insect. Something rumbled in the East.

The British prisoner packing the load shouted across to his friend on the other waggon.

"Hear that, Jack? Up the Bolshies!"

"Up the Bolshies!" the other roared back. "It won't be long now, Bert!"

But the Poles looked at each other with dubious eyes. The Russians? They had no delusions, Germany or Russia—what was the difference? They had tasted the methods of both.

The next day in the fields, they heard the very distant artillery. Jankowski saw Schacter's *Danziger Vorposten*, the headline underlined in red: EUROPE AT WAR WITH BOLSHEVISM! LUFTWAFFE STRIKES AT RED ARMY!

"If they come here, do you think it will mean liberation?" Stepha Markenski asked him, as they made their way to another field behind the half-loaded waggon.

"Who can say what it will mean?" he answered. "At least, it will be a change."

She stuck her pitch-fork into the hay and perched on the board protruding from the floor of the waggon; her legs dangled—her feet almost touching the dust.

"I had prayed that the English or Americans would free Poland. We don't want the Russians here, Anton —it won't mean freedom, it won't be any freer than it is now—if only it could have been the English or Americans! But the Russians, the Mongols——" she broke off, shaking her head.

"They are human," he said, "they are wild, but full of humanity."

"They are Communists," she answered, "they don't believe in God. Listen! Did you hear that? Surely the guns are nearer than yesterday! In a week this meadow could be a battlefield. They will send you to Siberia for not being a Communist," she spoke lightly, but her eyes told him that she, like the others, felt the tension and unrest.

"I would be a Communist, Stepha."

"Oh yes, I suppose you would. Why don't you register as *Volksdeutche* and become a real Nazi?"

"And be dragged into the *Wehrmacht*?"

"I must say a Mass for your soul, Anton," she said half-seriously, "one day I shall make a pilgrimage to Chenstohova, just for you. Is that the only reason you can find against registering as a German—being dragged into the *Wehrmacht*?"

"It's the strongest."

She took off her wooden-soled sandal and emptied out the dust.

"I can't understand what it is about you I like," she said with the ghost of a frown, "you are cynical, I should think you were treacherous, you're not particularly good-looking even; you are a pagan. Never before have I liked such a hateful person as you——" she began to pick scraps of hay out of her hair and the collar of her shirt. "Anyway," she said, as the waggon turned with a jolt into the next field, "I am not sure that I do like you. I suppose if the Russians come you will do your best to get out of Poland?"

"Of course."

"You won't stay and help in her reconstruction, to heal her wounds. But I shall, I shall work hard after this," she sprang off the board.

But their dreams of liberation faded. The sound of guns grew fainter; in four days it was heard no more and the *Vorposten* was already proclaiming the crushing defeat of a Russian army.

The rainy days of that dolorous Summer brought him near despair. The corn was cut and lay on the wet field.

ALMOST GLORY

They piled the soaking sheaves before the dawn, re-
building stooks that had collapsed during the night's
wind and rain.  Sometimes he worked with the British
prisoners; they talked about their homes, their football-
teams, their red-cross parcels or about France—the
brothels of Rouen and Calais.

Jankowski smoked their cigarettes and listened.  It
amused him to watch their eyes following the erect
figure of Stepha Markenski over the fields, to see their
futile rage when Tieson shouted at her.  Poor devils!
The things they had intended doing to Tieson when
'the Bolshies showed up'.  One morning they gave him
a cake of scented soap and two bars of chocolate for 'our
little Madonna'.

"Don't show the other girls," the wavy haired
prisoner told him, "it will make them jealous."

"But she'll share it with them anyway."

"Will she?  Well it doesn't matter—give it to her,
Anton."

A hundred yards away from them, members of the
Hitler Youth were singing as they marched towards
the woods.

Quite close to them, down the slope of the golden
harvest field, a familiar voice drifted.  As usual, the
lanky Berlin doctor who had once lectured at some
English University, had come out to announce the fall
of another Russian town, and as usual, he had become
involved in a political wrangle with the British prisoners.  He was on a familiar theme:

"Who are you to criticise?  Who are you to be so
righteous?  Have you given the youth of your country
something to sing about?  The boys and girls born in the
Reich now are born into a world of hope—of purpose——"

90

A slow, humorous voice was trying to interrupt: "Listen, cock, listen——"

But the earnest voice ploughed on.

"—they have a road to take, a faith they can devote their lives to. And you? What have you? Disillusion, age, decay warring against Youth. I know England— I've seen the hopeless lads at street corners . . . what do you do for them please? Have you one faith to give them, one clear road to take? They look back on the littered road of their own decay, we point ahead——"

"For God's sake!" the other voice broke in with sudden violence. "that patter gives me a pain in the neck—this bloody road you're on about, take it from me—it stinks, and all that youth patter . . . little cut-throats strutting around thinking they're God almighty. England? Cross the Channel and see, chum—not in a million years. You've given these poor devils a lot of faith in the Future . . . dragged out of their homes——"

The voices ceased abruptly and the little guard slouching behind took his hands from his pockets. Tieson's black dog had appeared round the corner of the barn.

In September, on a day when flags dropped from the low windows of Klein-Heinrichau, Jankowski sweated in the dirt under the threshing-machine. The chaff and waste mounted faster than one man could take it away, but with the sweat and dust in his eyes, Jankowski continued to drag the heavy boxes to the heap outside the barn.

As he jerked out the overflowing box from under the chute, he was vaguely aware of Tieson standing over him.

"I need somebody to help," he said, as calmly as he could.

91

Tieson kicked the empty box under.

"*Herr Gott! Los!* The machine will be blocked, you lazy hound."

Jankowski did not move. He watched the pile mount until the chute was almost covered. Cold fire lay round his heart, burned in his eyes, made his body tremble.

"Are you mad!" Tieson screamed. "*Los! Los!* Faster——"

Jankowski flung the box down with a force that cracked the sides.

"Faster?" he nearly choked over the word, "you dumb swine! Look at my face—look at the sweat! *Jesus Maria!* . . . faster . . .?"

He heard a vague, muffled voice saying: "Be careful, be careful"—the voice of his own clouded reason, or the prisoners shouting from the straw-stack or Stepha Markenski on the thresher? He never knew. He only saw the pale blur of a face, the lifted stick.

The fight must have been very brief; the machine had not even stopped; the waste, gushing out, had half-covered Tieson's left leg and was sticking to the blood under his eyes.

Jankowski staggered out into the sunlight, making his way towards the straw-stack. Stepha Markenski was following him, speaking in a voice he hardly recognised.

"They will take you away now . . . oh, Anton, why did you do it? Anton, I've hated you at times . . . but this——"

The flat lands reached away into the blue distances, never had it looked so wide, so free; wherever it was they took him, no breath of the spacious world would find him again.

Somebody shook him violently.

"What the hell are you waiting for, you bloody fool! You've knocked that madman cold—for Christ's sake! They're running up the road—Lenski, the guard . . . take that horse—have a shot at those woods . . . God it's a running chance!"

"Hopeless, you fool," Jankowski snapped. "No, quick! the horse out of that waggon—I can try if . . . that is——"

"Good luck, cock."

Between them they almost threw him up to the horse's back; he heard their great cheer as the strong muscles sprang to life beneath him.

He would last an hour, at most an hour, but he would reach the woods; already he could distinguish the birch-trees, the pines with the sun on their topmost branches. If only he could last until night!

He thudded over a field of stubble and reached the forest path, he kept to it for half-a-mile, the shadows were darkening round him. He slid to earth and ran into a plantation of small firs, as he stumbled on the branches stung his face, got into his eyes, but his thoughts caressed the only hope there was: the railway line, the Southbound frieght trains that ran through Pomorze and the Struga forest.

He found a deep ditch, matted over with brambles, and among its age-collected leaves he lay and listened. Somewhere above him a bird with a strange cry was circling, the first bird of the darkness. He heard the very distant, but clear 'pheep—pheep—pheep—' of a whistle.

He lay there until there was no sound but the old leaves creeping through countless unseen branches with a murmur softer than the lightest footfalls. A season was passing, leaf by leaf into the dark, wet earth; it was the most friendly voice he had heard for days. He found a path and followed it until it came out on a dim, vast plain. One black tree shuddered in the wind.

A train clanked through the night a long way away on the Gruziadz line, the weird shriek of its whistle was the cry of freedom itself. He walked on quickly, past great piles of stones, the light of the hidden moon had struck the jagged fringe of low-lying cloud and he turned often to look at it, it was beautiful, as if summer lightning had quivered over the skyline and been suspended there. In the dimness the loom of an immense cloud-bank reached away Southwards. There was no sound, but he fancied the muffled boom of the Eastern guns.

Freedom! The ghost of that great illusion was in the wind that blew over the plain and stirred the grass by the path, the great illusion for which men killed and died out there in the whiteness of Russian snows, under the insufferable heat of an African sun, on the pitiless oceans . . .

*"Halt! Wer da? HandeHoch! HOCH——!"*

Slowly, he put his hands up. They had sprung from behind the stones or out of the earth with their tall helmets, their sub-machine guns.

They had waited.

# CHAPTER SIX

A line of prisoners was working on the road, filling the ruts with broken bricks. Summer was dying, yellow leaves fell against the blue sky. Anton Jankowski thought of winter and its bitter cold. Half-a-mile down the road he saw the signpost to Lende and Keplin, pointing with hellish mockery—the road led somewhere, through fields and forests, through brilliant cities where laughing people sauntered home in the sun. To him it was a fragment of road suspended over Eternity.

*"Arbeit! Los! Los!"*

S.S. men strutted arrogantly along the weary line, smoking cigarettes and grinding the ends into the dust with the heels of their jack-boots, revelling in the stare of a hundred longing eyes. Once he would have attributed their senseless ferocity to a serious defeat in the East, or the outbreak of a revolution in Berlin, but time had cured the mania for seeking a wide significance in their moods. No doubt they were infuriated by having to watch a gang of wretched scarecrows on one of the last warm days of the summer, instead of loitering with their sweethearts by the river Linsk. But they would never know the longing, the heartbreak that was in the warmth of the sun, in the smell of the old leaves, in the glittering, murmuring life on the Allenstein road.

If only he could get a little peace—time to think and plan an escape, but he was always on the alert like a hunted animal; always some pain, some voice gnawed at his nerves. He could hear the injured whine of Wasserman, the little man from somewhere in Western Germany.

"To drag out the rest of my days," Wasserman was saying, "cursing the God I loved, cursing life . . ."

Jankowski tried to drown the voice by smashing in the bricks, but he could not, it seemed to envelope him like a substance, sickening, cloying—possessing his mind and killing his thoughts.

"Fools have said that a man can rise above circumstances," while he spoke, Wasserman glanced round continually, "there are circumstances like a ten-ton weight on the mind. Rise above! I have fought against it——"he turned his grimacing face towards Jankowski: a face impossible to imagine in repose. "I struggled up but my mind is crushed and they cannot free me now—press something against the flesh for a long time, when you take it away you can feel it still. The mind is like that. Why don't you ever speak, comrade? Dreaming of liberation or what? The word still means something to you because you've only been here nine days."

Jankowski toiled on.

The broken bricks arrived in waggons that were driven by Poles whose eyes were sympathetic. He hardly looked at them. What did they care? To them it was just another job, taking loads to a gang of prisoners on a road. Did they know that the road was invested with hopelessness, with its weary bent forms, the uncomprehensive stare of desperate eyes? Perhaps those who raised the dust with their cars made rapturous comments of the beauty of this road, on the birch-trees that graced it in summer and gave it a dreamlike perfection during a white frost.

"My memory is not what it was," Wasserman was saying earnestly. "My own part of the country—the memory of it comes to me in a few pictures, even that day seems a hundred years ago, the gloomy station,

made more gloomy by its atmosphere of constant fare-
wells. But I remember that soldier, the fairly old chap
who was saying good-bye to his wife and a small child—
very small, with a pinched, bewildered face, a face that
could have masked a vast stupidity or a vast wisdom—
you see, I remember these things; and suddenly it
howled, kept on howling——"

Wasserman paused while an S.S. man swaggered by.

"Its little spirit had succumbed to that atmosphere
of sorrow," he continued solemnly, "how it howled! I
shall never forget it. You think that there is nothing in
all this, you think it had the toothache or was just fed-
up with standing on a draughty platform? Ah, but to me
it was somehow symbolic, not long born but already
plunged into the madness and despair of war. You see,
I always see a little deeper than the rest."

He turned to Jankowski with triumph in his sunken
eyes.

"I know that you are planning to escape."

Jankowski glared back, longing to squeeze the skinny neck and cut off that voice. Why must this man
drone on? Why this eternal mania to impress his
fellows? Even here, on the brink of death, this shrunken
wretch was blind to all but his own cankering little
vanities. Had the voice conveyed hatred he could have
suffered it; it conveyed nothing but the idea of groping
towards an impalpable something, something that could
never be expressed, but could only be insinuated
through an accumulation of disconnected anecdotes.

"You cannot hear the guns from here, it's a little too
far, yet they are booming out death and chaos day and
night——"

The high tones, insincere, almost theatrical, were too
much for Jankowski.

"For God's sake!" he implored, "don't worry your-self—let them boom. If you only knew how sick I am of your voice—of every voice——"

He lifted his eyes from the road and the bowed forms that shuffled over it. He saw a little girl squatting on the path near the building where they stored the tools: she was brushing the flag-stones with an old clothes-brush, every now and then peering up through a profusion of pale hair and making happy, inarticulate sounds. She began to crawl away towards the corner and he watched the little body until it disappeared.

When he turned he noticed another man watching the corner of the house, as if eager for the child's reappearance. It was the man in charge of the party—*Scharführer* Ohlau, whom they called the 'Moon-man'. He stood on the bank that separated the road from the fields with his hands on his hips; while he watched he smiled wistfully. Ohlau was unique among the S.S. guards, he rarely raised his voice above a reproving '*Nah!*'. But Jankowski remembered the tales he had heard about the 'Moon-man', his spells of madness, during which the prisoners were afraid to lift their eyes from the road, or his genial moods when he questioned them about their families and homes, speaking as one human being to another. During such a mood his colleagues were appalled; to them this was the spell of madness.

Wasserman was talking again.

"There is a way, there is one way—don't look at me for God's sake, work as if I were not speaking but listen —every third day a van comes into the camp, you must have seen it, a little grey one that brings the rations—it is driven by a Pole——"

"Then escape!" Jankowski burst out. "Why haven't you escaped before?"

"Not so loud!" Wasserman glanced round furtively. "That regret is eating into my soul," he went on with passionate sincerity, "why haven't I escaped before! Why, why, why? As you see, it is too late for me now."

He ceased and bent over the shovel that seemed almost too heavy for him to lift. Jankowski's rage was swept away on a great wave of pity. He tried to speak, but what words could comfort this poor, God-forsaken-devil?

"Don't give up hope," he said at last, "no doubt you curse me for saying it, it is all I can say. Our bodies and minds will be healed one day—God knows why I say this, it must be the words of a girl I knew on a farm; I remember her speaking of some place above the forests and marshes, somewhere where there was no sign of human things; her words had more meaning than I thought——"

"She was a fool," Wasserman broke in testily, "a romantic fool, or she had never known a life like this. A farm. What wouldn't I give for one week on a farm!"

"She knew how to hope," Jankowski went on thoughtfully. "I remember when I met her after the first year of the occupation, after she had lost everything——"

"It is you who are the romantic fool," Wasserman interrupted with spiteful triumph, "but why tell me this?"

"She had lost everything," Jankowski repeated slowly, his eyes wandering up and down the ancient, tree-lined road, "her family, her home in Pomorze. She was one who would never give up hope. She was——"

He ceased. Why was he speaking of her? Did he hope to draw strength from the memory of a girl's fortitude? His eyes followed the road until it turned

South to Lende and Keplin; turned into a region he had never seen, would never see; turned away into light and life—and he would be trapped in this fragment of road until he was too weak to stand . . .

"*Los! Los!*"

Slowly, methodically, he crushed the broken bricks into the ruts. The guard who had shouted watched him for a while then turned away.

Jankowski stopped again.

The sun was going down towards the rim of a distant forest that reached into Pomorze. The waggon that had brought the final load of bricks rumbled back through the white dust. Furtive eyes began to glance at Ohlau who was still on the bank, thoughtfully pouting his thick lips, narrowing his eyes, tapping his gleaming jack-boots with a twig. He seemed to be absorbed by gigantic problems, but the wrecks who hungered for a sign to tell them that their work was done, knew that he was posing and that he was very conscious of them all and of his power. Because he knew their eyes were upon him he tried to look inscrutable, God-like.

At last, as if it had just occurred to him, he looked at his watch. He nodded to the other guards.

"*Feirabend,*" the word went down the line.

With his enigmatic smile Ohlau told five men to collect the tools while the rest of the prisoners were formed into threes by bawling guards and counted.

"*Marsch!*"

Clogs shuffled through the dust.

"Lift your feet! One—two—three—four . . . One—two—three—four. *Herr Gott!* the swines."

Frenzied yells could not keep them in step.

Jankowski stared at the pair of clogs in front, at the end of a foot-cloth dragging in the dust. He must keep his mind away from the long march ahead. He noticed scarlet berries on the road; they had reached the part where the mountain-ash trees began. There were miles and miles to go yet.

"Move! Move! You swines! Throw your legs up! One—two—three—four."

The S.S. guards screamed continuously, hysterically, like exultant boys who are half-afraid.

The clogs rose and fell. Still he concentrated on the man in front, on the end of foot-cloth dragging in the dust. He must keep his mind away from the long march ahead. His left instep was raw where the clog rubbed it; the rag with which he had hoped to ease it had slipped. Would they never reach the outskirts of Maskowitz?

Somebody clutched at his sleeve.

He was too weary to take any notice. The screams of the S.S. guards, the hunger, his bleeding feet, his aching limbs—these things seemed to reduce the Universe to a black tunnel of pain through which he struggled on and on, not because he saw light ahead, but because he was forced on by an age-old instinct of self-preservation.

His sleeve was clutched again; somebody was speaking imperatively.

"Please, what were you saying? It was you, wasn't it, back there on the road? Please, about that girl . . . the girl from Pomorze . . ."

Jankowski still concentrated on the flapping foot-cloth; he felt that if he turned or spoke it would break a spell, that he would never reach the gates.

"Tell me, tell me, that girl you mentioned, what was her name? Tell me, man."

An S.S. guard was yelling a few yards away from them.

"Swines! *Los! Los!*"

"Brother," the voice went on steadily, "was it Stepha Markenski?"

Stepha Markenski! The name belonged to another sphere. It had no meaning in this world of animals.

"Don't torture me! Brother, was it Stepha Markenski?"

Jankowski turned and was momentarily startled out of his weariness. Surely he knew those eyes!

"Yes," he said hurriedly, "it was. It was. It was she."

There was no reply. The man was falling behind again, going out of reach, and there were questions Jankowski longed to ask.

They were entering the little town of Maskowitz. He had a vague impression of shop windows and queues of women, of bicycles propped up against the pavement. A few people stopped and watched the column; their faces were expressionless. What did they care? But the town was a milestone on the march 'home', they had come three kilometres and they had two more to go.

Under the bridge, past the little *Lazarett*, past the saw-mill where the French prisoners of war worked.

"One—two—three—four!"

Past the shop with the long white loaves in the window—Ernst Schultz, *Backerei*. In half-an-hour he would be hurrying across the Camp with his *kaffee-ersatz* and bread-ration. In half-an-hour he could rest.

The road climbed towards the Camp. This was the final, terrible test of endurance. Sometimes his mouth fell open and his head dropped; then he would curse himself, compress his lips, lift his head.

The man was at his side again, touching his arm. The voice was indistinct:

"Is she . . . you were saying to Wasserman that she was . . ."

"Who are you?"

"She is my girl, my daughter——"

"And you have been here—in this place—since . . . my God——"

Jankowski fell into an appalled silence. He turned to look at the man about whom he had heard so much, but he was too tired and stumbled as he turned, Lucien; Markenski was blurred by dust.

"But was it so bad there, on this farm, was she so thin, so hungry?"

"No, no, no," he answered with a kind of desperation, "did I say that? Wasserman must have maddened me! Hungry? No, no, it wasn't so bad there at Heinrichau. I wish to God I was there now! Only wait a little longer, I shall tell you everything after roll-call, everything."

"Yes, but one more thing: does she know where I am, does she know about Maskowitz?"

"She knows nothing," Jankowski mumbled wearily, "after roll-call."

"What block are you in?"

"Three, but I shall be by the wire at the corner of the wash-house ten minutes after roll-call."

Again he concentrated on the pair of clogs that rose and fell in front.

At last, when he looked up, he saw the look-out posts perched above the Camp. Emaciated wrecks began to lift their eyes from the road, hungry for a glimpse of the gate whose image had kept them stumbling through the dust. The day was done; the gate into a concentration camp was the single goal of their lives, a hot drink, the bread-ration, sleep—a brief sleep.

The final checking-in outside the gate marked the limit of Jankowski's endurance. Ohlau strolled along the column with his enigmatic smile and his mild eyes played over the prisoners while he told them to get into an orderly formation; he was patient, almost benevolent, like a school teacher organising a children's treat. He seemed disdainful of the furious guards who shoved them into place.

Jankowski watched him, and the little man from the office, go down the column twice, three times. Couldn't the swines count? Or did they do this on purpose? He longed to sit down, his knees felt suddenly weak. Was it right this time?

"*Marsch!*"

When all the prisoners were through the gate Jankowski paused for a moment, but he could not see Lucien Markenski. Under his tired eyes the figures that shuffled away in their striped suits were invested with a baffling sameness. Some of the men who lined up daily in the hope of getting extra soup, were already going to the end of the queue that began at the cookhouse and straggled for a hundred yards across the sandy earth. Tins with long wire handles, old frying-pans, mess-tins, any vessel capable of holding soup they held in readiness. They had waited in vain as usual—S.S. men were already going from hut to hut and driving out the prisoners for roll-call.

On the other side of the wire that ran behind the wash-house of Maskowitz, a path had been worn by patrolling guards. Just beyond the path the ground fell steeply to the river Linsk three hundred feet below. As he waited by the wash-house after roll-call, Jankowski tried not to see the barbed-wire through which he looked; tried to cast his sight beyond the bleak huts. From the belt of reeds that followed the river's Western bank the land was flat as far as he could see in the fading light. The Linsk reflected the strange sky, he could follow its course by the traces of red in the fields and marshes, as if the dying sun had bled over the land.

Three belated yachts had sailed up from Maskowitz, a few people were still strolling along the river, mostly soldiers with their sweethearts. Sometimes they lifted their faces towards the grim Camp on the hill. Jankowski wondered whether they could see the men who moved behind the wire. Did they even think of them? He had never thought of them himself a month ago.

The yachts began tacking back towards Maskowitz. In the Camp behind him, men were still moving about, their eyes on the ground as if following the tracks of some fabulous beast. Dreaming of liberation, nursing hopes or fermenting hatreds, or merely passing·by in despair, with no thought but for to-morrow's bread-ration.

"Ah, I thought it must be you. You have been waiting? I am sorry."

"I came here directly after roll-call," Jankowski answered, turning towards Markenski, "I always do."

"Now tell me about her—I suppose it was just slavery?"

The voice was cultured and very calm, but Jankowski saw the look on the other's face, the tense, indrawn expression of one whose mind is clouded by pain, of one who has concentrated, fanatically, upon something within himself; a shred of hope, a philosophy, even pride.

"I can tell you that she was a Godsend in that place," Jankowski answered, "her dignity, her fortitude——"

"Ah, she had that," Markenski murmured, "but please tell me how she was—was she well, was the life so hard?"

He spoke without looking at Jankowski; with his hands behind his back emphasising the roundness of his shoulders. His eyes, staring at the water below, were the blue of his daughter's eyes: the blue that goes with dark hair.

As Jankowski spoke of Klein-Heinrichau, the place he had loathed mocked him; there had been enough bread there, and two soups a day, comparative freedom—tobacco! In retrospect even Tieson seemed almost considerate.

A low voice interrupted him.

"God—if I could have foreseen this. That sordid life; my poor little girl . . ."

The voice ceased and Jankowski too was silent;—there seemed no more he could say.

The skyline was already hidden by a mauve haze, but the Linsk still gleamed in the reeds below them. They heard movements in the huts, the sound of clogs on the wooden boards; occasionally beams from the search-light in the look-out post played along the wire.

"And I thought she was so safe in Cracow," Markenski murmured. "I had no idea, I never guessed at first when I heard you talking to Wasserman, but suddenly, on the march back, I remembered your words and I seemed to know it was she."

Jankowski did not answer. With his eyes on the darkening landscape he wondered how long he would have to listen—trapped and exasperated—to the pain in this other man's voice. And it was not his affair; he had no ties, no obligations, no land, no faith—not a single soul on earth. Why had chance thrust this upon him? This incongruous role in the human tragedy or farce or whatever it was?

Markenski talked about his 'little girl' as if he feared silence, feared some ghost it might raise. Below them a dinghy drifted with the current of the Linsk, its oars raised in the air like the feelers of some strange insect or hands lifted in prayer. A man on the bank stopped to light his pipe, shielding the match against the wind, then walked on, his arm round the waist of his sweetheart; three boys were throwing stones at something floating on the water. At Jankowski's side the shadow of a man talked on, his clogs protruding from under the frayed edges of those abominable trousers, striped blue and grey like the trousers of a dirty pyjama-suit.

Listening, Jankowski began to picture Malkow in the years before the war; above all he pictured Stepha Markenski. He could see her, slim and golden headed, on the tennis court or running into the long, low kitchen of the old house, with its twisted fly-papers and the cats jumping on to the table. Even as a little child he saw her, her little bare feet strutting through the warm, dusty sand.

"She believed," Markenski was saying, "through everything she will keep the faith—the faith that has been the only light in the darkness of these years; the only glimmer of hope has come from love."

"She had a great faith!" Jankowski exclaimed softly.

Simple and mysterious, her image had come back to him with the vivid, tragic force of something lost for ever, of salvation missed; leaving an emptiness he strove to fill by evoking yet more clearly her ways, the subtle inflection of her speech, the audacity and tenderness of her eyes—her personality enigmatic in its simplicity.

"I thought you were a foreigner at first, perhaps a Frenchman," Markenski remarked suddenly, "but of course, when you spoke——"

To Jankowski, this sounded like an invitation to talk about himself; dispassionately he began to do so. Before long there was a soft interruption from Markenski.

"So it was your father who escaped from Kassel? But I remember it all well—they called him the mad Englishman—and I have seen you before, my friend: the small boy with a queer green cap pulled over his ears, driving through Likora with his mother."

Markenski passed a hand across the upper half of his face, as if to brush something away.

"I used to see your chaise," Jankowski answered.

He began to talk of England, of his return to Poland and of the visits to his mother's grave.

"And you haven't been to Pallow for a long time," Markenski said slowly.

"Not once during the occupation."

"I was wondering—but of course, you must know all about it; I mean that Jewish gravestones have been smashed? I know because I remember we had some here on the road."

Jankowski did not reply.

"You are thinking of that stone?" Markenski said sadly, "please don't, it does no good—and after all so few have been smashed. I used to think of those things too, but now——" he shrugged, "but please tell me why they sent you away from that farm she was on."

Jankowski told of his attack on Tieson, of his arrest and the subsequent trial at Danzig.

"Your arrival here was inevitable," Markenski informed him, "this is the main Camp for a wide area, it is one of the best."

Jankowski wondered whether the reference to Maskowitz as one of the best camps was the truth or some pathetic attempt at sarcasm.

"How is it that you have lived so long in this place?" he asked.

Markenski looked at him and smiled faintly.

"I don't know," he answered, "the days pass, at the end of each day we congratulate ourselves for living through it—why congratulate I don't know; the animal desire to survive mingled with the human capacity to wonder, perhaps. Did she ever talk about me?"

"Very often," Jankowski said. "Like her, I suppose you hate these people?"

"Hatred? No, no, you see, I want to win, brother. Revenge, hatred—that will not do; I still remember that these people, these S.S. fellows, are just human beings —they have forgotten that we are, I know, but we must never forget that they are, for the love of Christ! When we do we are beaten; they have converted us—God knows too many of us are converted now. And how many of us never needed converting?"

A searchlight beam swooped along the wire and went out. The landscape was already dark, but for the Western sky and its faint reflection in the Linsk. Markenski was silent; it was the silence of hopelessness.

It was broken at last by a whisper.

"I cannot go on here now."

Jankowski did not answer; there was no answer to the quiet despair and conviction in the other's voice.

"I must get away, I must, she has no one."

"You mean?"

"That I can't go on here now, with thoughts of her slaving. I must get away."

"You mean escape? . . ."

"Escape," Markenski repeated with soft bitterness, "yes, but what earthly chance? But I must get out, if I were shot, well it wouldn't be so much—a bullet in me would only lay a ghost—but to drag on here with that thought? My God!"

Once again he passed a hand across the upper half of
his face.

"Oh yes, escape, it sounds easy. Three men tried to
dig under the wire once, and somebody else tried to
break away from a working party on the road; they were
caught and beaten to death. Yet there must be a way—
some way. Have you ever thought of escape?"

"Of little else," Jankowski answered. "What do you
know about the Moon-man?"

"Ah, so you think that Ohlau would be a help,"
Markenski said gravely. "My friend, that man is the
most ardent Nazi of the lot, but he is a weird devil—he
talked to me once, spoke of some great poem he had
written in his youth. I think he hates me now. He has
favourites and they have a chance of escape; he has
given men good jobs, especially the traitors, that's why
Vitek is our block-leader, he reported a man who stole
some potatoes from behind the cook-house. You see
how it is?"

"I see."

"I have sometimes considered a plan," Markenski
went on in his gentle, cultured voice, "I mean cut under
the wire at night. Trains run through that forest one
can see from the road where we work—you must have
heard them shunting and pulling out of the marshalling
yard at Tarnsee . . . ah, if we could only reach that yard,
brother; do you know that if you jumped a freight train
there and stayed on it for eleven stations, you would be
six kilometres from Malkow?"

"It would be hard to pick the right train in a large
yard."

"Yes, but half-a-kilometre North of the yard there is
a forester's house on the fringe of the wood, the trains
pass within four hundred yards of it and the freight

trains go slowly there because of a steep gradient. You couldn't go wrong if you jumped a Southbound train there."

"How would you cut the wire?"

"I have thought of that too, there is a young Pole in my block who works with the Lende party—I think he could smuggle some pliers into the Camp."

"But the searchlight," Jankowski persisted, "they sweep over the wire every minute."

"No, not every minute." Markenski's soft voice sounded almost like an apology. "Do you know, I have stood here at times and the light has not shone along this side for quite a long time? Of course, there is the patrolling guard; I know the risk is great, my friend, I know, I know."

Jankowski did not answer for a moment. He could dimly see the emaciated face, could distinguish the slight form in its striped suit. There was pathos in the spirit of this man, who had dragged himself through the hopeless squalor of innumerable days at Maskowitz and now talked of escape. Suddenly, with great clearness, he pictured Stepha Markenski riding beside him along the shore of the Struga lake and explaining that her father was a dreamer. Perhaps it were better if she never saw him again.

"You are not fit enough for escape," he said, "how long could you last without food, without shelter?"

"You don't understand," Markenski replied, with a faint suggestion of impatience, "I wouldn't care much what happened if I could only get out. As for death—it wouldn't be so unwelcome as all that, I am sick of it all now and I know I could never settle down to any sort of life again. The thought that Stepha was safe in Crakow kept me going. But now——"

111

"I understand."

The searchlight beam swept along the wire, rested on them for a moment then swept on again.

"I am tired," Jankowski said, "you must be too. It will be that cursed road again to-morrow; I shall see you. Try not to worry, she has food and shelter and there will be warmth there when the winter comes. That is something."

Markenski turned half-eagerly, as if about to speak, but he turned slowly away again. For a moment Jankowski hesitated, then he mumbled "good-night."

He made his way past the wash-house and entered his own block. He was tired, but he knew he would not sleep; he was not yet used to the stink, the lice, the footfalls of the patrolling guard; but the others in the hut slept like the dead, their unshaven features gleaming pallidly under the mess-tins and few belongings on the shelves. Only the long face of a Jew seemed to have retained a kind of idiot curiosity; the light fell on his glasses as he propped himself up on his elbows and Jankowski's eyes met the inscrutable, yellowish reflection; he could not tell whether the other studied him, watched every movement he made, or whether he was lost to the world, lost in a profound, hopeless meditation.

Automatically his hands began to go into his pockets, seeking the tobacco-dust which he knew was not there. But he had to do it. Even purposeless actions seemed to ward off insanity. There was not much time left now. The mind could rot and die, these men who slept round him were dead. There was not much time, liberation was a dream.

He thought of the Moon-man, that ardent Nazi who had favourites among the prisoners, who rewarded treachery . . .

# CHAPTER SEVEN

HE rested on his shovel and thanked God for the unexpected peace that had stolen upon the road. The S.S. men had lost interest in their charges; Ohlau scraped his nails, his head a little on one side, as if he listened to the voice that came from the white house further down the road:

> *"Und sollte mir ein leid geschehn,*
> *Wer wird bei der Laterne stehn*
> *mit dir, Lili Marleen?*
> *mit dir, Lili Marleen."*

The voice was sad, as if the singer had tears in her eyes.

The signpost that pointed to Lende and Keplin was now a yellow speck against the fields, beyond it, like a wreath of smoke or a shadow, was the forest which reached into Pomorze. Jankowski's eyes lingered over its dark blue rim; it raised maddening thoughts of escape. If he ever reached it they would not get him again. He looked at the dejected figure scraping dirt into the ruts a few yards away. Last week Markenski had talked of breaking out of the Camp, but since then he had been dumb, hopeless, too weary even to ask questions about his 'little girl'.

"Rest," Jankowski said with sudden exasperation: "take a break while you've got a chance."

Markenski rested on his shovel for a moment; made a vague gesture towards the down-stretching distances invested with remote peace by the Autumn sun.

"The world looks beautiful," he said softly: "dear

113

God! That wind—the freedom of it! My friend, I want
to tell you everything now. Come over here a little; we
can pretend we are moving these bricks over. I am going to-night. Directly darkness falls.''

"Going?"

"Going. Escaping, breaking out. It is now or never:
Winter's coming. I have planned it all."

"What is the plan?"

"It is really quite simple."

He began to tell Jankowski the plan. It was more
than simple; it was pathetic.

"What do you think of it?"

"Hopeless," Jankowski answered: "even if you had
the luck to cut through the wire——"

He was interrupted by an urgent whisper: "Work
on. Ohlau is standing a few yards behind us."

He worked on for a while, then glanced behind him.

Ohlau was startlingly close but seemed lost in some
pleasurable meditation. His thick lips protruded slightly; his eyes were on something in the middle distance.
His face was thoughtful and in repose, the face of one
who has watched all his life, with pity and understanding.

"He's dreaming," Jankowski murmured: "what are
you worrying about?"

"Work on," Markenski repeated imperatively, without taking his eyes from the road.

The dust drifted into Jankowski's face; he was surrounded by the sound of shovels scraping. There were
poison and despair in the warmth of the sun, in the
blueness of the sky. It seemed that the war, the battle-
fronts, the hopes of liberation had retreated far beyond
his horizon; that he would toil on until he had lost the
power to reason, until he was like the others with their
dull, uncomprehensive eyes. But at least, they were

past feeling the madness and frustration; they were dead; they were nothing but a line of striped suits against the dirty grey of a long road. Their haggard eyes were not human eyes; their bony fingers were not human fingers.

But they cherished memories, they were painfully eager to show the smudged, frayed photographs of themselves, their wives and children, as if to prove that once they had been dignified and respected. Wasserman was continually showing these testimonials to his vanished respectability. Jankowski had seen them, he was sick of seeing them—Wasserman smiling in a well-creased suit, Wasserman looking self-conscious in a bathing-costume, Wasserman and his ugly, genial looking wife with their house in the background.

Ohlau was watching him.

The knowledge came upon him like a cold feeling in the heart. He did not look round; with a vague unrest he began to shovel the bricks towards the middle of the road. Those insane plans of escape had been overheard? What would it mean?

For a while he worked on without a pause; then turned and looked Ohlau straight in the face. It was un-real and sinister—the S.S. man was looking at him with pity, with a tolerant smile. The look disturbed him more than one of rage or contempt could have done. He began to work again; the dust blew up into his face.

He heard Ohlau coming towards him over the bricks. He was tapped on the shoulder.

"Come with me."

The words sounded like a death-sentence. He stumbled over the ruts. Ohlau led him to the other side of the road and pointed to one of the drains that were cut in the bank. It had grown over and partly fallen in.

ALMOST GLORY

ALMOST GLORY

"This must be cleared," he looked at Jankowski with the ghost of a smile: "Don't hurry. Take your own time. But it must be done well. Understand?"

Jankowski nodded. He began to cut down the side of the trench, inwardly cursing the weakness that had made his hands tremble. Ohlau watched with his shining jackboots planted firmly on the road, his hands on his hips.

"So, so. Good. That is good," he said when Jankowski had cleared the drain. "That is neatly done. I believe there are three more further on. Come."

The voice was normal and kind, coming from an S.S. man it impressed Jankowski as might the outburst of a maniac. They went to the next drain. Without a word Ohlau sauntered off down the road towards the white house. Within three minutes he was back.

"Where do you come from?" he demanded suddenly.

"Pomorze."

"Pomorze? You mean West Prussia. There is no such place as Pomorze. That land is ours."

Jankowski did not answer. Men had been shot for uttering the wrong word at Maskowitz, for having the wrong expression on their faces even. He worked on, very conscious of the tall, elegant man whose shadow fell across the drain.

"Pomorze——! *Herr Gott!* The cheek of you Poles. But you seem different, you look different. You remind me of von Schirach."

For a while there was only the sound of shovels scraping over the road and a waggon bringing more broken bricks.

"Yes. The Corridor is ours," Ohlau continued forcibly: "It was and always will be."

"Of course," assented Jankowski, who was ready to swear that the whole of Europe was German and always

116

would be. What did it matter to him? An outcast without race or faith, whose only philosophy was the logical acceptance of a mad world.

Once more the harsh sound of scraping shovels filled the pause in a conversation which—to Jankowski—was sinister and fantastic.

"God, but I'm sick of this road!" Ohlau exclaimed with violence: "and all this lousy country round here, flat, ugly, God-forsaken. I think I only stick it because it's about the furthest I can get away from my wife. What a woman! God knows why I married her. God knows. What about you, von Schirach, are you married?"

"No."

"Ah, you see, I thought you looked sensible. You think Maskowitz is bad? Marriage is worse, believe me, my friend, my dear von Schirach. I believed in God before I married. I used to go to church like a good boy." Ohlau shook his head and sighed: "Yes, yes, away I used to trot every Sunday . . ."

Jankowski worked on silently, trying to piece together the scraps of information he had had about the Moon-man. Wasserman had told him that Ohlau's genial moods presaged a spell of madness.

"We shall be in Moscow before the Winter," Ohlau went on: "I have three brothers on that front. I shall thank God when it's over—at least I shall thank the Führer. I hate it, you know, the horror and the suffering; I hate to think of our boys out there. Yes," he continued with sudden enthusiasm, "but when the New Order comes, when all the damned Jews are kicked out Europe will thank the Führer. Look what he's done for us! The hope, the faith in the future, after the dust and chaos of the last war. You must admit he is a very great man."

"Very."

Jankowski repeated the word to himself with fury and disgust. Blind loyalties, patriotism, hero-worship, he met them everywhere, an impenetrable wall of insanity. Or had his own mind been twisted in its infancy? He had never found anything to worship in the out-worn farce of life; the most solemn hero was a pitiful jester, with bells in his cap, madness, mockery and despair in his most righteous utterances. Hero-worship, patriotism—he lived under the shadow of these things. They would kill him in the end.

A line of girls came over the slope of a field, piling sheaves. Everywhere over the hazy, golden landscape, waggons were going to and fro, bringing in the corn. The girls stopped singing when they saw the prisoners; they were Poles, it was the only way they could show their sympathy. Leaves were floating down across the road; twisting, catching the sun, so many were falling now, they invested the road with a vague unreality where it turned South for Keplin. Markenski had been right, it would be too late to escape in a month—in a fortnight.

Ohlau pushed the toe of his jack-boot through the fallen leaves; he picked up a twig and began to peel it; then he threw it into the middle of the road. The sudden, significant silence of the girls in the field seemed to have disturbed him.

"I think," he said slowly, "if I were given information about an escape——"

He broke off. He glanced at Jankowski, with the ghost of a smile.

Jankowski grinned like an idiot. His mouth was dry; he could hardly breath; he was being stifled by the beating of his heart.

"I have a reward for information," Ohlau went on in a hard, casual voice. "More than one reward. Six men work in the woods, cutting stakes; it is a good job. I gave it to them. Everyday they get extra soup, everyday they get a cigarette or tobacco—or both, my dear von Schirach."

"I have seen them march out," Jankowski muttered, without looking up. "Which wood is it?"

Ohlau pointed Southwards, towards the rim of forest. "They get a lorry at Maskowitz."

Jankowski began to scrape away the earth and leaves from the drain. Dry throat, trembling hands——! Where was his strength? The forest that went into Pomorze. Into Pomorze! He must be going mad. He was chained to the road, to a patch of road that fell into the abyss a hundred yards away. He had worked here for a month or a thousand years. But he saw the fringe of the Struga forest as clearly as he saw the leaves and mud at his feet; he saw the lizards wriggling over the warm sand and through the coarse grass. He could hear the bird whose clear whistle perfected the magic of the blue sky and the green pine-woods. Girls with scarlet bands round their blond hair were laughing on the Likora road . . .

"So Markenski wants to escape," Ohlau murmured thoughtfully, as if communicating with himself.

"Who doesn't!" Jankowski muttered recklessly.

Ohlau took no notice. He looked across at the girls in the field and waved. Not one waved back. He cursed them under his breath, glancing furtively along the road as if to see whether their blasphemous disrespect had been witnessed.

"Don't bank too much on the fact that you remind me of von Schirach," he said grimly, staring at Jankowski's clogs. "What do you know about Markenski's plans?"

"I know they are mad."

"I can believe it," Ohlau answered with unexpected gravity. He lifted sombre eyes to Jankowski's face: "Listen. I want to tell you something; give you some idea of the kind of man I am. Did you see those girls in the field—the way they took no notice? I dare say they are looking at me now; at the brutal swine of an S.S. man. They don't know me! Listen to this. I could blow you out like a match—you and that mad comrade of yours. Like a match, *mein lieber mann!* You know that."

He paused and looked towards the field.

"That is not my method," he declared at last. "All my life I have been cursed with a soft heart. *Herr Gott!* Do you realise I could have been great? Great I tell you! A general, a *Reichsleiter.* Anything! But I have always been damned by one small thing—I always see the other's point of view. Why was I cursed with that! It has paralysed me all my life; tied my hands; ruined me. Do you know, at times I have stood here on the bank and watched you devils working on the road and tears have trickled down my face? Yes, blessed are those who are blind to the other man's point of view for they will go far in life. They will go far. But I——"

As Ohlau turned, with a shrug of despair towards him, it occurred to Jankowski that 'the Moon-man' was the only possible name for this madman. He nodded solemnly.

"It is strange," he managed to say, "when I first saw you I thought you were that sort, that there was greatness in you."

"Yes," Ohlau assured him gloomily. "I am that sort, my friend, and I will die that sort, damned by my fellows

because I understood them too well. A little understanding is a blessing, too much is a curse."

He turned abruptly. Music was coming from the
white house; Ohlau stood and stared in that direction
with his hands on his hips. Jankowski bent down to
throw a handful of leaves out of the drain, his heart
seemed to pound louder than the sound of scraping
shovels or the waggons rumbling over the road.

"Of course he is mad—quite mad," Ohlau exclaimed
without turning round. "To think of escape. I hate to
think of those other poor devils who tried to leave our
little home at Maskowitz."

Jankowski looked down the road. He tried to pick out
Markenski from the line of prisoners; as always the
stooping forms were invested with a baffling sameness.
If only he could see him again. Why couldn't the man
look up! No. Those men were dead, forgotten, they
had no more significance in this life. Markenski had
said himself that a bullet in him would only lay a ghost.
Nothing could matter to those men now. But why
couldn't the man raise his hand—make some sign . . .

> *"Wenn sich die spaten Nebel drehn,*
> *werd' ich bei der Laterne stehn,*
> *wie einst, Lili Marleen."*

The woman was singing in the white house again, it
was the same song, the one the guards cheerfully
whistled, but she was putting the sadness of heartbreak into her voice.

Ohlau was right; Markenski was mad, nobody could
be sane after two years of Maskowitz. Of course, he
was an aristocrat, a patriot, one of those complacent
fools who drew comfort from imbecile notions of suffering for the Motherland, who took persecution by the

'brutal enemy' for confirmation that Poland's cause was God's.

The drain was finished, but he began to scrape his shovel along the bottom, as if he were still removing the leaves and loose earth. What of the girl at Heinrichau? She must believe, in her heart, that her father was dead. She would be used to the thought, as he had grown used to the thought of his own mother's death. What would she do if she saw her father now? He could imagine how her eyes would fill with the tears that glistened but did not fall. What sentimental nonsense. Like a hypocrite, he was trying to excuse himself. He was going to betray Markenski because it was the only chance of getting out of this hell alive.

But where was she now? What was she doing now? *"O Jesus, Jesus!"* he murmured in despair. With a low groan he turned. Again he strove to pick Markenski out from the others on the road. This was insanity. Who among that line of shuffling wrecks could be akin to her? What was there to evoke an image of purity, of youth, of vitality? Her father was already dead, one more grave in a land of graves and tears and hatred.

The woman had stopped singing in the white house, a gramophone was playing there now. Ohlau was still looking in that direction; he seemed to be listening; his hands were behind his back and his fingers were moving steadily, as if he were kneading something in the palms.

"That music reminds me of my youth," he said, in a sad, detached voice. ". . . the faces, the trivial scenes, the music I loved when the world was so different. I find no comfort in these things now. And that's what's so strange—the world is the same! The young, the ordinary looking youths we see on the pavements of

Maskowitz, perhaps they cherish the dreams I have cherished. Behind their ordinary looking eyes move the sparkling, priceless dreams of youth! Dreams that war against age and ghastly experience, fade in defeat; but they alone leave monuments to that divine, shifting beauty of Life. Have mercy on the young; on their dreams, remember . . ." he paused. His hands were still; his attitude expressed a profound dejection. "I think I lost my soul with my dreams."

Jankowski waited, reflecting with a queer lack of fear or emotion that this unique S.S. man had treated him to almost every mood but a spell of madness.

Ohlau swung round.

"*Nah.* Why aren't you working? Ach so, that one is finished. Good. Just throw that earth further back and while you work tell me everything about those plans. I said *everything*."

"It's not much," Jankowski muttered. "He's breaking out of the Camp to-night."

"Breaking out? But how? What the devil do you mean—'breaking out'?"

"I told you the scheme was mad," he answered sullenly. "I told *him* it was mad. He has some pliers. When the searchlight is out he will cut through and run for it. That is all."

"*Du lieber Gott!* Is it possible? Such madness. Oh, oh, oh, just like that—cut the wire and run for it. And then? Walk to New York or London, I suppose, in his clogs! And what time has he chosen for this suicide? What time. When is it to be? Come on, man, out with it."

Ohlau kicked the pile of earth in his agitation.

"Directly darkness falls."

"I want to meet him, that's all," Ohlau murmured thoughtfully. "I want to meet him strolling down that

123

path from the wire. My soft heart again you see—I told you I had a soft heart. What could be more merciful than a bullet? Ach, but he'll never get out! The patrolling guards, the searchlights beams—but I won't interfere—let him try. I shall meet him, the poor devil in his clogs——" Ohlau shook his head sadly. "The poor, mad fool. . . ."

Jankowski began to scrape the earth from the shovel.

"Think of the extra soup, von Schirach," Ohlau went on, "the cigarettes—no, I'll make it a cigar. Two cigars! And you will join the happy party of stake-cutters. I might be in charge of them myself in the Winter."

"What guard have they got now?"

"The little Otto—gentle as a kitten. But you're no fool, von Schirach, I knew you'd tell me. After all, you would probably have died slowly if you hadn't, though I hate saying it."

Jankowski continued to scrape his shovel; he felt an overwhelming desire to stay in just that position, his body crouching and his head down.

"A traitor!"

He looked up, startled. Ohlau was glaring into his face as if something loathesome were crawling over it.

"A traitor." The word was repeated in a scornful whisper.

Jankowski straightened himself; he glared back into Ohlau's eyes; he tried to fight the hate and desperation that clouded his reason.

"You wouldn't understand the word," Ohlau sneered. "But the treachery of you Poles serves the Reich, if it didn't——"

"Of course, the Reich," Jankowski repeated.

"Ah," the S.S. man murmured softly, with his ineffable smile, "I begin to understand you, *mein lieber* von Schirach. You—well, it doesn't matter, my heart is so soft, so soft! But do remember that I can put you out like a match—much more painfully of course. To-morrow we shall see." Still smiling he looked at his watch. "Go back to that suicidal comrade of yours. Dream of extra soup to-night, of cigarettes. Of cigars!"

He turned abruptly, smartly, as if he had been dismissed by a superior officer, and strode away towards the white house.

For a moment Jankowski glared after him.

"The Reich," he said aloud and grinned.

He put the shovel over his shoulder and went slowly back. His rage had left him; he even felt an illusion of freedom as he walked; he noticed the leaves, falling faster across the road; he noticed the sky was like a mid-summer sky—shining, spacious, remote. He did not look for Markenski, but joined two very old prisoners who were shovelling sand over the bricks. He would find Markenski by the wash-house of Maskowitz after roll-call.

Through the wire that evening he watched the river's barely perceptible motion between the wide marshes. It was abandoned. One man hurried along the bank as if to get home before darkness fell, a solitary figure that reached the bend and disappeared but revived a memory. So, as a boy, had he hurried home, to reach the warm room, the bright pictures, the certitude of an unshakable love, before the darkness fell. But he had left; like a fool he had gone, he had got lost. Every tie, subtle and profound, that had bound him to his God and his land, had been broken.

Somebody in clogs was coming over the sand behind him, but he continued to face the strong West wind that darkened the river, bent the reeds over, showed the glistening undersides of the willow-leaves. He looked far out, over the distances of Prussia under an evening sky that looked cold, with the shadow of the coming Winter. His thoughts went beyond, over this land and that land. Everywhere there were faces. He saw the women saying good-bye on the railway stations— Victoria, Marienburg, Moscow or Rome? What did it matter? The faces were the same; they had all caught that mysterious glow, a reflection from some well of pity and love that he had lost . . .

"It's you—thank God. Does he suspect?"

"I——" Jankowski broke off. The fatal words 'I told him' had almost forced their way through his lips.

"You think he suspects then? You are frightened to tell me."

Markenski peered into his face.

"Tell me, what did he say? Tell me, my friend, I am not a child."

"He might suspect——"

"When he took you away I thought it was all over," Markenski said slowly, after a long pause. "I prayed to the Virgin Mary . . ."

"You are not going to-night?"

"In about an hour's time. I've got the pliers—not much bread though, but I am going; nothing will stop me now. In one hour——"

Arrested by a sudden thought or a poignant memory, Markenski stared down at the Linsk. He was silent for so long that Jankowski turned. The other might have been standing on the edge of the world, so profound was his self-absorption, it gave the long, emaciated face a sombre nobility. The shadows under his eyes; the deep lines had dignity; they were the scars left by that insidious inner war—relentless, unceasing. And Jankowski suddenly knew that this man had not been beaten. This cultured dreamer, this pampered aristocrat had found something with which to fight the material degradation, the immitigable cravings, the bitterness of memories. Faith perhaps? Or an indomitable pride, or hope, or even the elemental desire to survive allied with a great vanity. What ever it was, he was not beaten. He would not be beaten—not until he was shot a few yards from here in an hour's time.

"My God," Jankowski whispered.

"They would have tried," Markenski said in a soft voice, "Leo or Stanislaw . . . Do you remember Kassel?"

"Kassel?"

"The man who used to have Struga, a captain in the *Wehrmacht*. He had a wooden leg. I used to see him sometimes, he had the most miserable face I have ever seen—close set eyes, a sort of bluish complexion. I remember, he used to go into the woods to shoot."

"I remember him."

"And his son Hugo—I heard somewhere that he is an officer in Kirschau now—he used to skate with Stepha and the boys on Struga lake. How Zygmus used to laugh at him! He used to write verses to Stepha too, sentimental German stuff . . . rotten stuff. My God——"

"I remember him," Jankowski repeated with exasperation, with finality. There was something most ominous and appalling about the trivial recollections of one who would be dead within an hour.

"Hugo Kassel," Markenski said slowly, "he might even be a hero now. Sometimes we see how stupid it all is—heroes, outcasts, the man who puffs out his chest to-day may be slouching along in rags to-morrow, an object of contempt."

"Well, I'm going . . ." Jankowski began.

"When the carnage is over," Markenski went on steadily, "when the ranting of hate-mongers is known for what it is, when the heroes go back to their ruined homes, from where will the light come then? From love, simple love—the love we despised."

"But the light never comes," Jankowski interrupted, in a loud, angry voice. "I'm going, I have lost sleep to make up for. Do you say your prayers? But of course you do, as she did. A loving God? Can't you see we are all damned?" his voice rose higher. "I realised it long ago, it's the basis of my philosophy. Damned. Damned!" the word gave him a kind of exultation; he had a wild desire to shout it across the flat land. "Well, I'm going——"

"Then good-night, my friend," the other said quietly, "I am sorry that you are not in the mood to talk. I had hoped——"

"Hoped? What had you hoped?"

"There are so many things you never told me. You realise, don't you? In one hour . . . that is final. It might be madness, suicide, but I am going. There are so many things you never told me about that place, that farm she was on. And to-night; I thought perhaps . . . you too . . . there's not much chance but I—well, it's a slow death here."

"You mean escape together?"

Markenski did not answer. There was a long pause.

"Don't go," Jankowski said at last. "Don't go! There's not a chance, I tell you. Not one chance!"

"You are not coming then?" Markenski said shortly. Jankowski turned away.

"One day perhaps, I don't know. God knows. Good-night."

He made his way across the sand. Men from some belated working party were leaving the cook-house and shuffling towards their huts, the steam from their dixies tinged by the red glare of the sun. Jankowski hurried on, his eyes turning towards the West. He knew these vast, October sunsets that flared over the flat lands; knew how quickly they died. Then the darkness fell. At the door of his hut he looked back towards the corner of the wash-house. Markenski had not moved.

He could not sleep. The strong wind played on the strands of wire outside the block. He heard the foot-falls of the patrolling guard, occasionally that most terrible sound from the other beds—the great sob that dwindled away into a sigh. He had heard it often during the night at Maskowitz, but he would never get used to it. It was inhuman, a voice from the depths of some eternal abyss of despair escaping through half-conscious lips.

Tears of rage and horror burned in his eyes as he stared into the dimness. He was trapped, a prey to virulent hosts of memories. He was lost and done for now. Not even a man. A traitor. There was nothing worse. There was nothing left now; he had cut the last tie which had bound him to the core of his manhood. That poor devil had been caught up in the same stream of disaster as himself; had shared the same mad hopes, the grey hopelessness. In one act he had killed the only flower that grew in this choking dust: that brotherhood which springs from something deeper than blood. An act of treachery! That was the final pollution of a soul gone bad.

He must forget it before it poisoned his reason.

Had he not acted in accordance with his own logical

129

philosophy of life? How could it be treachery? What
did the word mean to one without ties—without loyalties? He must think clearly. To lie awake; to drive
himself mad over the suicide of one ruined aristocrat!
The man was old too; had lived well for years, inevitably he must pay for that. Millions on the face of the
earth were born in misery; lived in it—died in agony.

He could not afford to lose sleep over the mere ghost
of a Lucien Markenski. The man might be dead now.
Of course—the sound of the shot had been carried away
by the wind! Markenski was dead. One more trivial
straw, caught up and swept away on the mighty whirl-
pool of human passions and unfathomable motives.

She would know nothing. She thought her family was
dead; she had never told him, but in her heart she had
believed it. He saw her clearly; they were piling
sheaves, and plovers were leaving the early slopes; she
was telling him how the white under their wings struck
an exquisite harmony with the white clouds. Meaningless pictures came and went across his memory, until
they moved, terribly distorted, before his eyes. This
was madness.

*"Jesu——! Jesu Maria!"* he groaned aloud. He
must fight her image or go mad.

He turned over and faced the window; the luminous
square did not banish her image—the youthful, vital
face, the parted lips.

He climbed down from the bed-boards; found his
clogs and groped his way out of the hut. Against the
wind he hurried towards the wash-house. He heard a
shot fired as he passed the cook-house, then another.
Between the wash-house and the last block there was
nothing but a stretch of reddish sky, latticed, desolate
in the inevitable wire. He went no further.

# CHAPTER EIGHT

OHLAU was facing the Allenstein road, watching the grey staff-cars, the Hitler Youths marching with their flag, the farm-waggons coming into Maskowitz from outlying villages, the army officers walking under the trees with tall, high-shouldered women in smart riding-boots; Ohlau contemplated these things, with his feet well apart, a hand in his tunic, his thick lips pursed. He seemed to meditate profoundly, but Jankowski knew it was a pose; knew how very conscious Ohlau was of what went on behind him.

Ohlau swung round. Jankowski met his eyes.

"*Los!*" the Moon-man roared, after a hard, casual stare.

Jankowski crushed the dirt into the ruts. The sun was warm on the back of his neck but in a month the trees might be white with frost. They were working under the mountain-ash trees, where berries mingled with the leaves in the dust of the road, the white house and the signpost pointing to Keplin were out of sight, but he could see the steeple of Maskowitz church, silver grey above the pale trees. The Southern skyline was still roughened by the blue rim of forest, it was a far off shadow now, hopelessly unattainable—a myth. But it remained, like the certitude of madness and despair.

"*Nab.*"

He looked up into Ohlau's face, his heart beat faster, hope sprang up under that enigmatic, but vaguely compassionate regard.

"*Nab?*" The word was at once an inquiry and a mild reproof. "*Nab*, von Schirach?"

"What?" Jankowski demanded hoarsely.

Ohlau was staring at the end of foot-cloth hanging from the heel of Jankowski's left clog.

"You must tie your feet up better than that. That sore instep will go septic. I shall see about some ointment."

He raised his eyes and looked at Jankowski with half-genial interest.

"So, so, von Schirach, my noble friend," he said banteringly, "you thought I had let you down, you wondered why I've not spoken to you before since that business——"

"He was killed . . . of course?" Jankowski mumbled.

He waited in vain for an answer. His reason floundered; was lost in the surge of a hope, tremendous, fantastic—Markenski had got away? Merciful Christ! Markenski had got away . . .

"So you thought I'd left you in the lurch with your dreams of extra soup?" Ohlau said. "That is not my method."

"Did he get away?"

Ohlau smiled and looked away towards Maskowitz where white pigeons were circling round the pale steeple.

"I hated doing it," he said simply.

He began to twist the faded chicory flower in his hand.

"That stake-cutting job," he murmured, "I remember, I remember. How I wish I could give you that job, von Schirach, how I wish I could get on it myself . . . the forest—ah, wonderful, the trees, the sun burning down on the fir-cones, the wild animals . . . I know, I know—I have studied nature—studied it, my friend. But I can't stand cats. Why is that? They remind me of my wife perhaps? What a woman."

"I would sell my soul for a smoke," Jankowski said.

"Would you?" Ohlau inquired gravely. He pondered, looking across at the fields of stubble glinting in the sun. "You wouldn't get a pinch of snuff for it," he said at last. "What makes you think you have a soul?"

"My mother told me so."

"Ach so. Well, don't you believe it. Soul?" he shook his head, "no, no, not you. How did you sleep last night?"

"I heard the shots."

"So," Ohlau murmured, "he heard the shots."

He was silent for a while.

Above the sound of the shovels scraping Jankowski heard the martial, staccato voices of the infantry on the Allenstein road. Three old women, gleaning in the stubble, passed into the shadow of the trees; they worked quickly, methodically, never looking towards the road. Ohlau watched them with a frown.

"Yes, they have a hard time these days," he said thoughtfully. "The women of Germany, trying to get food, trying to get fuel—they have suffered, they always suffer. We must not be beaten again—it would be the end of our land. We cannot be soft; we cannot—we fight the world. We have suffered defeat once, by suffered I mean *suffered*. We cannot be beaten again; they will exterminate us all, the Jews have it in for us, the Pig-dogs. It is our duty to be hard. We fight the world, and by God, we'll beat the world! Warsaw, Paris—Moscow next . . . to-morrow the world! To-morrow the world! Ah! *Sieg Heil! Sieg Heil!*" Everybody on the road looked up, startled by his roar. "The Third Reich, my dear man," he said in a subdued voice, "will not be beaten."

"God forbid——" Jankowski muttered.

Ohlau turned on him sharply.

133

"And who told you to stop working? Work on."

"That stake-cutting job—there is no hope then?"

"None," Ohlau snapped. "*Gott!* Haven't I told you? None. Smash those bricks up better or you'll puncture every tyre that goes over the road. You don't work as well as you used to—of course, you've weakened, I know, I can see, I am not like the rest—I understand you fellows——"

"You were cursed with a soft heart," Jankowski acknowledged solemnly.

Ohlau said nothing, but there was such an ominous quality about his silence that Jankowski involuntarily looked up. Ohlau was regarding him steadily, coldly.

"I see," the Moon-man said, "you are a funny man— a comic. But be careful, my dear man, be careful——"

"What's wrong?"

"Smash those bricks!"

Slowly, Jankowski began to scrape the bricks over and smash them up.

"But faster!"

Aware of Ohlau only as an agitated blob on the fringe of his vision, Jankowski worked on.

"*Mensch!*" Ohlau roared, "have you understood?"

Jankowski felt the jarring impact of a butt across his shoulders. In tight-lipped silence, he continued to scrape the bricks over.

Ohlau stepped back with a queer, sobbing intake of breath.

"Alright," he said, in a small, indistinct voice, "you work under Fischer to-morrow. And it won't be stake-cutting."

He turned quickly and went down the road, stiffly, with his shoulders hunched, like a boy that has been chastised.

As he worked, Jankowski's right shoulder stiffened until he could hardly use his arm. When he looked up he found that Ohlau was watching from fifty yards away; watching him tensely and the pale face was not quite sane.

The small party under S.S. man Fischer worked apart from the main body of prisoners; it had the heaviest task on the road—smashing boulders and slabs of sandstone, or anything else too large for immediate use. Fischer—skinny, vulturine, with expressionless eyes—was full of nervous energy. His high-pitched voice was fierce. Sometimes his friend Köller would stroll over from the main column and they would talk together, while the prisoners thanked God for the brief peace.

In a fortnight Jankowski had weakened; his nights were tormented by a gnawing dread of the dawn, of the march that was a prolonged agony. With a strange November sunset behind them they would march back under the bare trees. He knew every house on that long way now, every cottage. The same children played in the road each evening, the same women stood by the gates, the same spindly-legged boy with the long, red nose and the cap pulled over his ears, stood by the *Gasthaus*, waiting for something.

On the smooth surface of the Allenstein road, they would usually be passed by an Infantry company which would get the order to sing as it overtook the prisoners. Perhaps the officer in charge delighted to make the most of that great contrast, the lusty soldiers swinging along in step, the silent column stumbling on as if it were blind. But the soldiers never looked exultant, their faces expressed no emotion; to Jankowski this seemed a kind of sympathy.

The town of Maskowitz was nothing more than a

vague impression of shop-windows, smiling faces, serious faces; smart women lingered outside the cinema. The Poles, unloading wood in the saw-mill, would stop work and watch the column with pity. In the town he would try to keep his head lifted, but when they had passed under the bridge and were on the long climb to the Camp, he would march like the rest—head down, clogs dragging, his eyes fixed on the shuffling figure in front. Like the rest, he would not look up until he knew that he could see the square boxes of the look-out posts against the cold sky, then the high gates, the office and S.S. barracks, the squalid column of another party being checked in. He would strive to project his mind half-an-hour into the future, to the *kaffee-ersatz*, the bread-ration. To himself he would swear to save one thin slice of bread until the morning, but he knew in his heart that he would never have the strength of mind.

The evenings were growing colder, and he had no desire to stand by the wash-house and watch darkness fall over the distances of Prussia; he felt too tired, too weak. There was nothing to do in the evenings but eat his ration and flop down on the bed-boards; to stare into the darkness, recalling scenes and faces. The faces he had known best he would not see again. Were he freed to-morrow, he had no one to go to, no one could rejoice with him. It was as well that his mother was dead. But could even the dead quite escape the abnormal misery suffered and created by those they had known and loved? The Polish landscape, into which she had passed, seemed to brood on the dead. That placid, beautiful landscape. In its beauty was contempt for those who still struggled on its surface, for the ruin and tragedy, the sin and pain, the love and faith, the suffering borne together, the brotherhood.

# ALMOST GLORY

He had killed every chance of seeing Stepha again. Had he got away a month ago, he would have sought her; from her generous heart she would have rejoiced with him. Since the death of Markenski he had thought of her too much. After all, she had warmth at Heinrichau, enough food, comparative freedom, and the working day would be shorter now. But he could no longer picture her in that Prussian scene; in his imagination she was back in Poland, she too belonged to the passion, the colour and the sadness of that land. He could picture her riding home along the lonely shores of the Struga lake, the pine-trunks red against the pale blue sky, the forests still, the only sound a rumble of waggons on the distant Likora road, or the Malkow girls singing in the fields; perhaps the sound of the *Angelus*.

The memory of a dream was keeping him awake to-night. He tried to sleep and find again the freedom of that dream; he had been with Stepha and Radek, gliding through a forest on a farm-sledge, through the golden sunlight and the shadows, over the tracks of wild animals in the snow. The sky shining through the trees had seemed a fantastically blue, cold sky. At a headlong pace they had been fleeing from something. Radek had been driving, smiling all the time, his black hair blowing into his eyes; she had been sitting on the floor of the sledge, looking into the sparkling boughs, her lips parted. She had looked at Jankowski and smiled.

The dream had changed. She had sat beside him, her head resting on his shoulder, her hair touching his cheek. He had felt the heart-ache, the unrest, the sadness.

She had whispered fantastic words: "Why can't we glide on like this for ever? Just like this always, lured on and on by the blueness of the sky, comforted by the sun . . . for ever, on and on like a silver river, too swift and light to touch the darker things. O, Anton, why—I cannot even sing, Anton, if I started to sing I should cry——"

"For ever!" Radek had shouted joyfully, "but, dear little Stepha, how can you expect me to drive this un-tamed goat for ever? Make her see reason, Anton."

They had sped on faster and faster.

"Anton, you never say very much . . . at a moment like this—freedom, hope—surely, Anton? . . ."

In trying to answer her he had waked.

The vivid memory of that dream kept him awake, he still felt something of the heart-ache, the unrest, the sadness.

He lay and listened to the wind nagging at the strands of wire and whistling under the eaves, the voice of a cold and hopeless earth. He thought of Radek, some-where out there in the cold forests, but free, free to take any path through the dark woods.

"*Raus!  raus!*"

The guards were yelling in the first block.

Within half-an-hour he was hurrying from the cook-house with his tin of *kaffee-ersatz* burning his fingers, while all around him, in the half-light, men were shuffling towards their blocks, their eyes on their steaming tins. The first working-parties were already forming up by the gate.

It was light when the road party marched through Maskowitz, the workers were hurrying along the pave-ments, past the closed shops, under the Swastika flags that drooped like dark, dejected rags from the upper windows. The smell of baking bread was strong in the raw air.

They came out on the straight Allenstein road where

he saw the November mists lingering over the distances and softening the Autumn colours. On reaching the pile of sandstone dumped haphazard in the ditch and half covered by leaves, Fischer ordered his party of nine men to fall out from the rest of the column. As if weary, for once, of his own voice, he watched them in silence while they started to work, then he sauntered up and down the road, now and then glaring at them with a kind of thoughtful disgust.

"Rest whenever his back's turned, brother, it's the only way," Jankowski heard the deep voice of the man who dragged out the slabs for him to smash. "I know, I've been here a long time—rest, always rest. I know the tricks—that's why I'm alive," the big Pole went on, "take no notice of the others. Look at them! No life left in their bodies, no guts left, poor fellows—they wear themselves out, we know better, brother—here comes that wolf again."

The sun rose behind them as they worked, until it shone, without warmth, from a clear sky. As Jankowski finished crushing one slab of sandstone, Antek the big Pole would drag over another. From the main body of prisoners came the sound of scraping shovels and the shouts of the guards. Jankowski peered up again at the elegant figure a hundred yards down the road, but Ohlau had not moved from the bank where he supervised the clearing of a drain by the new prisoner from Stettin—a small man scraping feverishly at the earth, forced on by fear or by visions of extra soup, cigarettes —cigars. Ohlau contemplated his antics with a tolerant smile, sometimes pointing out a part that needed digging.

"My dear Köller," Jankowski heard Fischer's nasal voice three yards in front of him, "you've never heard me play the balalaika—you don't know what music is."

"The place for *Schnaps* is the Forester's," Köller, who had strolled over from the main column, was saying, "he always has plenty of cigarettes too, and bacon——"

"What do you think of his wife?" the nasal voice interrupted, "not bad, eh? Wait until he gets called up, he will be soon, he's about thirty-two. I think she fancies me, you know, she's got that look in her eyes."

"You?" said Köller, "bah! I bought some fine records in Maskowitz—I got that *Lili Marlene* I was after. I'm sick of this job—dead and alive place, I was in Vienna for a year—they live there, my fellow, even Marienberg is not too bad; I was there too—I wonder how my little Polish girl is getting on? She thought I was great——"

"My God," Fischer muttered, "did she?"

Jankowski lifted the hammer and let it fall on the slabs of sandstone. If only they would move on so that he could rest; he felt giddy and longed to sleep, to fling himself into the ditch whose shining grass and wild flowers were a yard from his feet, but far-off, unattainable.

But it seemed that they would never move.

"You've seen the photograph of my family?" Köller was saying, "this one?" he put his hand into his tunic and brought out a wallet, after much shuffling, as if there were some he did not wish to show; he produced a photograph of three girls and a young, handsome man. "That's Otto—he's in Africa—Rommel's division, I think he's a sergeant-major now. This is Erna—married a *Luftwaffe* man, a conceited ass but she adores him. These two aren't married yet."

"Pretty girls," Fischer commented, "I haven't got my snaps here or you could see them. I've got two sisters and three brothers, the brothers are all fighting, one's in the Waffen—S.S. Where are we going to-night, the same place? You know, I'm getting fed up with that chap who thinks he can sing—he ruins the place; I like a bit of peace sometimes, he doesn't know when to stop. I want to get off this party; it's no good —too much hanging around, and you never know when the *Scharführer* will go off his head—I suppose you've heard about that cursed poem he had published in the *Vorposten?*"

"I want to get back for Christmas," the other re-marked, "I've missed two already—that reptile Hein-rich hasn't missed one since the war started."

He drew out a handkerchief and began to rub his belt.

"I'm getting sick of the whole business—the war I mean; another winter at the Russian front won't be a joke. The Führer knows what he's doing, of course."

Jankowski grinned at the familiar words; they would be the epitaph of Germany; the Fuhrer knew what he was doing.

"It will be over by the Spring," Fischer said, "there's a great offensive coming off."

"How do you know?"

"Ah ha."

"These damn scarecrows work like warmed-up corpses—that little clown, he's always talking—you watch him."

"I haven't the heart to stop him," Fischer answered. "I give him a shout now and again." He put his hands to his mouth: "*Los! Los!*" he roared, "you're not here to talk!" he turned away with a laugh. "I'm pretty easy with them as a rule but without order God knows what would happen——"

"Look at that fellow, the one with a crab-like movement—they seem to have accumulated the dregs of Europe in this place; Jews, homo-sexuals, bandits—what a bunch! I wouldn't mind if they didn't get so lousy; I don't mind fleas, but lice——" he shuddered, "makes me itch to think of them."

"The Commandant does his best," Fischer remarked with a sigh, "trouble is he thinks he's dealing with soldiers——"

"I wish old Ernst was here," Köller said, "the very sight of that man's face makes me laugh—by the way, the Führer's sending a Christmas parcel to every soldier; I wrote and told them I'd get leave this year— I must, what a place to spend Christmas!"

"Ach, you don't know the ropes, man," Fischer's nasal voice broke in, "you can get a good time in Maskowitz—wine, cigars, women, why do you people always squeal about home? I could give you a time you wouldn't forget. Can you ride?"

"Yes, of course——"

"Alright then, I know a place where you can get the best horses. Do you skate?"

"Yes."

"Well, what's wrong with the Linsk?"

"Oh, I suppose if you know the ropes it's not too bad here—well, I must be getting back to the others. See you to-night."

Köller swung round smartly and marched off. Fischer went over to a prisoner working on the other side of the road.

"His back's turned, brother," Antek told Jankowski, "rest, always rest—I know the tricks . . . too late, he's coming back."

For a time they worked on without a word. Fischer watched them from twenty yards away.

"*Maria!* So we've reached these again——" with an anxious, half-disgusted look, Antek dumped a large fragment of granite at Jankowski's feet, "we had a load of them—I hated smashing them at first but one gets used to it, it is a tragedy or blessing, brother, that we can get used to anything——"

Jankowski understood neither the words nor the look until he saw the letters, half-hidden by the damp leaves clinging to the surface of the stone.

". . . there are plenty more bits of it here . . ." the words came to him, a faint, meaningless jangle of sound, ". . . don't be too squeamish, brother—there is nothing we can do—and he's coming, I tell you . . ."

The letters cut in the dirty granite at his feet vibrated, came to him in a stupefying uproar; through the crumbling floor of his own heart he fell into a timeless vision holding all his past—its happiest moments, its most sacred hopes—all that was good. He shivered violently, as with great terror or cold—it was the chilling of some ultimate warmth. That vision was ravished, trampled —held in desolate mockery for ever . . .

"But this is my mother's gravestone."

His sight was too blurred to distinguish the granite from the sandstone but he groped among the fragments with a vague notion of piecing them together.

"Can you hear? Work my lousy friend! *Herr Gott*——"

"*Jesus!* His mother's——" Antek whispered hoarsely.

Fischer laughed, then his voice rose to its harsh scream:

"Can you hear me! You swine, it should be your own stone, you cursed Jew! I knew there was something funny about you! Jew-pig—smash it! Smash it——!"

"Quiet, you fool!" Jankowski said hardly above a

whisper, "her gravestone," he muttered to himself, "smashed—smashed up. O the swines——" Suddenly he thrust a fragment of granite towards Fischer, holding it an inch from the other's nose. "Look what you've done!" he shouted furiously, "look what you swines have done! You swines—her stone . . . smashed——"

White faced, Fischer backed away, then slowly swung the machine-pistol from his shoulder.

"*Nah?* And what is the excitement here?"

His movement arrested by the soft voice, Fischer swung round.

"He's a Jew, *Herr Scharführer*—this swine here——"

"Go away," Ohlau ordered curtly, "you talk too much."

"*Jawohl.*"

Ohlau watched him go; he turned to Jankowski, there was no warmth in his ineffable smile.

"I have had about enough of you, my dear friend. Too much, even for my soft heart."

"Let me speak, *Herr Scharführer*," Antek begged hoarsely. "You are the kind of man who understands these things—this poor devil here—that's his mother's stone, his own mother's—it must have made him half-mad."

Ohlau looked at the fragment nearest his feet, twisting his head in order to read what was cut there. He frowned and pursed his lips, while he stared at the ANN and part of another A where the fragment had broken off from the rest of the stone.

"Of course—Anna," he murmured, and gently pushed the piece aside with the toe of his jack-boot, "they shouldn't do it," he said softly.

He glanced up at Jankowski, screwing up his face as with extreme irritation.

"Thousands have been smashed," he said sorrowfully, "thousands everywhere—this is not the only one; we have had loads of them on this road, from Klemba, from Pallow . . . it was never thought that this would happen . . ."

Jankowski hardly heard. Memories of the only place he had called Home crowded into his mind—the smell of burning peat, of hot coffee, the comforting sight of his coat hanging up to dry after he had worked all day in the fields, his few books on the table, the bright atlas he had loved to bring out in the evenings and study by the light of that lamp which had never burnt properly—perhaps that was why his mother's eyes had weakened; she had done so much spinning and darning and sewing by its light.

". . . it's no good worrying about these things," Ohlau was saying, "you see——" he broke off; frowning he looked at the ground between them. "It won't do," he murmured at last, "I am annoyed about this—I know how you feel—Jew or not, I know, I know . . . haven't I told you I'm not like the rest?" he demanded, with a kind of desperation, "I see your point of view—I always do, curse it! Listen. You will not be on this job again. Never."

With his foot, he began to push all the fragments to one side.

"They shouldn't do it," he said, "smashing gravestones—it will not do. Why don't they see that?"

Feeling sick and cold, Jankowski turned away. Through the fallen leaves on the side of the road, three children trundled an ancient pram stacked high with firewood; they heaved and tugged at the load with concentration and anxiety on their pinched faces. They passed with a significance he did not understand until he realised that the sight of their thin legs and pinched faces had gladdened him; he was glad they were struggling with that load. He would have liked to have seen them killed. Like a condemnation, with virulence in its fleeting futility, a sentence of Lucien Markenski's came into his mind: *'Hatred? Oh no, you see, I want to win, brother.'*

The men behind him were working again; Ohlau was saying: *"Nab,* von Schirach, forget it. Work on, we want to get this cursed road done sometime. You will be off this job to-morrow. Under that greenish brick by my left foot are three cigarettes wrapped in a bit of paper, there's a man watching us from that lorry. When no one is looking pick them up. You see, I am not such a swine. I see that you never bandaged that instep as I ordered—do you *want* it to go septic? See that it is done by the morning. *Nab,* I told you to start working again, my friend."

Jankowski picked up his hammer. Somebody had collected the fragments of the stone which had brought him back to Poland, and stacked them neatly on the edge of the ditch.

Ohlau turned to stare down the road.

"Where the devil has that sheep-headed Fischer got to?" he muttered impatiently, "it's almost *feirabend*— where is the fool?"

Mechanically, Jankowski lifted the hammer and let it fall, hardly knowing whether it was sandstone or boulders he smashed. He remembered his last visit to the peaceful graveyard at Pallow. It had been just before the outbreak of war; after walking down the hill he had looked back, the way the gravestone had stood out against the sky had pleased him. The recollection of all that was best in the past had been an escape, had held the certitude of its own warmth and peace. Into it now had crept the poisonous mockery—the cold. Even the dead could not escape.

What was there left? His very despair had turned to something too bitter, too vital to let him die in shame and obscurity. *'Hatred? Oh no, you see, I want to win, brother,'* the chance words of one who was dead lurked inevitably behind the smouldering, cankering fury that possesssed him . . . *'to win, brother.'* Then he had lost? No, he had never fought that battle, he had never loved his fellows as Markenski had done; he had never had the faith Markenski had had.

"So the fool has condescended to appear at last," Ohlau exclaimed, "wait until Bergman's in charge of this party—some of these fellows will see how soft I've been."

With a quizzical expression and with his hands on his hips he watched Fischer coming down the road. He turned to Jankowski:

"Don't look so grim, my friend, you work under me to-morrow—yes, the stake-cutting job. You will smell the resin in the pines, you will see the deer and wild birds—and I shall be as glad as you to see the last of this stinking road!"

"I shall be glad enough," Jankowski muttered.

Suddenly he saw the orange light of the setting sun on his hands, on the boulders, on the grass that had grown above the stubble, on the faces lined by suffering and turned to him with an envy that looked like horror. The light dominated the earth and sky then faded; he felt the wintry wind spring up and turned to face it. There was the line of forest, dark blue, like the beginning of a flood creeping over the horizon out of the pearly void of the Eastern sky.

# CHAPTER NINE

FROM the gate where he waited with the forest party, he watched the figures with their steaming tins leave the spectral outline of the cook-house and pass before the squares traced by the wire against the grey mist. Never before had they seemed so much like shadows; shadows that saddened unutterably by seeming to demand, for the last time, comprehension of their tragic and profound significance. He felt that he would never see them again.

Peering at the men with whom he waited, he was startled by one resembling Lucien Markenski in the half-light and mist, but there was no one here whom he knew or could trust with his plans. They would laugh at him or betray him to Ohlau. He felt the bread-ration in the pocket sewn on the inside of his left trouser-leg. Was he insane to hope of escape? Were he to get away without being shot they would soon pick him up. How long could he last in clogs, a striped suit—with a bread-ration!

But at the sight of the forest hope sprang up again.

The sound of the lorry that had taken them to the outskirts faded towards Maskowitz; there was a frozen calm in the forest. It was a different world—a world of countless boughs and green pineleaves, of light and shadow.

"For the love of God do not march in threes here!" they heard Ohlau's horrified voice behind them, "take your own time. Please do your best to look like human beings—I came here to forget the queues, the squalor—

148

have you no appreciation of nature? Look into the trees, look at the·sun on the branches, on the mist—never look at the ground in a forest for the love of God——"

Obediently the twelve men raised their heads.

For nearly a mile they followed the path through pine plantations in varying stages of growth; all the way Jankowski listened for trains on the Bromberg line, sometimes he heard the hollow *bup bup* of an axe in the distance. There was no other sound in the forest.

They halted by a pile of recently cut stakes.

"The Forester has marked the trees," Ohlau told them, "but you should know what to do. Don't wander: if I had to shoot anyone to-day it would ruin the pleasure of this place. There shall be a cigarette each and time to smoke it later in the day——" he paused.

There was a surprised, gratified murmur.

"And take your own time," he went on, "most guards would stand over you. That is not my method." As always, he seemed to imply some deep meaning— sinister or benevolent—in these familiar words.

He waited until they had started work, then strolled up and down the wide path with his cap in his hand, his head lifted.

"When does the lorry return?" Jankowski asked the Pole working next to him.

"Are you tired already?"

"Yes. When does it return?"

"This is not the party for you, comrade," the other answered without turning or halting the swing of his axe. "It comes at half-past three—we start walking towards the road at three."

"Is that train we hear on the Gruziadz line?"

"Where else?"

"How far is it?"

149

"Four kilometres perhaps, or three-and-a-half—I don't know. It's best to work and not talk too much, comrade—we don't want to spoil a good guard."

"Has no one escaped from this party?"

The other glanced hurriedly towards the path.

"*Maria!* Not so loud!" he looked at Jankowski with fear and real hatred: "Are you mad? For God's sake don't mention escaping. Do you want to get us all shot?"

"Most of you are dead already."

He worked on slowly. He must be away an hour before the lorry returned, which would be two hours before darkness fell. He watched Ohlau. The elegant *Scharführer* stalked along the path, looked into the boughs, breathed deeply like one released from the smoke and squalor of a city, sometimes he stooped for bits of moss; once be picked some faded flower and smelt it with a movement that looked like a prayer, but every time he turned his eyes darted over the prisoners. Hopefully, desperately Jankowski watched. He realised that Ohlau would have to be killed before he could escape.

Their plantation skirted a wood of ancient pines, rising like a cliff in the evaporating mist; at about half-past two the sun would sink behind them. Jankowski looked at the sky through an opening in the trees; he had the impression of looking up from the bottom of a well, he saw a solitary seagull drifting high above the forest; it was passing by in an upper world—a daylit world.

The sunrays weakened. Green twilight was already in the depths of the countless trunks.

"*Nah?*"

The familiar, long-drawn-out sound startled him.

Ohlau was standing five yards away, his hands on his hips.

"*Nab*, do you like this job?"

"Yes."

"It is the best in the Camp. I started it myself for the prisoners we can trust. Not many men would have thought of that."

He was silent for so long that Jankowski glanced up to see whether he had gone, but the Moon-man was in one of his peculiar reveries; his face, like a poet's with its sensual lips and melancholy eyes, was turned towards the path.

"I wonder who it is," he said softly, "it could be any-body—the Devil or Christ——"

Far down the path, where it almost faded into the green gloom of the forest, was a dim figure.

"There is something terrible in that sight," Ohlau went on, "don't you see? I am standing, thinking of nothing much, when suddenly the figure of a man comes into sight out of the half-darkness—somebody we have never seen before and will never see again; that figure suddenly becomes a symbol of our lives, that dim, indistinguishable figure of a man with thoughts and dreams and a destiny—a destiny unknown. We shall never know that man; he passes again into the half-darkness of the forest . . ." the detached voice became personal. "I am not explaining myself well but how could a poor, uncultured Pole like you comprehend?"

Jankowski could not comprehend, he could only detract—Ohlau was German; had the words echoed his own hopes and fears and confirmed a brotherhood, they would have been still incomprehensible, a sound that he could only relate to his hatred.

". . . how could you understand the terror—don't you

see, don't you see—I sometimes think of all those little destinies—no, those destinies as great as my own, or as meaningless—the shadows that come and go at Maskowitz—the terror, the horror . . . or is it the glory? I think of them, they come and go, those dim figures, the indistinguishables across the half-darkness of my memory. There was that little fellow who never looked up; he seemed afraid to take his eyes from the earth . . . from his mother earth . . . he should never have left that mother perhaps. I can't even remember how he died . . . they called him Kenar——"

"Kenar!" Jankowski exclaimed, "not from Pomorze?"

"How should I know? They called him Kenar, I know that."

"It couldn't have been the Kenar I knew——"

"It makes no difference," Ohlau answered sorrowfully, "he was the Kenar somebody knew. I see that you can use an axe."

"I used to work in a forest."

"When you were a boy perhaps? So did I once, and I often think now that I should never have left that kind of work. I loved the trees, the quietude, in those days I loved solitude and craved for it. You see, I was too sensitive, too eager to please, and I always over-estimated the other man's intelligence—I reverenced my fellows, in the company of others I did not speak, I did not think. I could not, you see, I seemed to be silenced by the presence of another mind, my own was so sensitive. I see now, it is only vanity that makes the company of others tolerable; we like to see a reflection of ourselves; we like the chance to be considered clever, virtuous or whatever it is—without that we die. But in those days I sought no such reflection. I craved solitude. I wanted harmony with the silent magnitude

of nature, to watch the sky—shining, magnificent—
through the trees, white blossomed trees that stirred in
sleep, to stand by those dark, old worldly rivers of my
land and dream . . ."

Raising his eyes from the chips scattered before his
axe, Jankowski saw that the sun was very near the top
of the pines. If this lunatic was not killed within ten
minutes it would be too late.

". . . but when I met my fellows," the dreamy voice
was saying, "they made a discord. They wanted to
drag me off to that cursed little *weinstube* at Haynau;
wanted me to come dancing, to play games. Curse
them, they killed my soul. I thought they were as
sensitive as I was, as easily wounded—I could refuse
nothing. And now you see me, an S.S. *Scharführer*.
What is a man when his soul is dead? I can only contemplate my gradual decay of body with what is left
of my mind. Nothing in me responds to the . . . to the—
you see, I cannot even give beauty a name because I
have lost it all. Don't bother to pray for me. My soul is
dead."

"It might live again," Jankowski put in hurriedly,
realising that Ohlau was addressing him directly from a
yard away.

"Not again," the Moon-man assured him mourn-
fully, "you have heard me talk about my wife, jokingly,
contemptuously? That woman, I felt, was my last
chance; with her I would find the tranquil seas again.
She would be the star. It didn't work, that was the
tragedy. Who knows, perhaps she felt as I did? Perhaps
she felt that I was the star. There was no star. She
hates me now. You are young, you might be lucky
enough to find the woman with the gift, the gift . . . I
mean of salvation. I never shall. There is a rhyme in

English that seems the epitaph of my soul—how did it go now? Moving with the river, fading in the river, slipping, dying, all away from me, sun-veined through the rushes, drifting ever, with one, once, far away I heard the sea. I knew not where it was and yet the sound was soft, as slumber keeping watch eternally, but very far away and never found——"

The sun was behind the trees. The lorry would be back within an hour.

"It is something to have heard the sea," Jankowski muttered, trying to keep calm, "but I don't like the poem. It is too obscure. What was moving with the river? Sun-veined? It sounds like bubbles to me."

"It is not obscure to me," Ohlau murmured sadly, "how many bubbles reach the sea I wonder?"

"None, if they pass through Maskowitz," Jankowski answered, "if they pass through Maskowitz——" he repeated slowly. He swung the axe short; it missed the tree and he lashed it at Ohlau's head. Too late, Ohlau had dodged back. He struck again and Ohlau fell, Jankowski was on him, wrenching the machine pistol from his shoulder, the Lugar from its holster.

He sprang back and held the Lugar a yard from Ohlau's bleeding head.

"Jacket, boots—off with them!" he snapped. "Faster ——!"

Dazed, Ohlau pushed across his jacket, then his boots.

"What are you going to do?" he asked weakly.

"Kill you," Jankowski answered, "if I had time I would do it slowly."

"But——"

Jankowski shot him through the head.

"Stand perfectly still," he said, turning to the prisoners, "does any Pole want to come with me?"

There was no answer. They stood and gaped at him.

Quickly, he put on the jacket and struggled into the boots.

"Who wants to come?"

No answer. He ran into the trees.

He was stumbling, his breath gnawed at his lungs, his leg-muscles pained . . . pained. It was no good. He was too weak. It was the lack of food, the lack of sleep . . . he could not go on. And he had come two hundred yards perhaps? They would use dogs and get him before darkness. But not alive . . .

Against a wet trunk he crossed his arms, letting his head drop against them. So he was done after all? Too weak to move.

He must force himself on. He could hear the trains. This was the forest that reached into Pomorze. The blessed darkness was falling; the lorry must have come and gone, it would be tearing back to Maskowitz. He must eat half his bread-ration and force himself on towards the railway-line.

He blundered on painfully until he reached a dense mass of firs, no higher than himself, growing on the fringe of a lake, dull and vast in the dusk. He lay face downwards on the dry ground beneath the firs; a water-bird made strange sobbing sounds a few yards away, and fell suddenly silent. He could hear the water lapping in the reeds and the trains pulling out from the marshalling-yard at Tarnsee. The gradient to the North of the yard could be no more than two kilometres away. When he rose to his feet it was too dark to see where the lake finished and the marsh began.

He ate the other half of his bread-ration. He felt better and there was hope in the darkness; they could only hunt him in daylight. He left the firs and went on slowly under the tall trees; he was conscious of that subdued whispering awakened by the last leaves creeping down over the woods. He remembered lying in the wood by Heinrichau and listening to the first leaves falling; he remembered the terrible voice crying '*Halt!*' on the path.

He stopped and listened.

For a time there was not a sound in the dark, wintry wood but the leaves falling, murmuring, and once more it was the most friendly voice he had heard for countless days. The rest had done him good. There was some age-old comfort in the darkness and obscurity; his heart was lighter. He breathed deeply, looking up at the flecks of sky that accentuated the darkness of the forest; he was conscious of the night that reached a million miles above the sombre trees.

Another train pulled out of Tarnsee and rumbled away Northward, there was magic and hope in the sound. It would pass within eleven kilometres of Heinrichau. He could think of Heinrichau now without emptiness and despair—she would forgive him when she knew of his great hatred. She must forgive. Keeping the sound of Tarnsee to his left he went on faster, oblivious of small boughs stinging his face. She would forgive him, and he was free. But how he had run. *Jesu Maria* how he had run!

Suddenly he laughed. Nothing could menace him here. He began to feel that nothing had ever menaced him, that the terror and pain through which he had come were all part of that spitefully comic game he seemed destined to play in obedience to some inexorable lunacy. The S.S. men and their dogs faded to insignificance, were somewhere swallowed up by the vast, mysterious night.

156

He heard the sound of a motor-engine. Headlight beams swept through the branches above him. A car-door slammed fifty yards away; an authoritative voice gave orders.

"Damn them," he whispered, in weary despair, "God damn them!"

He must keep his head.

The penetrating voice ceased and the car drove on shakily over the wide path. He could see nothing now, hear nothing. What were they doing? They had surrounded the wood and were creeping in on him——! No, they had no idea where he was. They were watching the paths. He must keep his head, not see terror in each tree, in each shadow. He would fool them yet in the darkness. But dogs?

Tensely he listened. Not a sound. The old silence had descended upon the forest. He had been away three hours or more—how could they know where he was by now? How could they watch every path? But they were thorough, well-organised; they knew the country. But he must not overrate their astuteness; he had almost blundered into them but if he kept his head he could beat them. Tarnsee was a kilometre away, perhaps, two at the most . . . they would be watching there of course; they would be patrolling the line. But he had to move or they would hunt him out in daylight.

He went on slowly, with the impression that each step might burst a fatal glare upon the darkness. By each path he listened, waited. Once he heard wild pigs crushing through the undergrowth, snorting as they ran; while he rested, cursing them silently, he realised that he was on the fringe of the wood—through the trunks he saw the open sky where the moon, like a curled wood-shaving, slipped slantwise towards a bare horizon.

He had almost blundered upon the line; he heard the trains shunting and the jangle of couplings. A high, plaintive voice called: "Franz, Franz," from the direction of the marshalling-yard and somebody crossed the line with a lantern.

He waited on, crouching low behind the little bushes, until the moon set behind the bare fields. Then, like the sough of the wind in telegraph wires, he heard the Northbound train coming. It was a passenger train. After it had passed two armed men—S.S. or railway police—went down the line. One forecast snow with dull persistency.

He heard another train pull out of the marshalling-yard. This was the one, a freight train, Southbound. It drew slowly towards him up the gradient. The locomotive laboured past and he ran, stumbling over the sleeper ends. He clutched the rail of the step behind the waggon and swung himself up; he crouched in the brake-cabin until the train gathered speed. He peered out over the trucks, and saw the sparks shooting into the night. But only for a moment—the air was like ice on his forehead.

The train frequently jolted to a standstill, and at the second station it waited so long that he was certain they were searching it, after missing him at Tarnsee. It had begun to snow; shivering with the cold he listened, while the snow-flakes whirled through the opening and wetted his face. The locomotive whistled and they clanked on. He rose painfully to stamp his feet and rub his hands between his legs. Five more stations . . .

The day was breaking when they passed through Magudken; enough snow had fallen to make the land as grey as the sky. He was in Pomorze. The train crawled across that familiar plain whose monotony was broken only by the dark patches that were isolated holdings; already the black smoke was rising into the grey light. He had expected to see some change, but of course there was none. The story of the occupation was not written on the face of the melancholy landscape; he would find it in the eyes of women—the mothers, the widows.

He longed to leave the train and go to one of those remote farmsteads, to eat something warm, and sleep, but the train would pass within five kilometres of the Naceks' home when it entered the Struga forest. They were the best people he knew.

It was dangerously light when he sprang from the step of the brake-cabin, but he was too cold and weary to care. When the long line of trucks was out of sight he went slowly into the trees. The snow, driving down through the pines, had picked the branches out in white and the trees were like gigantic fish-bones. What would the Naceks think of him? Perhaps they had gone, been turned out and replaced by Bessarabians; perhaps all the people he had known in Struga and Malkow were gone.

He forced himself on, through the spectral ranks of the trees, past the timber cut into metre lengths and stacked neatly on the side of the paths. He reached the fringe of the forest and saw the Naceks' house. He watched it until a muffled figure crossed the yard with a bucket and disappeared into the stable. Anna Nacek? He was not certain. But he could wait no longer. He crossed the fields.

She came out of the stable as he entered the yard.

"Anton——"

"Are there any Germans here?" he asked.

"No, no, only us—come in, what's wrong? . . . you look frozen, ill, and so thin! What's wrong, Anton?"

"I must rest——"

"Poor Anton, you can hardly stand—lean on me——"

They entered the house.

"It's Anton Jankowski, mother, he's ill——"

They sat him near the brick stove.

"Give him some of that soup, Anna. What has happened, Anton—we heard you were in Maskowitz."

"I escaped," he mumbled, "let me rest awhile and be on my way again."

"Where are you going?"

"I don't know."

"You are going to stay here, you stupid fellow—rest, get well again; you are not fit to go out, don't worry about anything, we shall look after you."

He felt the tears burning in his eyes.

"I don't know how to thank you. Why are you so good—so good, so kind . . . I can't understand."

"Drink up that soup—rest, don't worry."

"But why are you so good?" he persisted stupidly.

They did not answer, but took off his boots and rubbed his feet.

The soup was thick, hot; he drank it slowly, it was the best soup he had ever tasted in his life—never before had meat tasted like this, had peas tasted like this. Dimly he realised that he had put his arm halfway round the bowl as if protecting it. On the long tables in the huts at Maskowitz each man did that; there was no need to do it now.

He put the empty bowl on the floor and leaned back against the warm stove. All the hunger, all his misery, treachery, pain were made up for by the delight of that moment.

"Where is your father, Anna, and Franceska?" he asked. "Nothing has happened to them?"

"No, no, they went to Likora—to the miller's; they left very early."

"Do you ever see Radek now?"

For a moment they did not answer.

"He comes here often," the old woman whispered at last, "we give him bread."

"I must see him. Is he well?"

"Oh yes," Anna said slowly, "but he has changed— you will meet him."

"Do you ever hear anything of Stepha?"

"Stepha Markenski? No, no, Zygmus Radek has tried hard to find her, she was in East Prussia—on a farm, but she was sent away, no one knew where she went. The poor Markenskis! Such a tragedy, a family like that, so kind, so much loved and now——? It is a wicked world Anton, none of us are safe, every time the dog barks at night my heart goes cold, and it never seems to end, the war goes on——"

"It can't last much longer," he said, "the Russians are holding them, this winter they will retreat—ah, God, but I'm tired——! And Stepha, no one knows where she is—how shall I ever find her again?"

"Don't worry about her now, only rest, Anton, rest while you can. Did you like the soup? There was bacon in it, you know, you must have some more and some bread——"

"Somebody must know where she is . . . how could she just vanish like that . . ."

"There is no white bread now, Anton, sometimes you can get rolls in Likora—still the same baker, we give——"

"When can I see Radek again?" he interrupted gently.

"I don't know, but soon, sometimes he brings a friend—they are fine men. He stayed here once, he was ill, he slept in the barn; we made a place for him under the straw——"

"I must go there," Jankowski said, sitting up, "they might come here, they are after me you know."

"Mother is watching," Anna said, "not many Germans come here. But they searched the house once, Zygmus was in the barn. God was good to us that day."

"I have not been here for so long. How is Leo?"

"Quite well—he ploughs, and scythes too a little, he is a good boy."

"I must go into the barn now, I can sleep there, sleep, sleep and sleep."

"I see you have some white hairs, Anton, how long it seems since you used to come here as a boy."

"It was a different world," he answered.

He looked round at the same pictures, the same white cloth embroidered with yellow flowers, the First Communion pictures, the statue of Our Lady of Chenstohova; there was that ancient map even, on which old Nacek had shown them how things were going at the Front. Even then it had been a different world.

"Only your goodness——" he was going to say, "only your goodness remains," but he could not finish the sentence. He swallowed with an effort.

They took him to the place in the barn where they had burrowed under the straw and built a small compartment. They gave him a sheep-skin coat and two thick rugs.

"We shall come and see you later and hear all about your adventures—now sleep. We shall pray for you to feel better when you wake up, Anton——"

He did not hear Anna finish. Sleep overcame him.

He was awakened by the cocks crowing and the sound

162

of geese. He did not move but lay staring at the ends of straw protruding through the boards; his limbs ached but he felt warm, secure and comforted. The sun shone through the cracks and threw a golden line across the little compartment; he heard somebody drawing water and the sound of clogs moving across the yard.

He looked at the smart jack-boots and S.S. jacket he had taken from Ohlau; they were tangible relics of that nightmare of the past that struggled to assert itself— the shouting guards, the march, the waits on roll-call in the East wind, the grey-faced queues. And now, outside the cocks crowed.

He heard the clogs coming towards the barn and the big door creak open. The bundles of straw concealing the entrance to his hiding place moved and Anna Nacek came in; the steam from the bowl she held drifted into the golden line made by sun.

"How do you feel now, Anton? Did you wonder where you were when you awoke?"

"We don't wake in heaven every day," he answered. She laughed softly.

"Is it the soup or my face makes you say that?"

"There is an atmosphere of heaven here."

"Oh. Well, you must not get up, just drink the soup, all the family will be coming to see you soon. I shall bring some hot water for you to wash in."

"What time is it?" he asked.

"It must be past three, it's such a fine afternoon now, the snow has almost gone again."

"Could you tell my cousin Jan that I am here? How is he?"

"We see him sometimes," her round, jolly face assumed an air of gravity: "Anton, it is best to tell no one. We must be so careful. You must come into the

163

house to-night, the family are longing to hear about your escape. Oh yes, I almost forgot——" from the pocket of her apron she drew a cigarette-packet: "There are three in here—*Junos*. Father sent them, but be very careful of the straw."

"I shall take the greatest care."

With a smile and a warning shake of her finger she went out.

He rose shakily and peered through the cracks in the boarding, looking past the outbuilding at the plain of Palukin, surrounded by forests. This was the land he knew; its ties were stronger than he had realised. He stared at the distant homesteads, the clumps of trees; his heart was like an open wound of memory: the smallest things touched it and hurt in some way. A few leaves, black now, as though cut from smoked-tin, were still clinging to the deformed bush by the corner of the barn and shuddering in the wind. It had always been a dreary land in November, there seemed nothing to fight for here, nothing to live for even: barren fields swept by the East wind, everything under the shadow of war; where life itself was war almost; war against the sandy soil. A poor land, with bare-footed children beginning work in the fields. But never before had he felt its peculiar magic so strongly; its atmosphere of tragedy and ruin redeemed by love and faith.

The sun was going down towards the trees of the estate that had belonged to Lucien Markenski . . .

How could she ever forgive him? But he would redeem that treachery by revenging all she had suffered, by joining Radek, by fighting with the Partisans. When she heard of the smashed gravestone she would understand his hatred as he understood hers. He had much to revenge.

# CHAPTER TEN

SOMETIMES in the evening, when Franceska had cleared away the dishes and everybody seemed to be talking at once, old Nacek would say "Listen!" Staring into each other's eyes, they would hear the snow falling off the roof or the very faint murmur of sleigh bells on the Likora road; sometimes two sick ducks made soft, contented sounds from their baskets by the stove. After a dreadful minute Anna or Leo would laugh and they would all start talking again, whilst the old woman continued to spin or sew, listening dispassionately while the others told Jankowski about Radek's exploits, his astounding escapes, their own escapes when Radek was staying with them; the crone would nod her head sagely, implying that she had known such hectic times before.

When speaking of Radek, Anna would laugh, showing her two gold teeth, but the prim, blue-eyed Franceska only shook her head at the tales of danger and reckless-ness. Radek and his two comrades, Klemba and Darok, had apparently given the impression that the Struga forest was infested with Partisans. Perhaps it was? Jankowski could not tell, but the Naceks were con-vinced that every murder committed, every pig stolen, every attack on the police was the inspired work of the great Radek.

"But when will he come?" Jankowski would ask them, "I must see him. I want to join him. You have been too good to me. Look!" he would hold out his arm, "if I stay here much longer I shall be as fat as old Ambrose in Palukin."

"He will be here soon. He will come."

The lamp often went down while they talked. If anybody called they bustled Jankowski into the next room, where he waited in the darkness, listening to the voices, sometimes peering through the keyhole to see if it was anyone he knew. The Naceks seemed to enjoy this play-acting, spiced with danger as it was.

Late at night he would return to his little compartment in the barn, and lie and listen to the rats and mice rustling in the straw. He felt that he could wait no longer for Radek. What had happened to him? He might have been caught. But the Naceks always assured him that Radek would come; they seemed to know, almost as if they were in touch with him. But he could wait no longer. He must act.

He began to wander out at night, sometimes into the forest but usually to the Struga lake which was already fringed with ice. Her image lingered there, implacable, precious as the last hope of salvation. That insane *Scharführer* had been right when speaking of a woman with the gift of salvation. His desire for her had become an obsession.

One night Anna came back from Likora with news that an *ortsbauernführer* had been murdered in daylight while driving his waggon through the forest on the other side of Milunken. When they heard the news the Naceks looked at each other significantly. Jankowski knew that they were thinking of Radek.

"This will let hell loose," he told them, "the place will crawl with police. You are risking too much. I must go."

"Where can you go?" Franceska asked. "No, no, you must wait until he comes, Anton; the murder was a long way from here, the police won't bother us."

But he knew that the murder had troubled them. The atmosphere was not so cheerful in the evenings; while they talked, they seemed to be listening for a warning yap from the dog. The old man would get out his ancient map and gloat over the towns he had surrounded with red ink; the map had always comforted him, his round, blue eyes would brighten when he explained to Jankowski what might happen on the Western Front, but in the evenings now his mind wandered. Jankowski knew that the old man, like the others, was listening for the sharp yaps of the dog.

In the middle of December they heard that police were searching the houses of Malkow. Jankowski decided to go into the forests.

"If you go now you will freeze to death," Anna told him, as they sat late at night round the table. "Listen to that wind! The windows are covered in frost. Don't be mad, Anton——"

He listened. He knew she was right. But he knew that if he were caught here the family would be taken out and shot.

No one spoke for a long time. They could hear the snow being driven against the window by the raging wind; occasionally one of the ducks by the fire gave a low, satisfied quack. The lamp got low and the old man lifted it down to the table that he might study his map better.

"Somebody's coming," Leo said softly.

Conscious of the white faces, the wide eyes round the table, Jankowski listened. For a moment he only heard the wind roaring round the building. He listened in an agony of concentration. There was a lull; the dog was yapping madly. Before he could move somebody tapped on the window a yard from his head.

"Merciful God!" the old man whispered hoarsely, "it's Zygmus."

They all rose; Anna hurried out. They heard the back door open. A man spoke, then laughed; a moment later Radek came in, covered in snow. He was smiling, there was a bottle in his hand. Without a word he stepped forward and grasped Jankowski's hand.

"Well done," he said at last, "well done, brother."

The snow was thawing and dripping from his short overcoat, from the battered cap he had tucked under his arm. He had not changed, but seemed unnaturally alert; his eyes had the slightly tense look of a man whose life is continually in danger: the look of the hunted who rejoiced in the hunt.

"Sit down, hang your coat up by the stove, Zygmus," Anna said, "we must heat some milk up for him, mother, I can make some pancakes too."

Radek was still staring at Jankowski.

"I knew you had it in you," he said slowly.

"I have almost gone mad waiting for you," Jankowski answered. "Stepha left Heinrichau, have you found out where she is?"

Radek passed his hand over his eyes in a gesture of weariness.

"Not a trace. I have given up inquiring. Poor girl, God knows what happened."

"Have you been to Heinrichau?"

"No," Radek answered abruptly, "somebody did, somebody I trust. They knew nothing there; she had been sent away, why or where nobody seemed to know." He turned and put his bottle on the table.

"A present for you, *Pan* Nacek," he gave the old man a slight bow. "*Schnaps.* Ninety-two per cent. alcohol."

The family murmured in surprise, then all began

talking at once. The old woman, sewing by the stove, nodded.

"Wandering about on a night like this," Franceska was saying, "with a bottle of *Schnaps*."

"We must celebrate," *Pan* Nacek said cheerfully, "there is good news from the Russian Front, what's in the papers is all lies," he indicated a town on the map with the handle of a spoon.

Leo diluted the *Schnaps* with warm water and they sat round the table; they talked of trivial things, but Jankowski knew that part of them was listening for the dog, wondering whether he could be heard above the tremendous wind. Radek spoke of a pig he had stolen.

"They must have heard it squealing in Berlin. But we got away with it—Klemba is a genius with an axe— we slung it on a pole and staggered for miles, over ditches, ploughed fields."

Jankowski asked whether they had murdered anything worse than pigs.

Radek studied him intently.

"They did something to you in that place, brother. You have changed more than I thought it possible for anyone to change," he paused, "they have taught you how to hate."

"They taught me more than that."

"A hard school," Radek murmured.

Jankowski did not answer. He felt suddenly afraid that Radek had been to Pallow and seen the uprooted gravestones. And then he realised, with a kind of horror, that everybody in the district must know. He looked at the faces round the table, they must all know.

"Have some more *Schnaps*, Anton," Radek said gently, "don't think of Maskowitz, just thank your guardian angel that you got away."

"He never tells us much," Franceska murmured, "but there is hatred in his eyes when he talks of Germans."

"Yes, hatred," Jankowski said slowly, "and yet I remember Markenski's words——"

"Markenski?" Radek broke in, "was he there?"

"He was there."

"Is he still there?"

"He was shot trying to escape."

"Shot trying to escape," Radek repeated slowly, "Lucien Markenski? If you only knew how strange, how incomprehensible, how terrible that sounds, a man like that, so gentle in every way, shot while trying to escape! The criminal absurdity of it all. They are trying to kill Poland. Do you know, Anton, sometimes I wonder whether I carry on for revenge only, revenge, hatred. Where have we gone wrong, I wonder; I mean the whole world? I have got used to living like a rat, hiding, nerves always tingling; but sometimes I wonder, we are fighting for a cause, for freedom, but history reeks with the blood of those who thought they were fighting for a cause——"

"I am not the only one who has changed apparently," Jankowski said grimly, "of course blood has been spilled, the blood of Christ has never stopped flowing."

"I never expected to hear you say that," Radek answered in a startled voice, "but how can the blood of those who spill blood be the blood of Christ? Christ spilled no blood."

"No, but I for one, don't profess to be Christ."

"You do," Radek answered forcibly, "you spoke as if we were fighting Christ's war. But there is no Christ's war, only His peace, but we fight for our own little earthly lives, it's all we have. Do you think I like de-

170

railing trains, turning wives into widows, bereaving mothers?"

"Let us change the subject," Jankowski said shortly, "before we all march out and kiss the nearest Gestapo agent."

"It would surprise him. He might forget to beat us to death," Radek answered.

"He might not," Jankowski said; "when can I join you in the forest?"

"I must see the other two first," Radek replied, "but I think they will be glad to have you, I shall tell them that you are a very desperate character."

"But when shall I know?"

Radek silently twisted his glass of *Schnaps*.

"To-day is the sixteenth," he said, after a moment, "I shall meet you on the twenty-first. A mile from the Likora road, on the main path to Likol there is an old shooting-box. Do you know it?"

"The one Kassel used to use. I know it."

"I shall be there three hours after dark. Bring what you have. I cannot come here again until that murder has blown over."

"I shall be there three hours after dark," Jankowski said.

"Should you arrive first, make a noise like this when you see me coming," Radek made a clucking sound, "I shall do the same if I get there first. If I am not there by nine o'clock you will know something has happened. Good, so that's all arranged."

He looked at the clock.

"Five past twelve," he murmured. He rose with a sigh.

The three women went into the kitchen; Jankowski heard the rustle of paper and their voices speaking softly. When they emerged, Anna held a great loaf wrapped in an old copy of the *Danziger Vorposten*, Franceska had a small, square parcel and four eggs, each one wrapped in paper. From the stove they reached down Radek's coat, putting the eggs and small parcel into its pockets.

"One day, by the grace of God, I shall visit you all in daylight," Radek said, "in the sun; I shall help you mow the piece of ground, Leo, and help you chop the wood, Anna." He looked at the pictures, then at the fire. They watched him in silence, while the wind howled and snowflakes murmured against the windows.

He kissed the hands of the women and saluted the men.

"God bless you all and a happy Christmas."

Anna let him out of the back-door.

Jankowski returned to the barn soon after, but he could not sleep. Twice he rose and peered towards the forest, impenetrable in the darkness.

For five days he waited, scanning old copies of the *Vorposten*, looking through the cracks in the boarding until his eyes ached. At last the day arrived. He watched the pink flush leave the miles of untrodden snow, as the red sun went down behind the belt of trees.

Half-an-hour before the appointed time he said good-bye to the Naceks and went into the forest. The wind lisped in the higher branches as he approached the shooting-box. He paused and listened; occasionally he heard lumps of snow falling off the boughs. Slowly, he groped his way forward. Reaching the rough ladder he leant against it, and rubbed his hands together to keep them warm.

It seemed that he had waited all his life for this moment.

He peered all round him into the darkness, holding his breath at the slightest sound. Surely it was time now. Could there have been some mistake? Perhaps the Gestapo had found out! Radek might even be laying a trap for him; a man like Radek would not forget the things he had said against Poland. This was absurd. All that was changed now. He visualised those fragments of gravestones very clearly; he heard again the crunching as they were broken, each letter of his mother's name came forward out of the night, charging it with hatred.

The wind blew against his face. Where was Radek? Would he ever hear the signal in this whining wind? He turned his head abruptly. Surely that was the signal! He replied. Almost at once a dim shadow materialised a yard in front of him.

"Is that Radek?" his voice sounded very loud.

"Yes. The others will welcome you," Radek said softly as they shook hands, "did you bring the Luger?"

"Of course."

"And in that parcel, there is a blanket? Good, good. Come on then."

Radek led the way towards the path, walking with his slight swagger, and an alert motion of the head. Jankowski felt tense and exhilarated. They would never get him again, these woods were vast and wild, as Radek had said, they belonged to the Partisans after sundown.

Radek did not speak, all his directions were indicated by a movement of his arm. Jankowski had no idea where the secret dugout was. They followed various paths for three miles, then Radek stopped. They listened. There was no sound but the wind and the snow falling off the branches.

Radek whistled three times. From somewhere to the

left came an answer. They swung off the path into a plantation. Small boughs scratched Jankowski's face; he advanced with one hand protecting his eyes. Radek did not slacken speed. Jankowski blundered on behind him for about three hundred yards, then he saw a patch of the night sky. They advanced twenty yards into a plantation of firs no higher than their waists, then Radek suddenly halted.

He touched Jankowski's sleeve.

"Can you hear anything?" he whispered.

Beneath his feet Jankowski heard faint dance music, a fantastic sound in this wilderness.

Radek knelt, held aside the branches of a little fir with one hand, lifted something with the other. Immediately the music was louder. Radek shone a torch into the entrance, revealing a rough ladder made from thin pines.

"Go first," he whispered, "tread gently."

Jankowski descended on the wet, cold rungs for about twelve feet. On his hands fell pieces of earth dislodged by Radek coming down behind him.

"Just on your left there," Radek said softly, "there's a curtain, push it aside and go in."

Jankowski did so. He might have been in a small, windowless log cabin. An oil lamp burned on a table which hinged to the wall, on a primus stove a pot steamed, pictures of beautiful women cut from magazines adorned one wall, on another hung a rifle and a bow-saw, above them a large, brass Crucifix. Two deep bunks, one over the other, faced Jankowski. A man was half-lying on the top bunk, playing a gramophone. The lamplight brought out the shadows on his face; a long face, thick-lipped and hook-nosed, with a jutting chin. His smile was gay, reckless, vital: but Jankowski saw the lines of suffering, the marks under the eyes. By the Naceks' descriptions he knew this was Klemba, a miller's son from Magudken who had escaped from Stuthoff and whose entire family had been horribly murdered two years ago.

He said "Merry Christmas," as he shook Jankowski's hand.

The gramophone played the popular German dance tune *Lili und Louisa*.

"How do you feel, Anton?" Radek asked, reaching down three tins with wire handles from the shelf.

"More alive than I have ever felt in my life," Jankowski answered fervently, "mad, exhilarated! Thank God I can act at last."

"Don't I know that feeling!" Radek exclaimed softly. "Such moments are the compensation for this dangerous life we lead. Enjoy this one, Anton, you will never get such moments again; when the tears and the terror have left the land and the danger's gone, no moments will shine quite so bright. What water is so wonderful as that found after a great thirst, what air so fine as that breathed after long captivity? But I'm sad to-night, I can't help thinking of our little Stepha. Do you know this part of the forest well?"

"Yes."

"I think I know every path, every tree almost. I am at home here during the night, the few times I have seen it in daylight it has seemed a strange place, but during the night it is our friend. The police don't venture here now. Last winter we caught a policeman near Likora, stripped him, took his revolver and clothes then told him to run."

"And he broke all records?" suggested Jankowski.

"I don't know," Radek answered seriously, "it was too dark to see, but he did quite well."

"Does your other friend sleep here?" Jankowski asked.

"Darok? Not every night, he spends three nights a week with a girl in Palukin, but he's coming back early to-night. He's a strange fellow, God knows what race, half-French, half-Russian he told me; anyway, he came out of Russia. He lived in Kiev and first turned up somewhere near Brok. When you meet him you'll be surprised, perhaps disappointed; he looks like a particularly mild form of bank-clerk. He hardly ever speaks. But wait until you see him in action!"

"He is a terror," Klemba affirmed.

Sitting on the bottom bunk, sipping a tin of *kaffee-ersatz*, Jankowski almost forgot that he was twelve feet under ground in the depths of a wintry forest.

"We have started a little reign of terror on our own round here," Radek told him, "and what a place to operate from, too! As lonely as a Steppe. We wash at the little stream that flows into the lake; as you know, we live on what we steal from Bessarabians or Germans, or what our own people can spare us. By the way, an ardent Party member lives at Malkow now; he is on our list."

"Your list?"

"I mean we shall kill him sometime."

"But that means so many Malkow Poles will be shot."

"I know. That's why I said sometime."

For a time there was silence. The tree-trunks of which the little bunker was constructed shone in the lamp-light, the pictures of Klemba's favourite actress had crinkled in the heat.

"Darok's coming," Radek said.

They heard the clucking signal; a moment later there

was a movement on the ladder and a man pushed aside the curtain.

"Did you get any tobacco?" Klemba asked.

Darok removed his cap, showing a high, smooth forehead.

"The usual dynamite," he answered, his light blue eyes on Jankowski.

"I've smoked boot-laces before now," was the answer, "I bet our friend Anton has, too."

"Never," Jankowski answered, rising to shake hands, "only the elite smoked boot-laces at Maskowitz."

"We can make a four at cards now," Darok said, as he took Jankowski's hand. "I welcome you, brother."

He unwrapped his parcel of bread and a piece of pork and put it in a box under the bunk. He took off his short coat, like Radek's an army overcoat cut off above the knees. With a pale, studious face, he did not look like a desperate Partisan.

Radek divided the tobacco into four little piles, taking great care not to spill any. Soon the air of the bunker was blue with smoke, the faces content in the lamplight. Darok played a reeling, endless tune on a defective mouth-organ; he sat on the bottom bunk with his head down and beat time with his feet. He stopped abruptly and put the mouth-organ away on the shelf.

"What about that goose?" he asked. He turned to Jankowski. "Do you know, Anton, we've been planning to get a Christmas goose for six weeks?"

"What about Magudken?" Radek suggested.

"Good," Darok said, "to-morrow night then."

"But down to work now," Radek went on, "pass that paper and pencil, Franek. Did you say that the signalmen in Likora station were all Poles?"

"All three," Klemba answered.

Radek turned to Jankowski.

"We are planning to wreck one of those trains that take troops and munitions to the Eastern Front. We shall need your help badly, Anton; it is the biggest thing we have planned yet. If we cannot get the stuff to blow up the line, we intend taking the Likora signal-box just before the train is due; we would turn the train into a siding. Here——" Radek produced a piece of paper and smoothed it out on the bunk, "here it is, the signal-box not far from this plantation," he pointed to a dark patch on the little map he had drawn, "it's really quite simple if carefully worked out——"

While they talked and planned, Jankowski learnt that the men he had joined had no contact with other cells of the Polish Underground, but Radek strove to impress upon him that the real Underground was a mere irritant to the enemy compared with their own inspired onslaughts.

"I can't help thinking of that goose," Darok said.

"Then let's get it now!" Radek rose. "Come on!"

Within half-an-hour they were following the track to Likol. Jankowski realised that Radek had been unable to resist the temptation to show him what they could do. And he suspected that Radek's swagger was slightly exaggerated to-night.

"All these cursed Bessarabians have guns and fierce dogs," Radek said softly, as they came out into the open.

The small homesteads, scattered over the plain, were clearly visible under the half-moon. By the shape of a solitary tree, that stood where the track branched, Jankowski recognised the place. He had driven through here as a boy, on the way to Magudken.

The ground was frozen hard; their footsteps rang. Jankowski expected to be halted. These men were over-confident, mad.

178

"That's the place," Radek jerked his hand towards a building a quarter of a mile to their left. "It won't be easy, I know these devils. We must come up under the cover of that barn."

In single file, they went on swiftly down the narrow track.

"Good," Radek whispered, when they reached the barn, "have that stick ready, Franek, I hope your Luger's in good order, Anton. They lock the geese in that low shed at night."

While Jankowski watched the door of the house, and Klemba the path, Radek and Darok slunk towards the shed. Before they reached it the dog heard them; Jankowski saw its dark form streak across the yard. There was a thud, followed by appalling squeals. The geese shrieked and beat their wings. The house door banged as Radek and Darok dashed across the yard. Radek had the goose. They fled towards the forest, with somebody shooting blindly after them. Every dog in the district yapped or howled.

They were far into the forest when they halted.

"Wonderful!" Radek said. "But what a bird! Feel it."

All the way back they laughed.

"These little frays cheer us up," Radek told Jankowski solemnly, to accentuate the casual audacity of the raid, "but I don't know what Stepha would have done if she'd seen me hit that dog."

"No," Jankowski said, "she felt such things."

They said no more until they were sitting in the bunker.

"Before we sleep we must read the Lord's prayer of the Polish Underground," Radek told them gravely, "this occasion calls for it, we have a new comrade now."

He turned to Klemba, "you know it by heart, Franek."

Without a word Klemba rose from the bunk and knelt facing the wall where hung the rifle, the saw and the Crucifix. Radek and Darok knelt by the bunk; after a moment's hesitation Jankowski knelt beside them.

They made the sign of the Cross as Klemba began, low and passionately:

"Our Father Who art in Heaven, look upon the martyred land of Poland. Hallowed be Thy name in the day of our incessant despair, in these days of our powerless silence.

"Thy Kingdom come. We pray every morning steadfastly: Thy Kingdom come throughout Poland, and may in liberty and sunshine Thy Word of Peace and Love be fulfilled.

"Thy Will be done on Earth as it is in Heaven. Thy will be done. Yet it cannot be Thy Will to have murder and bloody licentiousness rule the world. May it be Thy will that humid prison cells stay empty—that forest pits cease being filled with corpses—that the whip of Satan incarnate in man stop its whizz of terror over our heads. Thy Will be done in Heaven and in the air, bringing us light and warmth instead of bombs and fear. Let aeroplanes be messengers of happiness and not of death. Thy Will be done on earth. Lord, look at our land covered with graves, and lighten the path of our sons, brethren and fathers, of the Polish soldiers fighting their way back to Poland. Let the Sea return the drowned, the waste spaces of land the buried ones, the sands of the deserts and the snows of Siberia give us back at least the bodies of those we loved.

"Give us this day our daily bread. Our daily bread is toil beyond any endurance—it is wandering and migrating and death in dungeons, death that comes

180

from the gun of the firing squad, from tortures in camps, death from starvation, and death on the battle-field. It is the torture of silence while our throats are choking with stifled screams of pain; our daily bread is a forced clenching of our fists and setting of our teeth in the hour that cries for bloody revenge. To this daily bread of ours, O Lord, add force and endurance, patience, and will power that we be silent, lest we burst out before the hour of destiny rings.

"And forgive us our trespasses. Forgive us, O Lord, should we be too weak to crush the beast. Strengthen our arm lest it tremble in the hour of revenge. They have sinned against Thee, they have trespassed upon Thine eternal laws. Do not let us sin against Thee with weakness as they sin in criminal debauch.

"And lead us not into temptation. Lead us not into temptation, but let spies and traitors among us perish. Do not let money bind the hearts of the rich. Let the replete feed the hungry. Let Poles recognise each other anywhere and at any hour. Let our mouths be silent while the torturer crushes our bones. And lead us not into temptation to forget to-morrow what we are suffering to-day.

"But deliver us from evil. Deliver us from the evil one, from the foe of our Polish land. Save us, O Lord, from the paths and misery of deportation, from death on land, in air and sea, from treason of our own.

"Amen. Let us again be hosts on our own soil. Let us rest our hearts with the calm of the sea and the beauty of our mountains. Let us feed the starving crowds in Thy sunshine O Lord. Let us establish justice in a righteous Poland: Amen. Give us freedom, O Lord! Amen."

# CHAPTER ELEVEN

LISTENING to the waggons of East Prussian refugees, Jankowski remembered that monotonous rumble, mingled with yells of encouragement to weary horses, that he had heard on the same road five years ago. He remembered the covered waggons, with pieces of furniture hanging from the sides, the old men pushing prams; these Prussian refugees were too much like that last host to excite him. They looked the same; no doubt they felt the same.

Behind him, in the kitchen, Anna Nacek was wrapping up a loaf of bread for him to take back to the underground bunker.

"Anton," she said suddenly.

"Yes?"

"Stepha Markenski is in Kirschau."

He stared at her. Without looking at him she nodded.

"Zofia Kot saw her fifteen months ago."

"No!"

"It's true. She was stacking wood in Bendimir's yard. I knew it would please you, Anton."

"But I can't believe it," he said stupidly.

"Zofia said she nearly fell off her cycle; she used to work for the Markenskis; she was on the Starogin road —the new *autobahn*."

"The new *autobahn*?" he repeated inanely, "but . . . then she is alive?"

"Don't stare like that, Anton, I'm not a ghost; I meant to tell you before, when——"

"In Kirschau! Well, thank God."

He went to the table and stared at the lamp-flame.

"But I'd given up hope a year ago!" he whispered.

"Don't worry, Anton, she hasn't forgotten you; no Polish woman could forget such a Partisan."

"Fifteen months ago," he said abruptly, "she might have left."

"Oh surely not; anyway, you could find out where she has gone. It was a saw-mill, she was on one of those wood-piles; Zofia heard her call——"

"I shall go to-morrow," he said, trying to restrain his excitement.

"Not in daylight, Anton; I am terrified about those police Leo saw."

"I know that saw-mill," he murmured, "I could be there by ten."

He picked up his cap: "I must get to the bunker and tell Zygmus."

Under the moon, along the stony track, he hurried towards the forest. The paper Anna had wrapped round the loaf came unwrapped and flapped in his hand; regardless, he hurried on, past the potato clamps, the dark stacks, and into the forest. He reached the path, high above the lake, where his parents used to meet. His father must have walked like this: senses alert, slightly exhilarated by the danger, with his heart full of hopes and memories. He branched left at the stream and followed its bank, walking faster, his feet making no sound on the turf, the paper flapping. What would Radek think?

At the next branch of the path he almost bumped into a man. A torch blazed into his eyes.

"*Halt! Ausweis!* Your papers."

"I have them here——" he slipped a hand into his jacket; whipping out the Lugar, he fired. With the explosion ringing in his ears, he dived to the left, tear-

183

ing through the pine-saplings that clustered round the large trees. Police-whistles shrilled behind him, then to his left, to his right. They had found the bunker. And he had left Radek and Klemba there. He ran on with a cold feeling at his heart. Darok would walk into their hands. He made for the rumble of waggons on the Likora road; he would mingle with refugees; but, crossing the Likol path a light shone on him; a great voice roared "Halt!" He dived back into the undergrowth as a burst of machine-pistol fire tore through the leaves. To his left, someone yelled an order; a body of men came running down the path.

Where now? The Naceks? No, they might trace him there. But he must get out of the area somehow. He crept back to the Likol path. He dashed across but was seen again. A whistle shrilled. There was not much chance now—this was an organised round-up. He made for the Likora road but he knew it was hopeless.

There were cars on the road; there was one twenty yards away; by the glimmer of its side-lights he saw the S.S. uniforms. He heard the voices, staccato, hatefully familiar. Keeping to the ditch he crawled towards them. Ten yards away he waited. Almost within his reach, one passed down the road. Another walked away from the car in the other direction. The man at the wheel lit a cigarette. Jankowski crawled to the running-board; reached up for the rear door-handle and sprang in.

"Drive!" he pressed the Luger into the man's neck, "alright, I shoot and drive myself——"

With a startled grunt the driver accelerated.

S.S. men came into the headlight beams, sprang away in time and fired blindly. Bullets ripped through the fabric.

"I itch to kill you," Jankowski said softly, "make for Starogin."

The driver was muttering: "What a fool, what a fool, a trick like that—*Gott*, what a fool I am . . . these cursed bandit-hunts! . . . I must say something when they catch us."

"You die if they catch us," Jankowski told him forcibly. "What did you swines find in the forest?"

"Christ! My neck, curse you——"

"What did you find!"

"A bunker; they blew it up."

"Empty?"

"There was a frying-pan, something else, too—a saw I think."

"A frying-pan?" Jankowski was hoarse with relief, "and the old saw——"

They swept through Likora, swerved into the Starogin road.

Jankowski laughed.

"A frying-pan! What a great police force."

They followed the road into the Starogin forest. He glanced behind. Not a sign of headlights. But they would be after him.

"Slow down. Turn into the first forest track."

They sped on.

"Slow down!"

"Oh no, my dear, we're going to Lieberschau."

Jankowski understood.

"So you think I won't shoot?" he jabbed the Luger into the other's neck, "that I'd prefer torture to hitting a tree at sixty-three miles an hour? Bonehead. Slow down!"

"Curse you, my neck——"

They slowed down.

"That track on the right; go down it for half-a-mile."
They turned sharply and the lights went out.

Jankowski fired, shattering the wind-screen; before
he could fire again he was flung back violently as the
car crashed into a tree. The driver had gone.

Bonehead? Jankowski sprang out; listened for the
driver fleeing through the forest. There was not a
sound. He left the useless car and hurried down the
track.

He would reach Kirschau before dawn; the image that
thought evoked killed his fear. What would she think
of him? Perhaps she would be working in the yard;
how he would surprise her! But in that image was
terror. She might ask him whether he had seen her
father. What could he say?

He sat on a fallen tree and put his head between his
hands. There was no hope of her forgiveness; he could
see that now, with her image so vivid in his mind. Faced
by the frankness, the simplicity, the courage of her
youth, what could he say? Murder, sabotage, days of
relentless struggle against the enemy, had he thought
that Stepha would forgive the betrayal of her father
because of that! She would not forgive. But he could
not lose her. His only hope was to lie.

He went on slowly towards Kirschau.

The track brought him out on the *autobahn*, wide,
white in the moonlight, reaching away through the flat
beet-fields. He walked faster, keeping to the edge of the
fields; the beet-leaves brushed against his trousers; the
wind soughed through the telegraph wires. He had
always felt elated, walking in the hours before the dawn,
when he had the spacious world to himself. But memories and ghosts were strong to-night. Faint tremors,
and rumbling in the East heralded for Poland—for

Europe, a vast, fateful change. He disdained it. He only wondered what she would think of him, and he felt the heartache, the longing, the despair of his quest for love and faith. He walked without lifting his eyes; the first he knew of the dawn was the pinkish flush on the cement of the *autobahn*. Larks sprang from the dew, mounted into the grey light.

Soon after sunrise, he saw the shining patch of river, broken by the bridge, and the church-spire, the factory-chimneys like sticks of schoolroom chalk, belching forth smoke which was tinged by the sun.

The dew dried; soon he walked on sandy dust. A grey staff-car swept down the *autobahn*. He half-expected to be questioned, but was too weary to care. He had seen Kirschau before, but not like this: it looked transformed, beautiful. And there was the thin, black chimney of the saw-mill where she worked; he heard the faint roar of the big saws, the high-pitched scream of a band-saw. Round the grey-roofed building he saw the neat stacks of wood in the yard, the workers moving about.

But on reaching the yard he did not see her. Three men in shirt-sleeves were pushing trollies loaded with tree trunks into the shed; girls were loading a waggon near the road. One had her back to him. Surely he knew that figure, that set of head, that hair! But she turned; her face was coarse, flat.

Two girls were walking from a stack of wood towards the shed. He went over to them.

"Does Stepha Markenski work here?"

The plump, sensual girl with a red scarf smiled at him; she was more interested in him than his question.

"Who did you want?"

"Stepha Markenski."

Again the voluptuous smile.

"Oh, Stepha? You've come too late for her—you're a poor cavalier," she turned to her companion, "you used to work with Stepha Markenski, Wanda, how long ago did she leave?"

"Last May, or June—over a year ago," she was looking at him closely, "are you Anton . . . Anton what was it?—Jankowski?"

"No," he assured her hurriedly. "Can you tell me where Stepha Markenski is?"

"That was it—Jankowski! She used to talk about him sometimes . . . but of course, I remember now—they took him away, Stuthoff I think it was. Don't tell me you're Leo!"

A tall, smiling foreman with his hands behind his back, came towards them from the shed.

"Have you any idea at all where Stepha Markenski is?" Jankowski almost shouted.

"I have her address."

"Thank God. Give it to me please."

"She wrote it down on a slip of paper when I met her near the bank; but I never went to visit her," the girl fell silent, saddened by the memory of this omission.

"Give this poor man her address," the plump girl said indignantly, "can't you see he's her lover?"

"I am giving it to him now; it was fifty-one Hermann Goring *Strasse*. Don't forget—Hermann Goring *Strasse*, it used to be Zygmount Street. Fifty-one."

"Fifty-one Hermann Goring *Strasse*," he repeated, watching the foreman approaching. "I shall remember."

"Come back and tell us if she's not there," the plump girl called after him, "there are plenty of ripe girls in the saw-mill."

He went on through the busy streets, under the blue sky; there was enough wind to move the curtains in the

188

open windows, to give a sheen to the plane-trees. In the summer sun, people loitered and laughed, undaunted by the faint murmur of guns heralding change. But over all was the uncertainty, the precariousness, the knowledge that soon this bubble might burst, leaving dust, rubble, window-holes staring at nothing; knowledge that seemed to crystallise the shifting, transitory fleeting of all life.

Kirschau had changed since he had seen it last; it looked like a German town; the names over the shops were German; the streets were named after high officials of the Third Reich; German soldiers strolled along the pavements.

He looked at the expensive houses in Herman Goring *Strasse* in surprise. No doubt that fool of a girl had made a mistake. He would have to be careful. Number fifty-one was as imposing as the rest. After a moment's hesitation he mounted the steps and rang.

An old Polish woman opened the door.

"Is Miss Markenski in?"

"Yes. What is the name?"

"Anton. She will know—just say Anton."

She silently closed the door in his face.

He stared at the polished knocker, the white doorstep. There was something wrong. It could not be the same Stepha Markenski. He had come for nothing. He heard hurried footsteps; the door flung open.

"Anton!"

"Why, Stepha——"

"Can it really be? After so many days!" she took both his hands in hers, "but this is wonderful—I mean, to see you again, Anton . . . I gave you up for lost. You understand, I gave you up for dead, Anton." Her great eyes were fixed on him with a look he could not understand. And her eyes had changed; they had hardened; there was something about them unhappy, disenchanted.

"Well please, Anton, come in—don't stand there; but you look worn out, where have you come from? You look like——"

"You mean I look like a bandit," he said slowly. The hall through which she took him, reminded him, by constrast, of the underground bunker.

They entered a wide room. The open window looked out upon Hermann Goring *Strasse*.

"Have a drink—not *Schnaps*, I'm afraid—do you remember that ghastly stuff the prisoners of war used to drink?"

She stood before him, calm, well-dressed, sophisticated.

"You have changed," he murmured.

"I suppose so," she replied enigmatically, without raising her eyes from the glass she held. "And haven't you? It has been a long war."

In silence, he looked at the thick carpet, the shining table.

"It all belongs to Hugo Kassel," she said slowly.

"And——"

"I live here. That's all, Anton."

"Then you married——?"

"No . . . why keep questioning? Anton, surely——" she broke off, looking at him steadily.

He smiled, the bitter smile of one who tastes poison.

"I came here for help," he said calmly, feeling utterly weary.

"Anton——"

"May I sit down, Stepha?"

"What can I do?" she asked eagerly, "I want to help, let me help you now—what is it? Food, shelter, clothes, tell me, Anton; tell me how I can help," she put her hand on his arm. He noticed that the nails were no longer broken; her hands were beautifully kept. It was somehow dishonourable.

"I am beginning to see now that you cannot help me," he went on, "you see, I want shelter from the police. I want it now." He looked at the large photograph of a German officer that adorned the sideboard. He turned and met her eyes.

"This is not the place to shelter from Germans," he said.

She did not answer. She looked at him steadily.

"So, you see, Stepha, I must go after all."

"Where?"

"I must think where."

"You are going to stay," she said.

"How can I?"

"Anton, do you think I could let you go? What do you think I am? Don't you understand, can't you understand—have some compassion, Anton. Please let me help you——"

"How can I stay? What would Kassel do if he caught me? Do you think *he* would understand?"

"I don't know, but he's away—he went to Poznan—I ask you again, Anton, I beseech you—let me help you. Anton—I——" she put her arm round his shoulder. "Don't be hard."

They were silent. Through the open window came the sound of waggons, the occasional honking of a motor-horn.

"Hard," she whispered at last, "you were always hard, Anton—and proud, though you'd never admit it. What can I do?" she said despairingly.

He went over to the window and looked down into the

busy street, his hands behind his back. She came and stood beside him.

"Anton, look at me—what's wrong? Why are *you* like this, you of all people? What has happened?"

He looked round.

"Like you Stepha, I have changed."

"Yes," she murmured, "of course, Maskowitz . . ."

Neither spoke for a long moment.

"We have come a long way," she said softly, at last, "who could have foreseen . . . they have made you hate."

He did not answer.

"I don't know what to do," she said, with a gesture of weariness. "It's quite beyond me, I had a different memory of you, Anton."

He watched the people passing down the street, the women in their summer frocks, the men carrying their jackets.

"Of course," he mumbled, "different memory—that was it."

"There's not much love left in Europe now," she said, "there's hatred in most hearts now-a-days, but I never thought to find it in yours; you seemed above that, or below it. But after all, you are like the rest, you are only human."

"Hatred is reached through love," he answered, "don't you of all people see that? When a beloved person is humiliated, taken away, hatred is born with the intensity of that love. But what happened to your love and your hatred?"

"I don't hate any more, that's all. The absurdity of it dawned on me long ago."

"Then you don't love any more."

"*Doch!*" she used the familiar German expression,

"the things I used to love I still love. But why are we talking like this? Tell me about yourself, where you have been—it seems you haven't prospered exactly, Anton."

"I am broke," he said with conviction, "can't you see that I am broke? No faith, no race, no philosophy, no illusions, why, I even stole these trousers."

"I think you could have stolen a better pair," she remarked, "poor Anton! But why tell me this? Haven't you always been, as you say—broke?"

Her tone was light, bantering; she was looking at him with a hint of mockery.

"Never so broke as I am now," he answered, "are you sorry I came, Stepha?"

"It is good to see you again, Anton; I have often thought about you, of your exhilarating bitterness, your contempt, of all the things you used to tell me on that horrible farm—what was it called? Heinrichau! I was very young in those days, full of faith, full of hope, full of charity—so young, I never missed my prayers."

"You are still young, Stepha; you must be twenty-three or twenty-four, as young as I was then."

"So much has happened. I wasn't strong, you know, Anton; you thought I was, I was proud that you thought so. But I never was—so much has happened; I lost so much, Stanislw, Leo, my father—I didn't have much left, Anton, only a few dreams; and they don't last well. I lost even you, I missed you, you know—so much—I could never find out where they had taken you. No. In those days there wasn't much left. I gave up."

There was a long silence.

"Do you understand?" she asked at last.

He could not answer.

"It has been a bad war, Anton—so many lives wrecked, so many hearts broken. Ah well——"

She turned and began to arrange something on a little table. Suddenly he saw her reflection in the mirror; tears were running down her face.

He could do nothing, say nothing; never before had he been so appalled by the impossibility of expressing his love, his craving to comfort her. He saw his own reflection, tattered, miserable. How would she ever know what he felt, how would she ever know that he had any feeling? How could he ever penetrate the wall of disenchantment, disillusion, cynicism behind which she lived? She had suffered greatly; she had been dragged, as he had been, over the sordid dust of life.

"I am very comfortable here," she said suddenly.

He looked up, startled.

"What do you think of my painting?" she asked, still with her back to him.

He looked at the water-colours on the walls, landscapes of forlorn skies, of waste lands.

"Only you could have done them," he answered slowly, "how Polish they are, too."

"They are not good," she said. "Anton, tell me how you came here, and in what way I can help you. Please sit down. You see, I forgot all about your drink. And food—you look famished. It's good to see you again; all my old friends have gone—so much has changed. One can hear the Russian guns now; do you remember at Heinrichau, how we heard them on that field, how all the prisoners started singing?"

"If only they had come!"

"The Russians? I dread them; they have done terrible things in the Baltic lands."

"So we read."

194

"Ah, 'so we read', how like you that is—still disbelieving; you haven't changed altogether, Anton. Have I changed so very much?"

"Not so very much." He did not look at her.

"Did you see Zygmus Radek again?"

"I've been with him since the end of nineteen-forty-one."

"No!"

"But yes."

"Then you joined him after all?"

"Over two years ago."

She looked at him, it was the inscrutable regard he knew. She sighed very deeply.

"So, so——" she whispered, "and——?"

"Our bunker was found last night."

She paled; she knew what the words implied. A convoy was passing; the petrol reeked; the tanks, motor-cycles, armoured cars roared.

"What happened?"

She listened silently while he told her.

"They might be caught——" she murmured at last.

"They would fight hard."

"I suppose so."

She turned and stared out of the window.

The convoy had gone; sparrows twittered in the plane-trees.

"What a day!" she said, "even Germanised Kirschau looks wonderful in the sun. Somebody is painting his door over there; I wonder how he got the paint—everybody is looking at him with sullen envy, with suspicion—they should shake his hand," she spoke hurriedly, drumming her fingers on the window-sill.

Lightly, her words dismissed the images of torture,

195

of death. He looked at the delicate line of her cheek, gilded by the sun.

"You are not perturbed about Radek and the others," he said softly.

"I am perturbed, very perturbed," she retorted quickly.

"You are not!"

"But I tell you I am, and please do not shout at me, Anton. I know how you feel, I know."

"You remind me of Ohlau," he muttered, "he knew how I felt."

"Who was Ohlau, Anton?"

"Somebody I killed two years ago."

"Somebody you killed!"

"Yes."

She looked at him steadily.

"It is hard to believe," she said. "Yet, I can believe it—you have changed so much, more than I thought it possible, Anton."

"Yes, we change."

"But so much!" she murmured. "I was thinking," she said, after a pause, "of that journey to Schonau—do you remember? We were in a farm-waggon; we had to lean against the cross-poles; the waggon bumped and jarred when we went through the villages, over the cobbles. I felt happy—the sight of the storks in the fields, the trees shining in the sun; we stopped to gather mushrooms, I remember. Anton, everybody we met on that road was friendly; they smiled and said 'good-morning', though there was more in it than that—they were trying to be kind. But I refused to smile because they were German; you said it was time I grew up. But perhaps you have forgotten all this?"

"I remember."

"Well, I have grown up."

He did not answer.

"I can't hate now.  As for love——"

"Well, as for love?"

She shook her head slowly.

"Then you may as well be dead, Stepha," he tried to be funny, but knew his smile was stupid, false.

"Oh no, and after all, I've heard you say the same, in fact you said it often at Heinrichau.  But now——"

"I love you now.  I loved you then."

"You never told me," she said slowly.

"No, what a fool I was!" he exclaimed softly, "I hardly knew it myself.  I knew the others pestered—told you they loved you, but I couldn't believe they had the same feeling as I have.  They desired you, it's hard to blame them."

Somewhere in the building a man was singing; with exaggerated anguish the voice rose, fell, and was silent.

"Pure love, faith, courage," she murmured sadly staring out of the window, "these things——" she broke off.

Neither spoke for a long moment.

"And you love me still, Anton?" she whispered at last, in a kind of wonder.

"Still?" he repeated, "Stepha, you don't understand, until I met you I was nothing; I was lost."

"Don't think of me as you thought of me three years ago," she said slowly.

"I must, because what we have done, what we haven't done, all that is meaningless to me."

She did not answer; her attention seemed arrested by something in the street.  She turned suddenly.

"I must get some food for you."

Without another word, she left him.

He stared at the door. The sound of her footsteps faded.

He turned; great blotches of sunlight were on the walls, the carpet. Going to the window, he looked across at the high, red-brick building where two women chatted from separate balconies, their bare arms resting on the parapets; occasionally they gazed over the roofs towards the Vistula and breathed the animating wind. Silver-grey, like the point of a dagger, the steeple of St. Mary's church protruded above the houses beyond the river.

He turned again into the room; like the world outside, it was instinct with death and corruption. No, it was himself; he was very tired—the lack of sleep, the hectic hours, finding her here—it had been too much. But how had he been fool enough to hope? What had he hoped for? Her love, her faith, and finally her forgiveness? What a supreme fool.

From the table he picked up an illustrated paper— August 20th, 1944. Was it two or three days old? His mind was muddled. He scanned the pages. Model was counter-attacking East of Praga, the Russians had captured Kossow. He put the paper down; the campaigns he had followed closely seemed remote, futile. He looked up at her paintings; one reminded him of something she had said at Heinrichau: 'a place I have pictured, somewhere on high ground, where one can see forest and marshes, but not a sign of human things.' Poor girl, how much she had suffered, and lost. What had he done to help her? His heart sank at the thought of Markenski.

The door opened behind him. He did not turn; he heard her put something on the table.

"Come on, while it's hot, Anton."

Still he did not turn.

"I hope you like my cooking—I've taken very special care over this."

He turned slowly and met her eyes.

"What's wrong?" she asked, "you like this, don't you? Scrambled egg, bits of bacon, too——"

"Stepha."

"What is it, Anton?"

"I betrayed your father in the Camp."

"My father! He's alive then!"

"No."

"Dead——" she whispered.

He looked at her and despaired.

"It was painless," he mumbled, "he knew nothing, Stepha." He heard again Ohlau's words, dreadful, mocking: 'My soft heart again, you see—what is more merciful than a bullet?'

"Poor old dad," she murmured, "may God in his mercy——" she could not finish.

He felt cold, sick with desire to comfort her. At last he turned away; he could hardly see.

"How did he die?" the clear words hurt him.

"He was shot escaping. I betrayed him."

"Betrayed him——"

"Yes, I had sunk very low; I betrayed him to an S.S. *scharführer*."

"You? I don't understand, betrayed him, what do you mean?"

"He planned an escape. I gave the plan away."

She did not answer for a long moment.

"But you escaped?" she whispered at last.

"Yes."

"But what a low, treacherous swine it is!" she said softly. "And you came here?"

"Yes, I came——"

"For a meal, perhaps?" her smile was dreadful, "or was it to make love?"

"I came, because——"

"But you won't escape again——" she made for the door.

"Stop!"

He had the Luger in his hand.

She turned, came slowly back.

"You couldn't shoot straight," she said, contemptuously, "your hands are trembling, so cowardly, ill-bred—you're a bastard, too, aren't you?"

He remembered the gravestone, the letters broken.

"I gave something to the Germans," he answered slowly, "haven't you?"

She regarded him silently; he put the Luger away.

"No, I couldn't shoot straight, Stepha. Get the police."

For a moment she did not move, then opened the door for him, her blue eyes full of tears.

He found his way out.

# CHAPTER TWELVE

THE roar of convoys on the *autobahn*, the hot pavements and weariness added to his despair. He sauntered aimlessly towards the town's centre. No street led to escape from her grief and scorn; like the corridors of a mad-house they trapped him with their walls, and from the windows she seemed to look down at him, her eyes full of tears. He must fight this impression of having fallen and been stunned. It was absurd. People were staring. No wonder; he was the man who had lost his all.

He laughed, startling an old woman.

His all. What had he ever had but illusions?

Outside the new Gestapo building in Bahnhof *Strasse*, he had an impulse to fire his remaining shots at the flag; to show his contempt, not for the Third Reich, but for life. He stopped and watched the flag ripple against the summer sky. Chilled by the thought that such an act would be interpreted as glorious, he wandered on again towards the public gardens. He sat on the first seat and searched his pockets for cigarette-ends. Nothing. He laughed again, raucously.

Two women, well-dressed, well-fed, obviously German, glared and half-rose from the seat.

He looked at them. They were offensive, intruding with their silly airs into his despair.

"Go away, I want to sleep here."

"Quite mad," one said dispassionately, "come, Ilse."

They went. He lay; flies settled on his face; seed-pods were cracking in the sun. He heard people on the gravel path, the clocks striking. He slept fitfully.

A single star, a few slate-coloured clouds in the
sheeny green sky, the outline of trees along Bahnhof
*Strasse* . . . it was evening. Hunger, like a monstrous
worm, groped and rankled in the pit of his stomach.
Instinctively, he felt for the Luger; finding it safe, he
rose stiffly and stretched himself. A blackbird sang in
the gardens, where a few lovers lingered; convoys still
rumbled on the *autobahn*. The sleep should have done
him good, but his head ached and there was the hunger.
Above all the hunger. When had he eaten last? Yesterday evening he had eaten bread and dripping in the
bunker, before going to the Naceks. Darok had been
playing *Lili Marleen* on the mouth-organ, flinging his
head back, as if overwhelmed by the beauty of his own
playing. Bread and dripping with hot *kaffee-ersatz*; then
he had left them, laughing over a remark of Radek's:
"We don't call them fleas any more—mechanised
dandruff you mean." And then?

He remembered. There was nothing left.

He began walking, but returned to the seat; there was
nowhere else to go. The birds rustling in the holly
bushes were suddenly silent; the last pair of lovers went
through the gates. No guns rumbled, but he heard the
convoys and troop-trains, a muffled roar that he had often
listened to on fine nights. In the winter too, the four of
them had listened, waited, the snow falling softly and
covering their shoulders, their caps. They had neither
moved nor spoken when they heard the train, but when
they saw the sparks shooting into the night they involuntarily shielded their eyes, covered their ears. Then
Radek's voice after the explosion: "I hope there were no
Poles on it." But there must have been some Poles on
the four trains they had wrecked.

It was getting dark. Putting his hand on the seat, he

found it wet with dew. Life seemed to retreat into itself, leaving hunger and the rumble of trains—a queer sound, ominous, tragic, reminding him of bare-headed soldiers with accordions, sitting at the open doors of cattle-trucks; whistling to the girls, or just staring out with the lost look of those returning from battles. There was defeat and despair in the sound of German troop-trains. The dreams had faded; the fight was ending. He had never known really what it was all about. But he could see them, those soldiers, throwing things out of the trucks; cutting up their bread-rations, holding steaming dixies.

Night falling, the sound of trains recalling faded dreams: it seemed symbolic. Something was dead.

Perhaps she loved Kassel. Why not? He had been a childhood friend; they had skated, ridden, danced to-gether; he might have been her lover then. No, on the Heinrichau fields she had talked with hatred and scorn of all Germans, and Radek would have told him had she loved Kassel; Radek had known the Markenskis well in those days. What did it matter? He would never see her again. For the rest of his life he would remember her letting him out with scorn and grief in her eyes.

Somebody coughed behind him. He swung round.

"It's alright, brother, I'm not Himmler," a voice said softly.

Jankowski saw nobody.

"It's alright I tell you, I'm not Himmler, or Hitler, Goebbels, Goring—who are the others—Bormann——"

Jankowski rose from the seat; he saw the silhouette of a trilby hat above the railings.

"I saw you sleeping here during the day," the man said, "so I came back."

"Why?"

"Because I am a Pole and a Catholic."

"Well?"

"Are you homeless?"

"Yes."

"I knew it. Come round to the gate," the man seemed irritated.

Jankowski did so. He distinguished a small, elderly man with glasses.

"Hungry, brother?" the voice was hollow, melancholy.

"Famished."

"I knew you were. I know the signs. It's the sort of thing I notice at once," his own powers of observation seemed to depress him, "of all the people who saw you sleeping on that seat I suppose I was the only one to notice that you were famished."

"I am still famished."

"My daughter kept telling me not to come back—said you might be a cut-throat."

"I might be."

"Well come then; there's no point in starving to death whatever you are. You are a Pole and we have bread."

Without another word he turned and began to walk swiftly towards Danzig *Strasse*. Jankowski followed.

"I hear Jassy has fallen," he remarked politely, as they turned down a side-street.

There was no answer. Jankowski wondered whether the Polish Catholic was deaf or absorbed in his own thoughts.

They reached a part of the town in which Jankowski had not been before, a disorderly mass of houses, interspersed with small yards, alley-ways. The place seemed dead; their footsteps rang on the cobbles. He could smell the Vistula.

By a broken gate the man stopped and touched Jankowski's arm.

"One moment," he hurried round the corner of a wall. Within a minute he was back.

"Good, but one can't be too careful these days."

Crossing a smelly yard, they entered a passage; the man closed a door behind them.

"Cursed black-outs!" he muttered, fumbling with the latch of an inner door. "So! Walk in—and push that door hard."

An electric-bulb, speckled with fly-droppings, revealed mildewed walls hung with oleographs of Our Lord. A girl, blonde, broad-hipped, was reaching a loaf down from the stove top.

"Didn't I tell you he was homeless, hungry?" the man asked.

Without answering, she pushed aside the old clothes strewn on the table and put the loaf down with a bump.

"You'd see your own countrymen starve, some of you youngsters. I wonder sometimes——" he turned to Jankowski: "I'm Ignacy Kuras. This is my daughter Agnes."

"I'm Anton."

Jankowski dragged his eyes from the loaf she was slicing and looked at her. Nineteen or twenty perhaps, but already lines went from the sides of her flatish nose to the corners of her mouth. Tall, a fine figure, but she looked languid, coarse, sensual. He turned to Kuras.

"You were a Godsend," he said.

"Far from it," Kuras answered, "but I smuggled tobacco once," he added sadly.

"And he can't even get a smoke now," the girl said

contemptuously. She gave Jankowski a long, pondering look, then went on slicing the loaf. Kuras brought a chair to the table.

"Eat and be merry," he said. "No dripping, Agnes?"

"Plenty," she said sarcastically, reaching down a cracked mug. What there was she spread on three slices and gave to Jankowski. He protested.

"Eat, eat," Kuras said.

Jankowski ate; they watched him silently, elbows on the table; pressed between their palms, their faces looked distorted, Asiatic.

"Coffee, Agnes?" Kuras whispered.

"It's on."

Above the smoke-blackened stove the faded oleograph of the Old God seemed to wage mute war with a frowning photograph of the New, which the artful Kuras had apparently hung up when the Germans came. One of Stalin might replace it soon, but the faded oleograph would not come down. What had Markenski said? 'The Faith which has been the only light in the darkness of these years.' He had said that she would keep her Faith.

A grey cat rose from the clothes on the table; stretched; yawned in Jankowski's face.

"They'll be here in a month—perhaps less," Kuras said thoughtfully, "a few traitors are shaking in their beds to-night."

"And your own son's in the *Wehrmacht*," the girl murmured.

He turned on her furiously.

"Could he help it? He did it for us; we'd have been shot if he hadn't gone."

"Perhaps some of the other traitors are thinking of others."

"But they're not!" Kuras hissed. "Look at all the women you see with Germans."

"Father and his friends are going to cut the girls' hair off," she smiled at Jankowski, "and then throw them on dungheaps or something. Nasty men. There's a girl in the chemist's where I work who goes with a German sergeant—he's very nice."

Kuras glanced at Jankowski.

"Well, he is, I can't help it," she went on, "he told Clara about the Russians—what they do to women. I'm frightened."

Kuras ignored her.

"You will understand," he addressed Jankowski, "that pro-Germans and every trace of Germanisation must be rooted out. As for the traitors—there's a place for them——"

Agnes giggled.

"In Red Army brothels."

Kuras rose from the table.

"It's no good trying to talk seriously with this girl here. Eat the rest of that bread, brother." He left the room.

"He's got some tobacco leaves drying in the loft," the tired, seductive voice broke into Jankowski's thoughts: "They are still green, but he can't wait."

"No?"

"No," her sleepy eyes did not leave his face, "well, I'm the last one to resist temptation. More coffee?"

"Thank you."

Kuras returned and, crushing the tobacco on the table, rolled two cigarettes.

"Yes, Poles must help each other these days," he said softly, "I'm very glad I went back, it must have been your guardian angel, brother. Did you hear about the bunker they found in the Struga woods?"

"No," Jankowski answered, "did they catch any-one?"

"Agnes saw two marched through Starogin this morning."

"What are you staring at?" she asked. "Haven't you seen any? One had his shirt torn right up the back, you could see the blood sticking to it. He was the dark one, the other was taller, brown-haired—but their faces were so bruised——"

Radek and Klemba.

"They almost caught another on the Malkow road— he shot his way out; killed three police," Kuras said.

Darok's girl would hide him in Palukin, but if Radek or Klemba gave way under torture she would not hide him long.

Jankowski rose.

"I shall remember your kindness."

"Where are you going?"

"I must go."

"But you said you were homeless."

"I am."

Kuras clutched his sleeve. "Then stay. Trust me— trust me, brother!" His black eyes were bright behind his steel-rimmed glasses.

Jankowski hesitated.

"I feel I can trust you," he answered, "I'm very grateful." He sat again at the table.

"Put sugar in the coffee, Agnes," Kuras said solemnly.

"It's already in," she murmured. "Where is our guest going to sleep to-night?"

"The little room. Where else?"

Jankowski did not sleep that night. Leaving the flea-infested bed he opened the window and looked over the roofs. A chilly wind, coming over the luminous mass which was the Vistula, blew into his face. It was hard to believe: this was Kirschau; Radek and Klemba awaited torture, death; Stepha lived a few streets away. It was too much like a nightmare. He heard the guns, growling, threatening now, beyond the horizon. They had come too late. Dreadful, farcical: he would be the hero when the Russians came, while she . . .

He must blot her from his mind. What were Radek and Klemba doing now? Hoping perhaps.

"I must get Darok," he muttered, "before it's too late."

But what could they do? Radek and Klemba were finished. Even so they must try. It would be the last fight. The greatest. He must act now—to-night!

He groped under the bed for his shoes, knowing it was too late. The rows of chimney-pots threw shadows on the roofs; he saw the cat slink across the dirty yard and spring to a window-sill. The Vistula was pink. Slowly, he took off his shoes, then sat on the edge of the bed; listened to the first footfalls on the pavements, the first waggons coming from the villages, or perhaps it was the Prussian refugees moving out of the town.

The door beneath his window slammed and somebody crossed the yard; for a time the footsteps echoed; before the sound of them had faded, the door of his room opened and Agnes Kuras entered.

It was obvious that she had just risen, that she had slept in the scanty pink slip she wore. She stood, swaying slightly, a few feet inside the room and watched him, her eyes misty, her thick lips pursed. She seemed half-asleep, but he sensed the tense, voluptuous passion of her beautifully-proportioned body.

"I thought you had gone in the night," she said softly, "you were moving about."

"I'm sorry if I kept you awake."

"You didn't; I awoke and heard you, that's all." She inspected him languidly: "But you haven't slept?"

"Not much."

"Was the bed so bad?"

"Very comfortable, thank you," he said hurriedly: "Do you know anyone in Palukin?"

"Palukin? Yes, Lena Tocek; do you know her?"

"No, but I must send a message to Palukin."

Swaying slightly from the hips, she watched him dully. One hand rested behind her head, the other clutched the loose folds of her slip, drawing attention to small, but prominent breasts. She seemed to have forgotten what they were talking about.

"Oh, I see," she drawled at last, "and you want me to go?"

"I would be very grateful."

"Would you? Well, I suppose I can go later on—I'm not working to-day," she said slowly. Her eye-lids drooped; she gave him a sleepy, quizzical look: "Don't you like me?"

"Why do you ask?"

"I just wondered," she pouted. "Do you always send women on messages when they come into your room?"

"It's a life or death message." But he spoke without conviction. A current of air was passing through the door and window; lifting her flimsy slip; revealing her shapely legs.

She saw him looking at them and smiled, then closed the door.

"I must keep out of the draught," she murmured, "I've only got this on," she lifted the slip slightly.

"So I see."

Looking at the floor, she smiled again, a small, secret smile, then sighed very deeply as if about to swoon, but again he felt the passion that burned in her body, that seemed to fill the room; seemed to mingle with his blood.

She sat on the bed beside him.

"Ah, the sun!" she whispered. Stretching her legs into the sunlight that was creeping over the floor-boards, she shook off her wooden-soled sandals. Her small feet touched the floor and she drew them back quickly.

"But the boards are so cold——" she said with a shiver, wrinkling her face.

Slowly, she drew herself back, until her blonde head touched the mildewed wall and her legs dangled over the bed near his own. Her blue, misty eyes watched him.

"Father's out," she whispered, "he won't be back until late, so I must entertain you, mustn't I?"

She lifted one leg into the sun and wriggled her toes.

"Mustn't I?" she repeated sleepily. The leg fell over his own; he felt its pressure increase. She drew herself towards him.

"Mustn't I?" her cool hands were inside his shirt; she pressed against him.

"I suppose so," he murmured, "like you, I have never been able to resist temptation——"

"Why should you?" she whispered, "why should you resist?"

As he turned, she pulled him down with her on the bed, wriggling her supple body beneath him.

"Why should you?" she whispered again, her lips seeking his hungrily.

He could not answer, but he did not forget them quite—the cells at Starogin, the house in Hermann Goring *Strasse*.

"You must not think too badly of me," she said, as she went downstairs ahead of him, her shoulder touching the wall. "There's not much else unrationed and up to pre-war standard." Was it Radek who had said that this phrase had become almost a slogan with such Polish girls as were fast?

"You are frank," he answered, remembering the flea-bites on the white flesh of her splendid body, the faint odour of dried sweat mingling with that of cheap scents, "but what can you know of pre-war standards?"

"Oh, I was seduced long ago," she said, with a snigger: "I don't blame the war for what I do—like some girls I know. But what can I get you for breakfast?"

"Don't worry, bread's a luxury to me."

"Don't lie," she answered, looking over her shoulder.

He said nothing until they were in the kitchen, where sunlight revealed more dust and disorder than the electric light had done. The grey cat had its face in the cup from which Kuras had apparently drunk before going to work; flies swarmed over the crumbs he had left.

"I wonder what happened to the two partisans you saw in Starogin," he said.

"Don't you know?"

"Do you?"

She lit the gas under the kettle before she answered.

"Yes," she said slowly, "I know because I work in Pilsudski Street, Weichsel *Strasse*—God knows what the Russians will call it. They'll be marched to the police station this morning for questioning—and again to-morrow perhaps——"

"What time?"

"Oh, about nine usually, after the Inspector's had his breakfast, I suppose. That reminds me——"

"What escort do they have, when they go for questioning?"

"Two guards, I think; but don't let's talk any more about it. It makes me feel cold, and rather sick. I see they are digging fortifications outside the town, all along the river—children, old men; they're roping in everybody."

"Can you take that message now?" he asked.

"Message?"

"To Palukin," he said sharply.

"Oh that——" she went to the window and looked into the sky, "it's going to be a baking day," she said, "and Palukin's almost ten kilometres away——"

He watched her.

"To a girl friend, I suppose?"

"No."

"Then who is it to? Why all this mystery? I like you, Anton, and I promised, but really——" she looked at him reproachfully. "You can trust me, you know," she added softly.

He wondered whether he could.

"Alright then, don't worry," she said quickly, "I'll take the message now—I won't wait. Tell me nothing unless you want to. I can see what you think——" she turned; lifted the kettle, then bumped it down again.

"I think you're a Polish patriot. We need your help?"

"My help? Who needs my help?"

"The two partisans."

"Of course," she murmured thoughtfully, "he's mad."

"But I know those men! I have been with them day after day for two years. Can you understand that? And now, leave them to die . . ."

She took his hand and looked at it, shaking her head: "I'm so sorry," she murmured, "I didn't know. Tell me what I can do."

He told her.

"You wouldn't have trusted anyone else, would you?" she asked, when he had finished.

"No, only you."

She looked at him, the tips of her fingers resting on the kettle-handle.

"Partisan," she whispered, smiling, "I might have guessed——" Possessive, exultant, her eyes did not leave his face.

"So you are a partisan."

"But get the message ready; I'm longing to go. There's some bacon I can fry you first." She hurried across to the cupboard.

He wrote a few words on a scrap of paper and gave it to her.

"But I can't understand what it means," she held it in front of the window: "The third bridge—what does that mean?"

"He knows."

"You've arranged to meet him, I suppose." She folded the message carefully. "Of course, you do know it's hopeless, don't you? I mean, to save them?"

"Yes."

They breakfasted in silence.

"I hope you borrow the old man's razor before I get back," she said, as she left for Palukin.

Sitting at the table, he tried to formulate a plan.

At a point between the prison cells and the police station two guards had to be killed and two prisoners armed before any witness had time to think. A perfect plan, speed, ferocity . . .

He could not concentrate. The distant guns made him wonder what Stepha would do when the Russians came. She must leave Kirschau; the mistress of a German major would get no mercy from men like Klemba, Darok, Kuras; even less from the women. He knew the Poles . . .

A perfect plan, speed—he must grasp the facts. The route from the cells to the police station was short—from the middle of the High Street, through Church Street, into Pilsudski Street. The High Street and Pilsudski Street were out of the question. He tried to visualise Church Street. The Labour Office, the Art School, a row of houses, the air-raid shelters. What cover the shelters could be! A fast car to get them clear of the town was essential: cars parked outside the Labour Office. But the distance between the shelters and the Office was too great. The attack must be sudden, deadly. A lightning start was essential. Therefore: the guards must be shot from the car itself, but a car going slow enough for Radek and Klemba to jump into. The fastest route out of the town must be known perfectly. But what of the mobile S.S. units? They would get on the trail quickly, and there were twelve hours of daylight. It was hopeless.

Those mobile units must be diverted.

He could not concentrate. It was the sound of guns; it broke into his thoughts, choking his mind with conflicting concerns. Surely Stepha knew what would happen when the Russians came? If only . . .

How could these mobile units be diverted? Until he

found an answer there was no hope for Radek and Klemba. Those S.S. units, he had seen them often, raising the white dust of the Polish roads with their cars. Hard-faced men in camouflaged jackets, armed with sub-machine guns. One Sunday in July the roads had been full of them—British parachutists were supposed to have landed by Konitz. The S.S. had surrounded a large area. They had found nothing.

That might be the answer—a parachute scare. If the S.S. were informed of a landing twenty miles West of Starogin?

He started pacing the room; the cat purred and rubbed against his legs; the flies pestered. Going to the window, he watched the white gulls swoop and twist high above the Vistula, hidden behind the houses. He heard the faint, threatening rumble of guns. The town had seemed lighthearted yesterday. To-day it looked doomed. Prostrate under the burning blue sky, it awaited what Allied papers called 'liberation', what the people he saw on the pavements called rape and chaos.

Before Agnes returned he had formulated a plan, but the more he considered it, the weaker it seemed. It relied on too many assumptions; that Kuras would risk his life, that Darok lived, that Radek and Klemba would be questioned at nine, that the Germans would be fooled with the parachute ruse. But what other plan would do? Darok would have no plan; he depended on luck, inspiration, deadly ferocity; he hated plans.

While trying to map Starogin from memory, he heard somebody put a cycle against the wall in the yard. It was Agnes. He met her as she entered.

"I was so frightened," she said breathlessly, "that you'd be gone, that somebody had come——"

"Did you see the Manias?"

216

She threw her blue scarf on to the table and flopped into a chair: "They didn't trust me, you know, but the youngest Tocek girl was minding geese in that meadow near the road; she told them who I was——" she handed him a fragment torn from a cigarette-packet. "I'd have swallowed it if they'd tried to stop me. Oh, but the dust—and all those convoys——"

Darok would meet him on the fringe of the Lieber-schau woods at midnight.

But he waited until long after midnight.

With his back against the boulder that marked the rendezvous, he listened for the signal. His mind began to wander. He recalled the time he had rested here as a boy. Where had he been going? He remembered that grass had shone, glinted; that the forests had looked dark under a blue sky; that he looked back at the footprints left by his bare feet in the hot dust.

Taking a handful of that same dust, he let it run through his fingers.

Where had he been going? Kirschau perhaps. He could not remember, yet he remembered the brown, thoughtful faces of children, looking into the pines for that bird whose clear call broke the stillness of the afternoon; he remembered the sheen on the clouds, the carriages passing.

Insidious memories. He must think, plan: time was short. The East glowed faintly; the mist on the meadow was luminous against the forest, like water under the shadow of cliffs. The guns seemed merely to flutter against the great silence.

What a fatal delay in his plans. And the long wait had given him time to realise the change in himself—the purpose, the fanaticism that had made him the leader of the others, had died; memories revived the old poison.

He sprang up. A dark figure, legs hidden by mist, seemed to float towards him across the meadow. Darok's queer, crouching walk was unmistakable.

"Ah, Anton!"

They shook hands.

"Thank God!" Jankowski said, "listen, there's not much time—the others are caught——"

"What a fight it was! And they nearly got me to-night on the Malkow road."

"They're in the cells at Starogin."

"Is there a hope?"

"I don't know. Come on; there's a father and daughter we must trust in Kirschau; they're waiting for us now. I'll explain while we walk. But there's not much time."

They hurried round the meadow's fringe, then took a path through fields of rye. Jankowski spoke softly, often glancing towards the reddening East.

". . and when she signals, we take a car from the High Street, slow down behind them in Church Street and kill the guards. We go for the *autobahn* when the others are in . . ."

Darok listened silently.

"Do you think there's a chance?" Jankowski asked finally.

Darok did not answer at once.

"No," he said at last, "anyway, we'll kill the guards."

# CHAPTER THIRTEEN

STAROGIN already looked like an evacuated town, the pedestrians had an aimless, half-hunted look. Jankowski was desperately conscious of the large, grey Mercedes parked under the trees near the hospital, and of Agnes standing at the corner of Church Street. The clocks were striking nine. Things suddenly became more vivid, intense: the grey street, the blue sky, the faces of people, the little yellow weeds which flourished in the chinks of the wall where he waited. He watched Agnes. She was scraping her nails, but he noticed her continuous glances towards the cells.

"I hate waiting," Darok said calmly, "it saps my strength. If that car doesn't start——"

"For Christ's sake——!" Jankowski muttered.

They watched silently. She had turned and walked away from them; gone a few paces; swung round again. The red-frocked figure had a frivolous, nonchalant air. Could she be revelling in the part she played? No. It was bravado; she was probably terrified.

"Now!" Darok whispered.

She was taking a blue scarf from her bag; she began to tie it round her head.

"Slowly," Jankowski murmured, as they strolled towards the car, "give them time to turn into Church Street."

Crossing the road, they went to the window of a music shop. With his intense awareness, Jankowski noticed small things, the crack in a bust of Beethoven, the name on a song-book, the price of gramophone records. He turned; sunlight reached half across the street where it turned beyond Church Street; on the shady side a little procession was approaching. Radek and Klemba were shuffling along near the gutter, their bare hands drooping slightly, on the pavements two guards strutted a short way behind them. Sombre, ominous, the procession disappeared into Church Street.

Without a word they turned and walked to the car.

Quickly, surely, Darok lifted the bonnet, made some rapid adjustment, then put it down gently.

"Alright——"

Jankowski climbed into the back seat, Darok into the driver's seat.

Somebody was yelling. Jankowski had a vague impression of faces at windows, of people waving, their mouths open. Darok laughed; waved back. They roared down the High Street.

"Take the inside guard," Jankowski said, as they swerved into Church Street. Agnes was standing in a shop door-way, her face white, her mouth open.

"Slow down," Jankowski said. "Now."

They fired simultaneously. The outside guard dropped. The other twisted round; they fired again and he fell.

"Get in, boys!" Darok yelled.

But Radek and Klemba were on the pavement, wrenching at the machine-pistols. A woman with a pram screamed; fled.

"Get in!"

Jankowski had the door wide for them. They dived in and Darok accelerated. They swung left at Pilsudski Street, smashing a cycle that had been propped against the pavement. Jankowski was very conscious of the two tattered men panting and muttering at his side.

"How do you feel?" he asked, as calmly as he could.

"Ah, *Jesus!*" Klemba said hoarsely.

Radek was staring at the road.

The tyres screamed as they swung right by a church.

"They should be on our trail in ten minutes," Darok said. "Or less—thank God Germans are slow to recover from surprises."

They swept down a dusty avenue; tall, white houses showed behind the trees.

"*Jesus, Jesus, Jesus——*" Klemba was muttering. Suddenly he grasped Jankowski's hand. "I thought it was all up——"

"Not yet," Jankowski answered, "we're making for the *autobahn*, then for the forests East of Kirschau. There'll be fighting."

The avenue brought them out on the *autobahn*; stretching wide and white for miles across the flat land. The beet-fields spread away on either side, like a sea islanded by the large farmsteads.

They swept on. A convoy came from the other direction, an endless stream of grim faces, of vehicles covered with dust.

"Look out for the signpost pointing to Largantau," Jankowski said, "we turn right there."

"Pray that Kuras has started that parachute scare," Darok replied. "If he hasn't——"

"How did you know about us?" Radek asked.

Jankowski told him.

"It must have been our guardian angels, Franek," Radek said to Klemba. "I had a feeling——" He too, grasped Jankowski's hand. "We can never thank you two."

"The fun hasn't started yet," Darok said.

"What's your plan?"

"To reach the forest," Jankowski answered, "aban-

don the car and trust to luck until dark, then try to
reach Kirschau where Kuras will hide us."

"What made you go to Kirschau in the first place?"

"I heard that Stepha Markenski was there."

"Was she?"

"Yes."

"God!" Darok muttered, "are those two going to
talk about that girl at a time like this?"

Radek smiled. "You've never met her," he answered.
"But how is she, Anton?"

"Changed."

"You sound grim."

"If we reach Kuras," Jankowski answered, "I'll tell
you a story you might not like."

Radek frowned, said nothing.

Jankowski looked at him, and at the others. The mad
hope, the exhilaration of the moment had been swept
away by the thought of Stepha. He faced a dull, yet
vaguely sinister reality. He saw that Klemba was half-
asleep, his head in his grimy hands, but his fingers kept
twitching. Radek was leaning back, his bare arms
folded, his legs crossed; his dirty, ragged clothes, the
great bruise under his left eye contrasted strangely with
the smart, red-leather upholstery of the car. The
machine-pistol was in his lap. He smiled faintly.

They were charging the empty road at eighty-six
miles an hour, yet Darok appeared to drive with an
attitude of elegant boredom, his left arm resting on the
window space of the door, his cap well back on his head.

"If we can reach the woods——" Radek murmured.
He glanced behind. "They will never catch us up, but
the police at Ripno will have orders to block the road."

"They won't get me again," Klemba said softly. He
too, glanced behind, furtively, as if ashamed of the cold

dread that was stealing over them. They had begun to realise the chances were slight.

"I can see a yellow speck by a clump of trees," Darok said, after a moment. "Can that be the signpost, Anton?"

Jankowski peered over Darok's shoulder.

"Yes. We turn right there."

He looked behind. The road was empty, spinning and hurtling away from him. The dash-board clock showed twenty past nine. The Germans, once started, acted with energy, speed; by now all their available forces must be in operation; they had twelve hours of daylight.

"I can see the forest already," Radek shouted joyfully, after they had turned into the inferior road. "We'll make it—by God, brother!"

Jankowski saw the dark belt of forest which began abruptly and reached Eastwards. But there was something between, a large farmstead, or a village. Yes, a village; as they swept nearer he saw the grey church steeple rise above the trees, he saw a large barn with a stork's nest on the end of the roof, the smoke from the chimneys went straight up into the still air.

He looked behind, but saw only the dust they were raising; in this flat country such a cloud of dust would be seen for miles.

"I know this village," Klemba said, as they swept past the first cottages, "it's Loniew—my father knew the miller in the old days. What a sour old devil he was too!"

Darok did not slacken speed. Flaxen-haired children ran to the gates and stared after them; hens fled from the road. They swept over the cobbles, through the speckled shadows of the trees.

"We'll make it!" Radek yelled again. *"Jesu Maria!"*

They came out into the sun again. The pale green of the sugar beet spread away for the forest's deeper green. The empty road stretched ahead, white, dusty.

"Can you boys stand a shock?" Darok asked.

"We've stood a few in our time," Radek answered. "Why?"

"By the feel of this thing, it's running out of petrol."

"Impossible—the gauge says half-full——"

"It's no good, brother. She's running out, I tell you."

"Yes, she's slowing down," Klemba muttered. "So we're done?"

"Stop," Jankowski said, "look at the tank; if it's empty we must run for it."

Darok pulled up at once, almost flinging them through the wind-screen.

The tank was empty.

Hurriedly, they took off their boots; tied the laces together and slung them over their shoulders. They ran for the woods. Jankowski felt the fine, sandy dust round his toes, the boots knocking against his back and shoulders. The forest seemed far away.

"And we didn't see if there were any cigarette-ends," Radek grunted, "in the ash-trays of that damned machine."

"Save your breath——"

Jankowski listened for the sound of motor-engines, but heard only the heavy breathing of the men running at his side. Glancing behind, to see how far they had come, he saw a splash of brilliant light, where the sun reflected on the wind-screen of the Mercedes. It blinded him to the road beyond.

He felt conspicuous, felt that they were being watched through binoculars. It was hopeless, tragic. But he

wanted to laugh. Running for their lives. He looked at
the others. They would not see the joke; they had the
aspect of shy, rare night-birds, discovered in daylight.
It felt like that, too. Blindly, instinctively they sought
cover. But they looked comic. The lanky Klemba with
his swinging stride, his chin jutting out, the machine-
pistol clutched in one hand. Radek, his dark head held back,
trousers tucked to his knees, his worn boots almost
slipping off his shoulder. And Darok, nimble, pale-
faced, his light blue eyes fixed on the woods.

The sun blazed into their eyes; warmed the dust
under their feet. Suddenly childish anger, bewilderment, passed over their hunted faces. They had heard a
faint rumble of Russian guns—a cackling laugh from the
gods. It unnerved them. Far off Allied guns, torture
and death waiting in the dust and the sun.

"March, march, Dombroski——" Radek sang, with
a sobbing intake of breath. "How far have we come,
Anton?"

"A mile," Jankowski grunted, "or more——"

He glanced behind. The Mercedes was over a mile
away; the road to the village was otherwise empty. But
cars, looking like a row of beetles, moved on the distant
*autobahn*. Within ten minutes . . .

They would not even get a chance to fight.

"If we reach the woods," he panted, "we must
separate. Or go in pairs. More chance."

"Or fight it out," Darok said, "make a stand together. Ambush the first car—fight it out——"

"Wouldn't last five minutes——" Klemba grunted.

"If we reach the woods," Radek managed to say, "I'll
be too surprised—to fight—anything out——"

How far away were the woods? A mile? Surely not.
Just over half-a-mile. He saw the red pine trunks

plainly; saw three birds flying over the trees. Less than half-a-mile.

Radek's boots slid from his shoulder; thudded in the dust. The laces were untied; he knotted them while he ran, cursing softly.

The white road disappeared into the dark forest. Jankowski heard the 'bup—bup—bup', of an axe; saw the wood-piles on the fringe. The Mercedes was out of sight; the road was empty as far as he could see.

"We'll make it——" he croaked out.

They were running in the shadow of the forest, the dust cold on their feet.

"Left," Jankowski grunted, "into the undergrowth."

The leaves were cool, still wet with dew. They plunged on, carrying their boots in their hands.

"A short rest," Klemba said, "I'm beat."

"Half-a-minute then——"

They flopped down. The place crawled with ants; flies pestered.

"Thank God," Radek grunted, his face buried in the weeds, "they would have shot us out there like hares— like rats. Mown us down——"

No one answered. The stillness was profound, until one became aware of the flies droning, the faint barking of a dog in the village.

A car changed gear on the road.

"Here they come," Klemba whispered.

While the car drew closer they stared at each other. It passed down the road a short way away; before the sound had faded, they heard others.

"Surrounding us," Darok said softly. He regarded his revolver blankly, as if surprised to find it in his hand. He began to move the safety-catch to and fro. The metallic 'klik—klik—klik' sounded very loud, nerve-racking.

None spoke: there was nothing to say. They thought of the hard-faced, energetic men who were springing off lorries, out of cars. There was terror in the golden flecks of sunlight, in the stir of a leaf. Slinking from the road's vicinity, they reached a glade; its wild strawberries and thin grass were loud with crickets.

They stopped dead. A man was squatting by a stunted silver-birch with a broken trap in his hand. His shot-gun and forester's rucksack lay beside him. He looked up slowly; Jankowski met his eyes, blue, thoughtful. Without surprise he regarded their bare feet, their weapons.

"I'm Polish," he said.

Jankowski hurried across to him. "Can you hide us?"

"Police?"

"Everywhere——"

He shook his head slowly: "I'm sorry, brother—I've a wife and two children. Make for the Largantau woods —it's denser there——" He jerked his thumb over his shoulder.

"Too late!" Jankowski snapped. "We hide now or die—painfully."

"Yes, brother, yes—but I've a wife, two little children; I cannot——"

"Listen you," Darok broke in, with cold ferocity: "So you're a Pole, eh? Yet you registered as German, or you wouldn't be a forester. I'm Russian," he tapped his own chest and glared. "You hear the guns? The Russian guns? They are coming, and when they come they'll cut registered Germans into small pieces——"

"Never mind that," Radek interrupted, "this man is a

Pole at heart. I can see it in his face." He addressed the forester: "Will you let the Germans take and torture us because we have fought that one day Poland may live again? The day will surely come when you, and for that matter, your wife will be asked 'what have you done for Poland?' What will you answer? 'I did nothing. I could have saved four patriots from the Germans but I did not. I have a wife and two little children and I was afraid.' "

"I am not afraid," said the forester, his grave blue eyes watching them steadily, "as for the Russians——" he spat; rose to his feet. He turned to Jankowski: "I've helped more than one partisan," he said, "the *Ortsbauernführer* suspects me. But I'm going to help. For God's sake don't mention me if you're caught. There's a disused bunker—three British prisoners of war hid there for a month in the Spring. Follow me at a distance." Picking up his rucksack, he walked swiftly across the glade and into the trees.

He was hard to follow; the green uniform blended with the forest, but occasionally he stopped and listened.

"As for the Russians——" Radek murmured, glancing at Darok. Full of renewed hope, they chuckled and grinned; Radek most of all. He said it again and spat.

The lower branches of the plantation were broken off and covered with a feathery, powder-green growth; the forester was twisting and stooping in the vague passageway of trees ahead. He stopped suddenly; his immobility made him harder to see. They stopped too; listened. A far off dog yapped, there was no other sound.

"What the hell——" Klemba muttered.

The forester knelt. Approaching, they saw him feeling among the pine-needles.

"The bunker," Radek whispered.

When they reached the forester, he was gently raising the camouflaged lid.

"This bunker was made three years ago," he said solemnly, "but they never used it—they had a larger one in the Lieberschau woods. They used to go to the English prisoners at Neudorf for food—they showed three prisoners where it was; the prisoners escaped and lived here for a while——" he spoke in the mechanical voice of a tourist's guide, "they used to give me their English cigarettes. What tobacco that was!" he exclaimed, with sudden enthusiasm, "Players, Goldflake—what were the others?—State Express, and the little fellow . . . ah, Woodbine——"

"Police and S.S. have surrounded the wood," Jankowski said, "time is horribly short."

"Yes, hurry," the forester hissed, "take these matches; try to keep them dry—it's damp in there. Hurry-hurry—I'll make it so that a hawk won't see the entrance. But for God's sake——"

Jankowski did not hear him finish. He followed the others down into the black dampness of the bunker. It reeked of carbide. The forester replaced the lid; Jankowski heard him patting down the pine-needles.

"Strike a match," Radek said, "and we'll go up in smoke."

"The place is full of tins," Klemba muttered, "strike a light, Anton, or we'll cut our feet to pieces."

The match revealed wet, glistening walls, tins with bright labels which had crinkled. A candle was stuck on four twigs that had been driven into the wall; by its light they saw what the Englishmen had left. There were cartons from the British and Canadian Red Cross, one was full of carbide, the others of empty tins.

Jankowski read the labels—Meat Roll, Tomato Juice, Dried Egg, Klim.

"I thought the English never prepared," Radek murmured.

"When they've decided to act they prepare better than any," Jankowski answered. "They are never ready for the merely obvious, that's all. Anyway, one of these was a Scot." He had found an old letter-card addressed to John Blair, No. 5769, Stalag XXB; it had a Perth post-mark.

There was the bottom-half of a kit-bag, which had apparently been used for water; it had the name Jack Eaves on it. Somebody had begun to make a table of small pine-trees. On one of the bunks was a book called 'Monkey Puzzle', some sheets of a pad with the score of a game—Jack 24, D.V. 21, Jock 21. There was an improvised carbide-lamp—a Red Cross tin with a hole in the top and the bottom stopped up with a damp rag.

"How did they get this stuff here?" Darok wondered.

"Gradually," Radek answered. "On most of these farms the English prisoners get out at night. They slip bars from windows, dig tunnels. Oh, they get out alright, to sleep with their girls, to trade chocolate for eggs. The Naceks knew two. You can see what happened to these three—their food gave out and they started to eat grebe-eggs. Look at these shells! There must be a lake——"

"I don't like that forester," Klemba said suddenly, "he'd sell us for a cigarette-end."

Instinctively, they looked at the entrance, where they saw a thin line of light.

"They trusted him," Jankowski indicated the names on the pad.

"And where are they now?"

Jankowski shrugged: "The bunker is not blown up."

"Anton's right," Radek said. Sitting on the bunk, he regarded Jankowski. "You're a queer devil,", he declared softly. He turned to Darok: "I saw him smiling—when we ran like hell for the woods. Smiling——"

"Lose everything," Jankowski answered slowly, "and you see the funny side. God smiles in your face—you smile back. It's a good joke."

"No time to see the funny side if they drop a grenade down here," Klemba muttered.

"Grenade?" Radek said cheerfully, "we'll catch it and throw it back. If only those English boys had left coffee, fresh water——"

"How long do we stay?" Darok asked.

"We must get food to-night," Jankowski answered, "the moon sets early; it's a dense forest."

"Kuras?"

"Where else?"

"With food, we could stay here until the Russians come," Radek said.

"I'm half asleep," Darok yawned, "I'll try this bunk for a while. And I'll say a prayer."

"If we only knew those S.S. bastards were past——" Klemba blurted.

No one answered.

"God, but I'm getting a jumpy fool," Klemba went on wearily, "lived this life too long——"

"Sleep, Franek," Radek told him gently. He indicated Darok: "He's like a log already—doesn't know what nerves are."

Klemba lay; his face looked shadowy, hollow-eyed in the candle-light. His hands were twitching.

Radek sat on the end of the bunk, near Darok's feet.

"I'm longing to see her again," he murmured slowly,

231

staring at the tins, "Stepha, I mean. Do you think she would spare us any food?"

"Are you going to see her?"

"Of course. How was she?"

"Quite well; she lives with Kassel."

"Kassel? Who the devil's he?"

"I thought you knew him. Hugo Kassel."

"My God——"

They were silent. The candle sizzled and spluttered.

"Stepha," Radek whispered, at last, "with that ass."

"Is he an ass?"

"Worse. A German ass. Did she ask after me?"

"Yes."

"And what about you?" Radek asked quickly, "was she glad to see you?"

"I think so."

"I think so, too," Radek murmured thoughtfully, "she had a great interest in you. When we were at the Naceks' she was continually asking about you. God knows why."

"God knows," Jankowski answered, but he felt a stealthy elation.

"She had romantic notions about you," Radek went on softly, "still has, perhaps——"

"No. You see, I betrayed her father."

Radek did not answer; he continued to stare at the tins. Grease from the candle was dropping near his feet.

"It was at Maskowitz——" Jankowski murmured.

"I see," Radek whispered, "and she found out?"

"She found out. I had to tell her, just as I have to tell you now."

"Three years ago I would have killed you," Radek said softly, "but now——"

"Well?"

"It would be fratricide."

There was a long pause. Klemba muttered in his sleep; the bunker had an air of midnight, desolate, sinister. And somewhere above them the wild strawberries, the burning sun.

The candle spluttered; went out.

"God! What a business——" Radek muttered, with a deep sigh. "So she hates you now?"

"Yes, she hates me."

"And she's hard to forget," Radek went on softly, "she's too rare to forget. A charming, original mind, a generous heart, above all—lovable. It was her simplicity, honesty—in a world of deceptions, innumerable lies and falsehoods, of faces concealing the hard crust round their hearts, left by the years, of corruption which begins like a petty irritation but turns into a force, a raging fire——" he paused.

Jankowski heard Darok breathing, Klemba muttering.

"No," Radek went on sadly, "even the lowest blackguard keeps a place in his memory for something he believed true, incorruptible. Even you, brother, who told me once that you were three parts rotten."

"She meant more to me than that," Jankowski answered, "you see, she meant everything. She means everything. You don't understand, sometimes we meet one, caught up in the same stream of disaster as ourselves; we see our own sorrows on the face of that one, our own hopes. I would have died for her because my heart went out to her great suffering, because I knew she was good, because she was gentle, because until I met her I was nothing, I was lost in life. Who can say that Hell and Heaven are not on earth? Only the dead souls. That was Heaven, the sun on her hair, the way she walked——"

"You speak as if she were dead," Radek interrupted gently. "But I understand. Didn't I love her too?"

There was no reply. Somewhere above them, men were bawling to each other in German.

The bawling grew louder and ceased abruptly, leaving a silence that was stifling, charged with terror. Jankowski stared at the edge of the trap-door, where light filtered through the covering pine-needles. His scalp tightened. They were round the opening. He sensed them a yard from his head.

"I can't——" the voice was small, faltering, like a frightened child's.

An indrawn breath, then a whispered: "Quiet, Franek!"

A moment's unbearable silence.

"I'm going up——"

"Fool!" Jankowski hissed. "Quiet!"

A movement by the bunk. Klemba said loudly: "I'm going up——" He sobbed. "Into the daylight, into the air——"

"C'est fini," Darok murmured.

"Give me a gun!" Klemba shouted, "let me get out——"

Jankowski struck a match; sprang, but fell over the half-finished table.

Klemba was out. Light poured through the opening. He saw the sky through a net-work of branches.

"They've gone," exclaimed Klemba from outside.

Radek dropped his machine-pistol and put his head between his hands.

"My nerves will be the next to go," he said weakly.

"Get him down again, for God's sake, Anton."

But Klemba refused to go down. His nerve had gone completely. Repressing an impulse to knock him out and drag him down, Jankowski told the others to stay in the bunker. He replaced the lid; camouflaged the entrance, then with Klemba hid in a denser part of the forest.

"They won't return, Franek," he told Klemba, "they haven't got the men for a thorough search. I know how you feel too well. We'll join the others at dusk."

"Lived this life too long——" was all Klemba would say. He lay, face downwards; he had been one of the bravest men Jankowski had ever met.

Jankowski slept.

There was a haze over the forest; a heron flew across the greenish sky. Awakened by ants, and hunger, Jankowski rose. Klemba was leaning against a tree.

"You see," Jankowski said, "we're safe. They never came back."

"In half-an-hour we'll be safe," Klemba answered, "when it's dark. Let's go back to the others."

They found Radek waiting near the bunker.

"Darok's after bread in Largantau," he told them, "I waited to get Stepha's address from you, Anton."

"It's fifty-one Hermann Goring *Strasse*. Don't mention me. Tell her you got her address from Bendimir's saw-mill. Franek and I'll try Kuras. We should all meet again here before dawn. We can find the bunker by this stump."

They parted with Radek on the outskirts of Kirschau.

Kuras's house was dark and silent. As he slunk across the dirty yard, Jankowski prayed that Agnes had not been suspected in Starogin. He waited a moment by the wall. Suddenly he distinguished a face at the upper window.

"Anton——?"

"Yes," he whispered, "and a comrade. Everything's alright."

She let them in. The night was warm, but she was shivering slightly in an old coat. Kuras was striking matches in the kitchen. Glasses off, sleepy, unkempt, he groped his way to the electric switch. The sudden light awoke the flies, the grey cat. Agnes hurriedly arranged her hair in the yellowish mirror.

Jankowski introduced Klemba, who impressed them by his size, his fierce, reckless face.

"If I'd been younger, I'd have joined men like you," Kuras said. "I smuggled tobacco once, you know."

Agnes lit the gas under the kettle.

"But how did you get away, Anton?" she asked, "I saw the police, the S.S.—it was terrible——"

He told her.

"If you're hiding in the woods," Kuras said, "we can give you bread."

"Don't leave us now," Agnes put her hand on his arm, "be here when the Russians come—stay until then, Anton!"

"I shall come back."

"But I'm frightened——" she turned towards Klemba. "Stay, we could hide you until the Russians came."

"We can hide one," Kuras said.

"Then stay, Franek," Jankowski told him.

Klemba hesitated. "What will the others think?" he murmured.

"They'll wish you well, brother. You know that."

"Then I'll stay."

Jankowski left soon after the bread and *kaffee-ersatz* had been cleared away. Slinking through empty streets, he felt that he would never see Klemba, Agnes and

Kuras again; they would be swallowed up in the chaos, the change heralded by the faint guns. The breeze, blowing across the Vistula, moving his hair into his eyes, stirring the plane-trees' leaves, seemed a live thing in a dead city. He hurried past the saw-mill on the town's outskirts; crossed the *autobahn*, and went towards the woods. Perhaps Radek had not returned to the bunker? Stepha would hide him . . .

But Radek and Darok were there.

"So the Deadly Four of the Struga Forest are getting disbanded," Radek said, when he had heard about Klemba, "and our little friend here is forsaking us, too," he indicated Darok. "Somebody has offered to hide him in Largantau――"

"It's the sound of Russian guns," Darok said, "that makes people so friendly. Look at this!" He pointed to five great loaves on the bunk. "I staggered all the way back――"

"But we must all meet again, whatever happens," Radek exclaimed. "In a free Poland the four of us must meet—in Warsaw!"

"Warsaw's flat," Darok said.

"We'll rebuild it, brother!"

"Who knows?" Darok murmured. "Share out the tobacco—a last smoke together, then I go; if only Franek were here."

Radek produced a small quantity of tobacco, screwed up in a yellow packet.

"Hugo Kassel's," he said softly, "the poor fool! Yet he won after all, with his precious verses, his serious, stupid, dog-like devotion. He wasn't such a bad ass. He's dead, you know, Anton? She showed me his name on the back page of the *Vorposten*――"

"What will she do?"

237

Silently, Radek divided the tobacco into three little heaps.

"What can she do?" he said at last, looking up. "She'll stay—it's Kassel's house. Every week she's going to send that moon-faced crone to the edge of the woods with bread. She doesn't know you're here. She mustn't be there when the Russians come."

"Will you go again."

"It's a great risk. I want to. But what an astonishing girl she is—when I asked if I would see her again, she said I might see her barefoot, with a few geese, among the parching grass, the chicory-flowers. . . ."

## CHAPTER FOURTEEN

THE rain had frozen, buds and branches glinted in the moonlight; ice fragments on the Largantau path crunched under Jankowski's boots. The forest was an island in the inferno of thundering guns, bombs, the ceaseless roar of vehicles.

"They're held on the Tucheler Heide," Radek explained, for the fourth time, "but they're pushing west towards Konitz. We can hold out."

"We must get bread," Jankowski said. "We must get a hot drink."

They emerged from the forest, the east wind met them out of a lurid sky.

"Should have stayed in the bunker——" Radek complained, shivering in his thin jacket.

"And starve?"

"Stepha might send the old woman out to-morrow——"

"We can't rely on that again."

They plodded on, holding their collars up. The rumble of waggons which had not ceased for weeks, was louder. They heard yells, three rifle shots.

"General Disorder reigns soon," Radek muttered, "then we come into our own."

Jankowski said nothing; optimistic forecasts were getting on his nerves.

"Don't worry," Radek said, in a low, scornful voice, "you won't lose her."

Jankowski shrugged; plodded into the freezing wind. His head still ached with the smoke of the fire they had tried to light in the bunker, or perhaps it was the effect of hunger, sleeplessness?

"I watched her face, when I told her you were probably dead," Radek's voice came muffled through his gloved hand. "She doesn't hate you, brother——"

Jankowski watched the glow on the skyline, where some great fires flared.

"You met her through me," the muffled voice continued, "remember?—on the Malkow road, before the war—with Leo, or was it Stanislaw——"

"Get her out before it's too late!"

"Before it's too late——" Radek repeated slowly. "Yes, I've heard them talk, those so-called patriots who've got to behave like swines to prove they're Poles, and she'll never realise the danger. Starogin's evacuated——"

Jankowski did not answer. What chance had Radek of reaching Kirschau now? Five times during the last week, they had almost been caught by patrols.

Radek halted. "Listen! We can't leave it longer. I'm going——"

"To-night?"

"Now!"

"Wait. Where could you take her?"

"You won't lose her," Radek said bitterly, "I'll bring her back, I tell you——"

"Bring her back . . . yes, and then?"

"You won't lose her!" Radek shouted furiously. "Can't you see—there'll be chaos, we could take her West—mingle with refugees, reach the British, Americans. There'll be hell here again when the Russians come through . . . well, I'm going. Come on, come with me——"

"She'd never come with me."

Radek put his hand on Jankowski's shoulder; sighed deeply.

"When I've spoken to her, she'll forgive you, brother. She has forgiven you already in her heart—one day you'll understand why. I'll bring bread. Take these matches; try to light that fire again in the bunker —there's some bits of straw under the entrance. Anton, good-night. Good luck, brother."

Radek had gone; his footfalls faded rapidly, leaving only the rumble of waggons, the thunder of guns. Jankowski turned his back on the east wind, the glow of fires. He dreaded the night, it was troubled with fear, unrest. The persistent grinding of waggon-wheels was getting into his brain. He stopped; listened, concentrated on the sound with a queer notion that there was something in it that he had missed. The dull roar of that fleeing host surrounded his island of branches, of buds sparkling in moonlight. Something he had missed. For a moment the sound seemed of the earth, and the misery of all those people awoke a universal unrest, insinuating despair into the creeping wind. But he could listen no longer. He was unwell. The months of waiting, with a little bread, an occasional hot drink, had weakened him.

He would try the fire again; boil up those *kaffee-ersatz* dregs and surprise Radek who might be back before daylight. Back with bread, perhaps tobacco! He tried to dwell on these things, but could not keep away from the thought that Stepha might be there. She would not come. It was unwise to nurse such hopes. It would be enough to thank God for if Radek returned.

But reaching the bunker, Jankowski melted snow in a Red Cross tin and by the light of burning straw, attempted to shave. With the old open razor Darok had left, he tore and scraped at three weeks' growth of beard. His own face looked back at him from the tin-lid

they used as a mirror. Yes, he looked very much the
traitor, the cut-throat. Or was it the gallant Partisan?
No, not that—his hands were trembling; he could
hardly shave. Whether he was mistaken for a gallant
Partisan or a treacherous cut-throat depended on who
looked at him. He would never be recognised as a mere
human fool, trying to sublimate a shivering sojourn in
an unhealthy bunker. No: he was already doomed to be
hanged or fêted. He clung to this conceit, tried desperately to consider which was the greater imbecility. The
attempt was weak, useless. He could not keep away
from the thought of Stepha.

Radek had spoken of going West, of mingling with
refugees and reaching the British or Americans. That
was typical of Radek, to have an outlandish inspiration
and follow it through fanatically. Of course, he loathed
the Russians, and Stepha feared them. It was easy
enough to mingle with refugees in the chaos, and there
were many people wanting drivers. But refugees were
freezing to death.

Jankowski laughed; he would be neither hanged nor
fêted. He would freeze.

The straw went out suddenly, leaving darkness; he
struck matches and stuck them into the wall. He
laughed again. He would freeze! Freeze to death. But
even this prospect could not cool his feverish excitement. Within eight hours she could be here. Less, six
hours—five hours. He put the razor down and started
to tidy the bunker.

He scraped twigs from the floor; lit a fire under the
bunker's entrance, but smoke filled the place. Coughing,
shivering, he emerged into the open and was met by the
thunder of an artillery barrage. The battle raged a few
miles south; again the Red Army attacked the line

between Konitz and Graudenze. They might break through to-night. He started walking aimlessly towards the Largantau road, but remembered that there was no water left in the bunker. He returned for the kitbag and began the weary trudge to the stream.

The journey for water exhausted him completely. Wrapping himself in the blanket Agnes Kuras had given him, he lay on the bunk. He was shivering.

"I must be careful," he mumbled, "lived this life too long—I'm unwell . . ."

He must have slept; his head was throbbing painfully, his limbs ached. There was a lull in the sound of guns. He sprang up suddenly. Surely that was voices! Radek's laugh? He hurried out of the bunker.

Nobody. The wind was creeping through the frozen trees, there was the waggons' everlasting rumble, a desultory boom of guns. The moon had set. If they were coming, they should be coming now. It was a forlorn hope. They would not come. No doubt Radek was already caught.

But he relit the fire, fanning the smoke towards the entrance. He boiled up the *kaffee-ersatz* dregs; cleaned three drinking tins. He sipped a little himself and kept the rest bubbling on the fire. Whoever came from Kirschau on a night like this would badly need a hot drink. The fire went down; he put the last of the straw and twigs on. He went outside for a while; listened. The forest was surrounded by sounds, but this made it seem the stiller by contrast. He felt the touch of the creeping, impersonal wind. What could he do if they never returned? Panic stirred in his heart. No, that was unthinkable. Radek was not the man to be caught and hanged like a dog.

But Radek did not return.

For long Jankowski sat in the bunker, watching the cold daylight come through the square of the entrance. It fell on the few things Radek had left. For five months they had lived like rats in this place; getting on each other's nerves; arguing about fetching water, stumbling over each other in the dark, cursing, laughing. So Radek was caught after all? After all those optimistic platitudes: 'I can smell the Russian tobacco, brother— it won't be long now! or 'God, how we'll celebrate, Anton!'

The bunker was haunted. Slowly, Jankowski crammed the few things they had accumulated into the kit-bag. He thought of the frozen miles between himself and Kirschau. He would take her away; tell her to forget, for a while, what he had done. The artillery barrage started again, making the earth tremble. He must reach her before it was too late. He could not even wait until darkness fell. He trudged towards the Largantau road.

The continuous stream of waggons had torn holes in the road's surface; weary horses strained madly, as if sensing a natural disaster. Boys, old men, women stood in the waggons; cracked their whips, swore, entreated, sometimes springing off to urge their horses on from the road. Families were sitting in uncovered *leiter-wagenen*, sheltering under blankets, under damp straw, their belongings hanging from the sides. Their faces were drawn, expressionless, contrasting strangely with the despair and panic of the drivers. Jankowski passed a spot where Russian planes had machine-gunned the road; waggons had turned over in the ditch. Things, familiar in a home, looked strange scattered over the road —broken gramophone records, candle-sticks, tins with 'sugar' marked on them, books, an old straw hat lying in the snow. He found a jar of home-made jam, which he ate while he walked; most of it was frozen. He felt conspicuous; of all that host he seemed the only one making for Kirschau. But the refugees' eyes seemed sightless. Some way ahead, he saw a long column approaching, flanked by armed men. Stupefied by cold and weariness, he stumbled on. Too late, he realised the danger—the armed men were S.S., the column consisted of tattered civilians, prisoners of war in a varied assortment of uniforms, deserters from the German Army.

Jankowski hurried across the road, where a family of refugees were struggling to put a wheel on a waggon.

"Let me help."

They stared at him as if he were mad, then went on cursing and straining at the wheel. He helped while glancing at the faces of the men in the column. He did not see Radek. The column passed. He went on again.

"*Halt!* You there, with the bag—come back!"

He turned slowly. Tense, hard-faced, an S.S. man stood a short way behind him.

"Come here."

Jankowski went back. Light brown eyes, like pebbles, inspected him quickly. The man exuded a cold ferocity.

"*Ausweis!* Papers——"

"I'm looking for them now. That's why I've come back a little way——"

The other laughed shortly. He looked at the name on the kit-bag.

"Ah ha—English?" he relaxed; smiled, "a 'Tommy'?"

"Prisoner of war," Jankowski said.

The other looked at him curiously; shook his head.

"Ah, you English—why don't you help us keep the Asiatic hordes out of Europe? You'll be next——"

"I don't know," Jankowski said woodenly, "I'm not Churchill."

"No, he looks a bit better fed," the S.S. man stroked his chin. "Why are you here?" he snapped suddenly. "The camps are evacuated."

"I drove refugees."

"Where are they?"

"They ran out of food. Told me to go."

"Fall in with the column. Move!"

"But my——"

"Move!"

They had to trot in order to catch up the others; Jankowski felt stricken. The sub-machine gun was a yard from his shoulders. He was done—finished. There was no hope now.

"*Du Englander!*" the S.S. man bawled at a man muffled up in a British Army overcoat. "I've caught a comrade for you."

The man turned.

"Take it easy, chum," he grasped Jankowski's arm, "so the bastards have picked you up too?"

Panting, staggering, Jankowski could not answer for a moment.

"Take it easy, boy——"

Jankowski asked if there was a chance of escape.

"I'm all in," the Englishman said. "Dysentry. Bastards picked me up at Neudorf. No grub—but the first chance I get I'm off—rather freeze in a bloody ditch than carry on with this lark——"

They dragged on, past road blocks, over-turned waggons, dead horses. Jankowski kept his eyes fixed on the man in front. He had the vivid impression that he was back at Maskowitz. They stumbled over the ruts, the frozen snow.

"God! But I was on a smashing farm," it was the weary, but calm voice of the Englishman, "ran the place, I tell you—old man was in Russia . . . I lived like a rajah . . . used to give my Red Cross chocolate to the Frau—smashing bit of stuff! Boy, did I go down the slope! And you should have seen the farm—never known a place go to the dogs like it . . . she used to ask my advice, *mine*, mind you—I didn't know the difference between a cow and a hole in the ground before I was nabbed in France——" He paused; swung his haversack over his other shoulder. "A towney—that's me. I told her it needed rest—the soil I mean. Let it go to grass, I said, and that pig should be killed . . . and killed soon. The soil needed rest alright. So did I——"

An intense bombardment started in the south-east.

"Roll on those Bolshy bastards!" the Englishman burst out. "But she was a smashing bit of stuff," his voice was suddenly calm again, "she was, really—felt sorry for her in the end—so good to me, worshipped the ground I trod on. God knows why . . . s'pose I was different. Poor old Marie——"

There was a dry rattle of machine-gun fire behind them. It grew louder; a plane roared.

"Joe's boys. Blind bastards think we're infantry—" Jankowski never heard him speak again. The plane was on them. Jankowski was flung into the ditch by stampeding men; they trod on his hand, his legs. The S.S. fired, yelling like mad-men. Men screamed at bolting horses. A few yards down the ditch a woman held up a headless baby; looked at it with inane curiosity. The column had scattered. S.S. men lay in ditches and methodically sniped at figures stumbling over the white fields.

Jankowski slunk along the ditch. The plane roared back and he fell flat in a bulging snow drift. Bullets tore into the ground a yard from his head. He had been hit! No, he could run. His run fell to a faltering stagger. He looked back. The road was littered with corpses, dead or dying horses, broken waggons. A staff-car had come from the other direction; a man in uniform screamed and waved his arms, trying to clear the road.

Feverishly, Jankowski searched wrecked waggons for food. Finding a lump of bacon, he left the road and followed a line of telegraph poles across the fields. He forced himself on. He thought of marching songs, counted his steps, made an objective of each telegraph pole. He fought the painful wind, called it foul names, cursed it passionately.

Kirschau burned. Bombs fell on its Eastern outskirts, the station was a heap of twisted girders. Exhausted, battered convoys poured West down burning Danzig *Strasse*. The public gardens were full of refugees, the lawns a morass of mud and snow. Jankowski picked his way over the dusty debris that had been the busy, cheerful Kalisz Street. He turned into Hermann Goring *Strasse* and came to fifty-one. He looked up at the curtainless windows. She had gone. No, a chimney smoked. He stumbled up the steps; banged on the door.

The old woman opened it furtively, there was a rosary in her hand. For a moment she regarded him without comprehension, then smiled.

"The Anton? So you've come——"

"To take her away——"

She looked at him steadily, absently, as if his agita-

tion had reminded her of something. He pushed past
her into the littered hall and called Stepha's name. No
answer. He called again, then went through the house.
There was nothing there but rolled-up carpets, boxes.
The crone was waiting for him in the hall; she watched
him approach and shook her head sadly.

"She has gone. It's no good looking, my son. I'm
glad she's gone."

"But alone——"

"With the young officer, the partisan—

"Radek."

"She went with him, but they did leave something for
you—for the Anton. Wait——"

He hardly heard her; he was vaguely aware that she
had clattered off in her wooden-soled slippers. Then
she was back again, thrusting something heavy into his
hands. "Don't look so sad, son—it is war, it's always
the same. Take this bread, they left it for you, for the
Anton—coffee, too. You will need it. I'm sorry to
lose her, too, she was good-hearted, kind always . . .
no good ever comes of war, even the things she left me
—the new linen, the china——"

Jankowski sat on the stairs; put his head between his
hands. A moment's rest then he would go.

"But that is what she said," the crone was saying,
" 'tell him, if he comes, that I found forgiveness was not
so hard, tell him that,' that is what she said, we were
standing here—I saw her tears," she paused. The house
shook in a shuddering blast of artillery.

"They're coming," the old woman croaked, "the Red
Army . . . but they wouldn't harm an old, old woman—
a true Pole?"

"Don't worry, mother," he muttered thickly. He
rose. "I'll take the bread."

He was slouching in the gutter, staring at refuse, muttering; he sought the streets where acrid smoke lingered, where people searched for the remains of their families under ruins; he hungered for the sight of pain and misery, as if it could save him from his own despair.

A furious battle raged a few miles beyond the Vistula; shells had landed among the squalid houses, the small yards, the dirty alley-ways where Kuras lived. The wind, coming over the river, blew dust into Jankowski's face, sent scraps of wall-paper whirling over the rubble. He went along the high wall where snow had drifted, through the broken gate and into the yard.

Agnes was holding up the corner of a sack, while Kuras tacked it over a shattered window. She heard the footsteps and turned, then dropped the sack.

"But it's Anton!"

"Yes."

She adroitly pulled blonde curls from under her woollen cap; brushed the dust and snow from her sleeve. "Thank God you've come."

They half-dragged him into the disordered kitchen, where Kuras bombarded him with questions, statements; the man could not keep still, but bobbed up and down before Jankowski, his face twitching. Yes. Franek had gone; they had tried to keep him, done their best—it was a question of food—it was always a question of food now. Poor Franek, he had been like a son, but what else could they do? Always the guns, the guns, the guns—for weeks, months the Russians had been held . . . oh, it was all over now! Russians had crossed the river a few miles down. People had seen the tanks. Perhaps by to-night . . . Merciful God, what a time they had had! Police had come; it had been the evacuation order; they had started packing. Then what had happened? Why, the police had gone, fled, run like rats out of the town. The *Burgermeister* had shot himself . . .

Jankowski listened. Kuras waved his arms; had an imbecile cackle for the most sombre incidents. Jankowski was conscious of Agnes's misty blue eyes watching him.

Kuras thanked God he had come—they were a little uneasy, not frightened but nervous. Three years ago they had registered as Germans. Had to, or starve. Then the son had been called-up for the *Wehrmacht*— God alone knew where the poor lad was now—but he had never killed a Russian, he had fired over their heads. There were letters to prove this. He would get those letters—some had 'Long live Poland' at the end. That was proof. He would get those letters.

Kuras hurried from the room. Agnes rubbed up against Jankowski like a cat, like a child, and with a child's innocence questioned him about the Russians. Was it all true, what the Germans said, did the Russians really commit atrocities? Had German soldiers really found raped and bayoneted women when they re-captured Goldap? She was so terrified, she had not slept for five nights; lay shivering all night, thinking of the Mongolians.

Jankowski looked at her. In that place which had already an odour of death and ruin, she was like one prepared for carnival. She had taken off her coat and woollen cap; her other clothes, the short yellow skirt, the white jumper, looked gay and smart; seemed designed to exhibit the superb contours of her breasts and thighs, and her face was made up with powder, lipstick, eye-black. He suspected that the slight trembling of her body was not through fear, but suppressed excitement.

But he consoled her as if she had been a delicately nurtured virgin. What did it matter? It pleased him to please her; inwardly he thanked God that he had found her here: somebody he knew, who welcomed him, made him feel human. He tried to console himself—the best and purest love dies, and its death must bring a sorrow like madness. He had Stepha's forgiveness, but somebody had said: "Things do not come at all, or if they come, they come not at that moment when they would have given us the fullness of delight." What was her forgiveness? She forgave, but remembered with contempt, pity.

That night the cold was intense. Between the roar of guns, he heard the waggons; he thought of that machine-gunned road, the misery and chaos. And Radek had taken her into that hell. They would never get through. Russians were north-west of the town; a battle raged, shaking plaster from the ceiling of the little room.

The next day undefended Kirschau was 'liberated'— swarms of drunk Mongols looted, raped. With Agnes and Kuras, Jankowski went through the public gardens, where refugee families stood in silent groups while the contents of their waggons were flung into the snow, and their horses taken for the Red Army. An old woman, crouching under a blanket, cursed the *Wehrmacht* for pulling out of the town in the night. They went on past the remains of soaking eiderdowns, lidless suit-cases, broken jars, torn photograph albums until they reached Bahnhof *Strasse*. On all sides they heard sounds of smashing glass, shots, the roar of tank tracks. They stood by the public garden gates with a group of refugees, towns-folk, liberated prisoners of war. On the other pavement a little soldier, with a happy smile, fired his sten gun straight into the air. Three white-faced members of the *Deutsche Madel* were being hurried into a looted shop by a group of laughing, excited Kazaks. Units of the Red Army were pouring into the town in every kind of vehicle. An Englishman in a tattered battle-dress muttered: "Gengis Khan with Yankee guns, Gengis Khan . . ."

While their homes were ravished the Poles watched —silent, enraged, helpless, as they had been when Germans swept into Pomorze. The *Wehrmacht* had been orderly, European. These were wild Asiatics.

"Look at them," Kuras murmured, "if they had only been Ukrainians——"

"Where can we go?" Agnes asked despairingly, "I'm afraid to go home—they might be there."

"They'll be gone by to-morrow," Jankowski said, "then it might be Ukrainians, Russians——"

"God knows where we'll be by to-morrow," she sobbed, "they have taken all the German girls away——"

"But we're Poles!" Fury twisted his heart, distorted his vision. For five years Partisans had suffered for this! Greatly suffered and died, to see their homes desecrated. The Allied press, with fatal ignorance or sinister hypocrisy, would proclaim another town's liberation by the 'glorious Soviet Ally'. Were Poles expected to be grateful?

"Let's go back," he said hoarsely.

As they hurried down littered side-streets, past looted homes and shops, Jankowski thought of Radek and Stepha. They would not get through.

The poor quarter where Kuras lived was quiet, but

terror had spread its sickly squalor over familiar alley-
ways.

"Nothing to loot here," Kuras muttered, fumbling
with his door key. He looked old, round-shouldered;
Jankowski suspected that he was thinking, not of loot,
but of the future.

Agnes buried her face in the fur of the grey cat.
Jankowski lit the fire.

"I dread night," Kuras said, staring out of the window.

But the night was strangely calm. The fighting had
faded northwards. With Agnes, Jankowski stood at the
window of his room; gusts from the Vistula moved
snow and grit along the window-sill, against the broken
panes. The town's calm was sinister. They heard an
occasional rifle shot, a scream, bursts of drunken singing.

"Come to bed, Anton," Agnes whispered, pulling at
his hand, "don't keep staring over the roofs. Whom are
you thinking of? Come on, to-morrow we might be cold
——" she shuddered. "They might come before dawn."

But for days the quarter of cobbled yards and alley-
ways remained a backwater. As Kuras had said, there
was nothing to loot there. But the people breathed
fear: the next day—the next moment might bring dis-
ruption of families, humiliation. Every day Jankowski
foraged for food in the town's centre, searching abandoned houses, shops. All young Germans, men and
women, had been marched East, leaving children and
old people wandering the streets. Jankowski walked
between the gaunt, high ruins which looked as if they
would be left for ever, mighty monuments to hopelessness. He went to fifty-one Hermann Goring *Strasse*,
went through its wrecked, looted rooms. What was the
good? As if she would return where she was known as
the mistress of a German major.

He went down Bahnhof *Strasse*, to the indoor riding
school which the Germans had used as a billet for
refugees. The windows were shattered, but it was still
full of German children and old people, of liberated
prisoners of war, of Poles and Russians on their way
home from German factories and farms. People lay on
the straw as if they had come in to die. Some families
had hung mirrors on the walls, made shelves, clothes-
lines.

Jankowski looked at every face. He had been mad to
hope. The four Poles opposite were sharing out
tobacco dust. An old German stared past Jankowski.
What did he see? His eyes seemed empty, staring out
of a soul abandoned by hope, resentment. Defeat. Did
he see it as a material defeat of armies, or a defeat of
great illusions, a defeat which would rankle on until he
died?

The old man said suddenly: "That's why we never
gave in before——" he swung round towards a French
prisoner of war who was stirring something in a dixie,
"you have cursed us for fighting, in your blindness . . .
it prolonged your suffering. Do you still wonder why
we fought? You have seen our women dishonoured,
humiliated; you have seen them marched down the road
into slavery; you have seen the look on their grey faces
as they turned their backs on the ones they love, and
you watched them and——" he could not go on; he
stooped suddenly and tugged at the strips of blanket
wrapped round his feet. "They took my boots——"
he said in a small voice.

The weary-looking Frenchman raised his eye-brows;
went on stirring the dixie's contents. "It's the war,"
he declared thoughtfully, "you should have seen my
Abbeville. If you must follow maniacs like Hitler——"

he pursed his lips; shrugged. Very gently, he touched somebody covered by straw and old coats. "Look at my friend here." He shrugged again.

The person under the straw moaned; tried to raise himself. He said weakly: "The horse is dead, Stepha."

For a moment with a feeling more like an awakening than surprise, Jankowski stared into the dulled black eyes of Radek.

"Hullo, Anton——"

Jankowski knelt: "What happened, brother? Where is Stepha?"

Radek tried to raise himself, but fell back. Weakly, he wiped the straw and dust from his hair and unshaven face. With the ghost of a frown, he shook his head. "I don't know."

"Where did you leave her?"

Radek put a hand across his eyes; screwed up his features as if in pain; Jankowski saw a deep cut across two fingers; it was dirty, uncared for. Radek sighed; moved his head round, his hand slipped partly away from his closed eyes: the gesture spoke a great weariness, utter despondency: "She left me," he explained thickly. "Stepha left me," he repeated distinctly, in a kind of wonder.

"But why? Where did she go?"

"She told me she was going back," Radek mumbled, "it sounded like a bad joke on that frozen hell of a road. Poor girl, she must have been mad . . . it was by Berent, she told me we were running away—like rats leaving a sinking ship, she said; we had been driving refugees, people from Goldap, Insterburg, two horses had died . . . when I saw Stepha last, she was hurrying away, she looked strange, lost——"

"Why didn't you stop her!"

"I called, went back, but I never found her. She was not the only one lost on that road. Yes, I went over that way again, miles, miles, miles—frost-bite, dysentry; this Frenchman saved me—found me in a ditch outside the town. Can you forgive me for not taking her back to the bunker? I meant to, Anton, I swear; but when I was with her I hated the thought of losing her. God, you must have cursed me, brother!"

"I'm going to take you to Kuras," Jankowski said, at last, "Agnes would like to look after you. I shall leave you in good hands, brother."

"And you?"

"I'm going away."

"You are leaving Poland for ever?"

"Yes. I have a craving to leave, brother; I suppose I shall be driven by God knows what ghosts. I returned to Poland six years ago to see my mother's grave; the stone was smashed so I must replace it before I go. That's all I can do—replace a cold stone whose very meaning seems blotted out by blood and ruin and passion and hatred. But a stone is something we can replace."

"And where will you go?"

"England perhaps, if I can. I've connections there and I'm half English, but I wouldn't stay long. We might meet again."

"No!" Radek declared with surprising strength, "I'm staying. She was right when she spoke of rats leaving the sinking ship."

"The ship sinks whether the rats leave it or not."

"But I want to fight on, until I die, to fight on, not in this war or that war . . . but what greater glory is there than to die fighting in the everlasting war, the fight against injustice, ignorance, hate——"

257

"Man easily forgets he's fighting that war."

"Man forgets easily. Too easily," there was the coldness of despair in Radek's voice, "but I shall think of them when it's wet and cold . . . the solemn little children we passed in that hell, no summer will melt the icy memory of that road, it will be haunted for ever," he put his hand across his eyes, "the days and days we passed over it! The hopelessness, the chaos, ah well———"

"It is war," Jankowski murmured gently; never before had he seen the high-hearted Radek in such a mood.

"Yes," replied Radek slowly, "it was war. Somewhere, in the warmth and shelter, people were reading of glorious battles, gallant counter-attacks; brass bands were playing somewhere, sergeant-majors were as smart as ever. But war to me is a small girl helping along an old woman bent up with the cold, the rags round their feet dragging in the snow. No Glory."

Suddenly tense, he lifted his head and looked straight at Jankowski with an air of baffled concentration, as if he were trying to remember a message of tremendous importance.

"Brother, her head was resting very lightly on my shoulder—she might have thought it would tire me otherwise, I don't know, but the touch of it—gentle, almost imperceptible—with the cold, the terror, death, you know that was———" he smiled, as one who meditates on a great triumph, "well, it was—almost glory. She wore that reddish cap, a kind of hood with a white fur fringe; I remember it got soaking wet and dirty. What an amazing girl she was—where women were getting raped and murdered she worried about that white fringe—'do you think it will dry white again, Zygmus? . . . surely it's not ruined for ever?'"

# EPILOGUE

# EPILOGUE

HOSTS of birds were passing across the sun which had given a pink flush to the thawing snow on the plain. It seemed to Anton Jankowski that the firs by the Pallow graveyard got no nearer, that the sound of sleigh-bells was in the snow all round him, like the elusive music of crickets in summer grass.

What would this journey be but another change of scene on the homeless passage of his life? He had said good-bye to those with whom he had shared hopes and disasters. The Naceks, Radek, Agnes Kuras and her father had all wanted him to stay, but he would go and never return. Those hectic years had been swept away into an episode, rounded off, neatly encompassed by Jan Domohoski's welcoming and farewell handshakes. He was left with an ineluctable memory.

He passed the Struga lake. The greenish sheen of water gleamed in the reeds; water birds were diving, leaving ripples. Her image lingered. The belt of reeds, the stunted bushes, the few boulders seemed to jar the incurable wound. He walked on more slowly, bowed by the implacable memory of salvation missed.

He climbed towards the graveyard. Why had he come back? There was nothing here. He went through the space in the wall where the gates had been, down the overgrown path and to the grave. For a while he looked at the grass showing above the thawing snow. The rising wind brought the faint sound of guns; the madness and slaughter had swept on to the Pomeranian coast; the ancient plain looked as it had looked when he had left Poland for England twelve years ago.

Scenes rose in his memory.

He saw the sandy hill, the sombre huts, the look-out posts of Maskowitz, the men who walked with their heads bowed, the Linsk flowing between its wide marshes. By the corner of the wash-house he saw a slight figure silhouetted against the last glimmers of the evening sky. From the haters, the crude patriots, Markenski stood out as the man who had won. "Man no longer fights the evil in himself, but the good, brother; for the sake of some cold creed he tries to smother the warmth of pity in his own heart." That was true, like many of the other things Markenski had said.

Looking at the grass and weeds which covered what he had known and loved in his childhood, he felt no bitterness or hate over the stone, broken through some purblind motive of revenge. He sought for a pattern in the trivial scenes that came into his memory. He saw again the bent forms on the road, the smart S.S. men, the white house with its Swastika flag drooping from the window. The road was still there, but now the bent forms would be German, the men with the guns— Russian or Polish. The flag had changed. Everything else was the same.

The terror of loneliness was on the horizons of the land which was fading into the night. He would never return. He had loved here, he had hated and what had it taught him? That the hate had been born of ignorance; the love of understanding. He had not had more than his share of tragedy. That was worth knowing. He had escaped for ever from his cynicism and bitterness, and who would expect to escape from the world's despair and unrest? Or from its colour and beauty, from its love?

It was getting dark. He would erect a wooden cross and go.

Somebody was hurrying through the space where the gates had been.

"Is that you, Anton?"

"Stepha——"

He stared at that face, so familiar, but still enigmatic, strange.

"I knew, that is I waited——" she stood, looking at him shyly, yet with exultation. She was ragged and out of breath, bare-headed. It was a dream, madness, but she could never be anything else but beautiful.

"Anton, have you nothing to say? No greeting, not even a handshake?"

"Stepha, why did you come back?"

"I had to," she answered, after a pause, "you see, I imagined all kinds of things were happening—to you, I mean, Anton."

"But when I saw you last——"

"I hope you've forgiven, as I've forgiven—you see, I had to come back; I felt the promise of something precious would be lost—it turned into a kind of panic. Can you understand that? I knew you'd come here—I knew, so I've been staying in the cottage there." She nodded towards the Kilana track, "this part of the land is my home, you know."

The lighted cottage window was a sign of life on the grey, vast plain that reached to the forests where the 'mad Englishman' sought freedom twenty-nine years ago.